CW00819575

Finding Sarah

A PHOENIX TO BEHOLD

NINA PURTEE

PORTO BANUS
PUBLISHING

Copyright © 2024 Nina Purtee
All rights reserved
First Edition

PORTO BANUS PUBLISHING 2024
St Pete Beach, FL

First originally published by Porto Banus Publishing 2024

This novel is a work of fiction. Any references to historical events, real people, or real places are used fictitiously. Other names, characters, places and events are products of the author's imagination, and any resemblance to actual events, places or persons, living or dead, is entirely coincidental.

ISBN 979-8-9898529-4-9 (Paperback)
ISBN 979-8-9898529-5-6 (Digital)

Acknowledgments

It is with heartfelt gratitude that I discovered the two brilliant female artists to draw Sarah's inspiration from...Rosa Bonheur, born in France in the 1800s, and Rachel Ruysch, born in the Netherlands in the 1600s. Sarah feels a kindred spirit with these artists, and much of her success in this fictionalized work is a result, in part, of their influence. As an author, they gave me a wealth of material to draw from!

Although Sarah's involvement in conservation efforts is presented in a fictional manner, the Grumeti and Peregrine Funds are real and worthy proponents of conservancy. In Tanzania, during the 1990s, when Sarah's story is set, the Tanzanian government managed the Grumeti Fund. Today it is managed by Singita. Peregrine, located in the United States, is dedicated to the preservation of raptors, which gave me the inspiration for Sarah's incredible raptor series.

My sincerest thanks to my supportive beta readers... Katherine, Ana, Bonnie, Hyeyong, and Charlotte...who watched me sift through all the possible ways of telling Sarah's story until I finally found the right path. Their unanimous support let me know this was the path able to take Sarah to a higher level. And, as always, to my friend and editor, Susan Schader, your perspective, guidance, and suggestions are so appreciated!

Out of the ashes rises the phoenix to discover the beginning of new skills, capabilities, wisdom, and experience. It will take courage and commitment to make the phoenix soar.

Chapter 1

Happiness, so easily taken for granted, can be shattered in an instant. Anyone who looked at pictures from my early childhood, growing up on the shore in Brighton, England, would think I had a charmed life. It was...for a while it was true. I was an only child with doting parents. They would have done anything for me. Daddy would take us to the beach on Saturdays where we would have a picnic, build sandcastles, and play frisbee.

My mum was always humming a tune and constantly taught me new songs to sing with her. My grandmother, Nana, referred to her as Mary Margaret, but my daddy always called her Maggie May. I particularly remember her garden, which became our special place. She would tell stories, and we would pick flowers. Every morning, she would pack my lunch and take me to school and then be the first in the carpool line to pick me up in the afternoon. Little did I know all of that was about to change.

My tenth birthday was in the middle of the summer, so as usual, most of the kids from school were somewhere else on vacation with their families. To compensate, my parents gave me a huge paint set that included pads of art paper and a whole array of watercolor paints, along with an assortment of brushes. To be honest, I remember at the time being rather intimidated by it all. It seemed like a messy sport, and I wasn't sure I could even draw, much less paint. Somehow the paint set worked its way to the back of my closet, and there it stayed.

School started and I entered fifth grade. Many of the same classmates from the year before were there. I particularly remember my new teacher, Mr. Armstrong. He pretended to be very strict, but inside I could tell he was a softy. It made me work extra hard to be sure he was proud of my work.

One morning, I was hurriedly trying to polish some homework while Mum packed my lunch. It was raining that morning, and she tried to get me as close to the front door of the school as possible. We were late, so there wasn't time for our normal goodbye kiss. Mum said, "Hurry now, love. Have a good day!" We waved goodbye, and I went in sure Mr. Armstrong would be pleased with my work.

Since Mum was always at the front of the line to pick me up, I tried every day to get outside early enough so she wouldn't have to wait. This particular day, the rain from the morning had still not let up, so I remained under the awning looking for our car. When I didn't see her, I reasoned she had somehow gotten delayed somewhere in the rain. I sat down on the bench and said goodbye to my classmates as they one by one were picked up and left. I kept watching, knowing she would turn the corner into the school any minute. The thunder seemed to get louder as the number of kids dwindled. I remember the thunder frightened me as much as sitting on that bench alone, waiting.

After a while, Mr. Armstrong was walking to his car and saw me. "Sarah, what are you doing all alone out here in the rain?"

I said, "I'm waiting on my mum. She should be here any minute." At that moment, a particularly loud burst of thunder made me jump in fear.

Mr. Armstrong asked if I had my phone number. Handing it to him, I said proudly, "My mum told me to always have it in my pocket."

Starting to dial, he smiled at me. "That was very smart of her!" Someone answered on the other end, and I could hear Mr. Armstrong say, "Oh no, I understand. No, she is right here with me. Would you like me to bring her home? All right. We will leave now." Stooping down, he looked at me and held my shoulders. "Sarah, there has been an accident. Your mum is in the hospital. I am taking you home. Your grandmother will be there. Looking at him through the eyes of a ten-year-old, trying to absorb what he was saying, I had no idea that was the moment the world as I knew it ceased to exist.

*****

Nana was crying when she opened the door to Mr. Armstrong's knock. He put his arm around her, and they stood over to the side talking quietly. I was standing there watching them feeling alone and afraid. Why had no one picked me up? Finally, I spoke up. "What happened to my mum? Where is she? I want to see her. Where is my daddy?" I'm not sure I realized I was crying, but I was trying so hard to understand.

After a few more words, Nana saw Mr. Armstrong out and took me to the sofa. She had her favorite handkerchief in her hand and wiped her eyes. She held my hand and took a deep breath. "Sarah, after your mum dropped you at school, she went to work as usual. At the cafeteria during lunch, there was an accident in the kitchen. There was an explosion, and your mum happened to be close by. The explosion caused a fire that swept over my dear Mary Margaret. She got burned badly, Sarah."

I tried to comprehend. "Are the doctors fixing her? Can I go see her?"

Nana hugged me tight. "Sarah, sweetheart, your mum's face burned badly. The doctors are trying to take care of her, but she does not look the same. The way she looks might frighten you."

I somehow knew I needed to see her. "Nana, I have to see her. It was my fault we were late, and I didn't get to kiss her this morning. Please take me to see her. I'll do anything. Please!" I was sobbing by then.

Nana finally gave in and drove me to the hospital. We went in and I saw Daddy. Screaming, I ran to him. "Daddy, is Mum all right? Where is she? I need to see her."

Looking over my head, he sternly stared at Nana. "Why did you bring her here? She should not see Maggie May like this."

Desperate, I pleaded, "Nana told me she was burned and wouldn't look like herself. I need to kiss her to make her feel better. Please, Daddy! Let me see her." I watched Daddy go talk with the doctor, who shook his head. He obviously didn't like the idea of a ten-year-old seeing a burn victim. Somehow Daddy made it happen, and he held my hand as we went to her bedside in the ER. Her eyes were closed, and there were wet bandages on her face and arms. As I got closer, she must have sensed I was there and slowly opened her eyes to see me. I will never forget her look of pain and helplessness. I looked for part of her hand that wasn't bandaged and held it. I don't know how I stayed strong when I saw her because her image that day will stay etched in my memory until my last breath.

"Mum, we didn't get a chance to kiss this morning." I watched her and understood I could not reach over and kiss her face, so I took my free hand, kissed it with my lips, and gently touched her mouth under the bandage. A tear began to roll down her face. She raised her arm slowly, and I let go of her hand. She must have been in horrible pain, but she brought her hand to her mouth and reached out to me touching my lips with the part of her hand that wasn't burned. The doctor came to say it was time to take her to surgery. He let Daddy stay a few more minutes and walked me back to Nana.

Mum did not survive the surgery that day. I had gotten my kiss, knew how she felt about me, and never cried another tear nor did I smile for a very long time. At her funeral, Daddy couldn't stop crying. At one point, he looked down at me and shook his head and then said between sobs, "Sarah, you look so much like my Maggie May. I don't think I can bear to look at you every day knowing I will never see her loving face looking at me again." I looked at him feeling nothing but numb. My father packed up and left that night.

Chapter 2

I'm sure my grandmother never expected to be raising a ten-year-old at this stage in her life. Nana did what she could to find some normalcy for me but without any warmth. She was grieving too. She told me my father got a job in Southampton, but I never forgot what he said at the funeral and knew deep down he left because of me. Mr. Armstrong could have been a shining light. However, because I moved in with Nana, I got assigned to another school, so I walked into a fifth-grade classroom filled with strangers. I rarely smiled and had a hard time making friends. My performance at school suffered.

I suppose Nana asked for help, since soon after I moved in, a caseworker began coming to check on me every Friday after school. Her name was Amelia. I thought she was pretty and all grown-up, but in reality, she was a freshman in college working in Social Services as a volunteer. She always wore her dark-brown hair in a ponytail. I remember she was extremely kind to me, and we would take long walks to the beach. Of course, I realize now she was trying to get me to open up. I had buried the loss of both parents so deep I could barely function.

Who knew one Friday would stand out as important? Amelia asked me, "Sarah, do you have anything special from your parents that reminds you of good times?" I thought and thought. The reminders of good times broke through to my heart, and the tears finally began to fall down my face. Then I remembered the paint set from my tenth birthday and the loving looks on Mum and Daddy's faces when they gave it to me. She nodded. "Perfect, why don't you get it and let's bring it on our walk today?" Amelia helped me carry all of it, and we went to a nearby dog park and set it up on one of the picnic tables.

Amelia helped me unwrap a canvas and sharpened a charcoal pencil. "Sarah, have you had any art classes in school?" I told her I had put it in the closet because I didn't know what to do with it. Amelia said she was taking an art class in college and was learning herself. "My professor started our course by explaining how a true artist looks at a scene in a unique way. Your eyes see the scene with depth. The talent comes in seeing the layers that make up that dimension. Instead of a canvas, why don't we begin with the sketch pad."

For several weeks, Amelia and I would just take the sketch pad and charcoal. We discussed shadowing and creating roundness. For the first time since losing my parents, I felt a connection with something. I overheard Amelia discussing my interest in art with Nana. There was some talk of insurance from Mum's death. I guess there was an allowance coming each month from Daddy, but the school year had turned into summer, and he never came to see me or even call. I think it might have been more of a convenience to Nana, unable to keep up with a preteen for the whole summer. Whatever the reason, she enrolled me in a full-time summer art school. Amelia promised she would be back in the fall once she came back to college.

I did not have friends to play with, so when I wasn't learning more about art in class, I would take my sketch pad to the beach and sit among the sand dunes to draw. I turned eleven that summer. Focusing solely on art, by the end of that summer, I had learned enough to start experimenting with the various tubes of paints. My art teacher told me I had promise, and I decided, other than Amelia, art was the friend I was missing. Maybe it couldn't speak to me out loud, but it spoke to my soul, and when a painting turned out well, I understood I had its approval. It was like a secret that no one else knew about, and I could not wait for Amelia to come back to college to share the secret!

I finally showed Nana one of my favorite paintings of the summer. It was of a golden retriever that came to the dog park every afternoon with its owner. It was the first time I painted a living thing and not just an inanimate scene. I particularly liked the dimension I achieved in his rounded body. Nana actually smiled and told me she was proud of me and that she had a secret to share with me. She went to her closet and took a shoebox off the shelf. I opened the lid, and inside was filled with dollar bills! "Sarah, this is your very own art savings. Every month I add what

I can to it so you never have to run out of supplies or if you want to take an extra class. You have talent, sweetheart. I really think you will grow up to be a fine artist."

When I hugged her that day, I remember thinking that was our first hug since the funeral. Nana never talked about what happened to Mum or the accident. I didn't want to hear it anyway. We simply fell into a pattern of routine. Later, looking back, I had no idea how much she was hurting, too, over the loss of her daughter and of her independence, as she was now forced to raise her granddaughter.

Chapter 3

For two more years, the school year would come, and Amelia was with me every Friday. I don't think she missed one Friday during the entire school year! Her dependable presence had such an influence and was a shelter for me during those days. I was still dreadfully withdrawn and resistant to joining my classmates in any after school activities. I was happier to ride my bike alone to the beach and set up my paints unnoticed in the sand dunes. Then, for some reason, Amelia got this idea I should join the drama club of all things. I thought she was crazy to think someone as shy as me could get up on a stage in front of people!

She brought it up for three straight weeks until she came up with a different tactic. "Sarah, do you want to go through your life with everyone around you thinking you are the sad and lonely shy girl always hovering in the corner? What if you could magically change your face and turn into someone else? To you, it might be pretend, but if you got good enough at it, those around you wouldn't know it wasn't the real you. You might have fun putting on whatever personality you wanted for the day! Go try it. See if you can do it!" I signed up for drama class the next day.

Entering eighth grade, I was now thirteen years old. I'm not sure what I would have done without Amelia. She helped me buy my first bra and told me what to do when my monthly cycle began. I still had not heard a word from my father (it was impossible to think of him as "Daddy" anymore). His abandonment on top of the tragic loss of my mother created a wound in me that was far too painful to even acknowledge. Honestly, my true self was in shambles.

The day I attended my first drama class, I sat quietly in the back row paying close attention to the teacher. Her name was Miss Martin. During one of her first lectures, she said, "For an actor to truly be great, he or she has to cultivate the ability to morph into the character they are playing." She brought an actor in from the local Brighton Playhouse to demonstrate. We were all given a copy of a play that involved a scene including a duke, his butler, the wayward son, and the chef preparing the dinner for the evening. I was captivated as he took on the individual's characteristics, dialects, and mannerisms and made each character come to life.

Miss Martin continued, "An actor needs to have the ability to fill whichever role is needed at the time." I worked with the class on facial exercises that would eventually become facial expressions. With her direction, we learned the deliberate decision to slouch or stand up straight, how to cock our heads to emphasize the meaning behind the words we said. She told us, "Think about all those actors and actresses who go onstage every night. Do you think they don't have a bad day, feel sick, experience heartbreak? Of course they do, but they show up night after night to perform."

I practiced hours and hours in front of the mirror to master the change in my demeanor. I think I must have made Amelia laugh a few times! I tried it on Nana, too, and even had her wondering if I had magically turned into someone else. I got my chance to try it in real life very soon.

That was when the principal of my school somehow learned I could paint. Probably Amelia told her, but I'm not sure. She asked me if I would paint a floor-to-ceiling mural in the main hallway and that the board requested a jungle theme containing a series of animal species with the whimsical subject of showing the animals in various stages of learning. I knew it would be more challenging than any artwork I had done before and I would need help. I went home that night with a dozen books from the library to work on ideas. They were not all books with pictures of animals. Some of them were about the personalities of famous painters. I quickly skipped over the brilliant but outlandish ones like Van Gogh and Dali to find a personality I could identify with.

That was the night I discovered the French artist, Rosa Bonheur, born in the 1800s. Little did I know then that she would be an artist I held in high regard to this day. Two things stood out to me when I read about her that made me choose her. First, Rosa's mother died when she was eleven. We had that in common. And her mother taught her to read and write by encouraging her to draw a different animal for each letter of the alphabet. *It was like a light bulb went off inside my head!*

The more I learned about Rosa, the more I was amazed at her "I don't care" attitude. She never wanted to be stereotyped and always moved to her own unconventional manner. I studied how she held a stare as if daring anyone to object to her current whim. I practiced for hours, mustering Rosa's strength of will. When I walked seemingly confident into the principal's office in my new attitude, thanks to Rosa Bonheur, to explain the animals and alphabet concept, she loved the idea!

Chapter 4

Now that I had the project, I had to figure out how to get help. I didn't have friends at school who would willingly work on a project for me with my normal personality, meekly keeping to myself. I kept asking myself, what would Rosa do? It was almost as though she whispered in my ear. *Entice them. Make them want to come to you! Come on, Sarah, show them how good you can be!*

I tried to think like she would, unafraid and clever. We needed a competition...something that students would seriously want to win. I brazenly pitched my idea to the principal, and after giving it thought, she reached out to the board for approval. Once I got the nod, I prepared for the contest. First, I made posters announcing what was at stake. The board had agreed that once the mural was complete and they approved it, each student who participated in producing it would get an honorable mention and extra class credit in art. Students ready to move up to high school loved the idea of the extra credit and honorable mention!

Getting the animals for the alphabet was the first step. Forty classmates signed up. I had forty bits of paper, one through twenty-six and the rest blank. The twenty-six who got numbers got to draw for a letter in the alphabet. Once they had a letter, they had to find an animal name with that first letter. Their job was to gather photos of that animal from different angles and think of something they could do as schoolwork. Then they would assist me with that section of the mural.

Before I knew it, kids were inviting me to sit with them at lunch and inviting me over after school. I knew they just wanted me to pick their choices. When some of them wanted to become friends, I was sure they really wanted to be friends with my Rosa personality, not me, so I never went all in on friendships. Amelia was amazed at what I had done and actually came to see the finished mural at school. The principal loved the community effort and told me the mural would be a permanent part of the school going forward. It turned out to be a great collaborative effort between the twenty-seven of us, and there were a lot of fun parts of the mural. It got a great response from the principal and the board!

Taking on some of Rosa's bravado, I finally felt like I found a way to plow through the pain. Unfortunately, it was short-lived. Right before I graduated junior high, Nana became seriously ill. Her doctor told me she would need to be moved to a nursing home to receive the care she needed. I wouldn't turn fourteen until the middle of the summer, so as a minor, the authorities had to figure out what to do with me. It could not have been worse timing. I naturally looked to Amelia for what I should do, but this was the year she graduated from college. Her days here in Brighton were ending.

Amelia told me before she left, "Sarah, I want you to know. Every year that I came back to Brighton, social services offered me different children to mentor, but I would have none of it! You are my little sister! If you have to live life imitating Rosa, do it! But live life! Push through it. Remember, I'll be just around the corner if you need me." As I grew older, I realized I was too young to understand I should have gotten her forwarding information, and when I finally asked later, social services never would release it.

My new caseworker was older and exceedingly serious about her job. I remember her asking me so many questions and making notes in the pad she kept by her side. They moved me to a shelter farther from the beach and my school. I begged them to let me at least say goodbye to the principal and some of the few friends I had made while painting the mural. I can't remember that caseworker's name, but her supervisor drove me to the school herself to say my goodbyes.

The principal took me out into the hallway to study the mural. She took my hand and said, "Sarah, look how far you have come! Your talent is magical. Children who come to this school in the future will see your painting every day and identify it with the school. Don't forget the impact it will have on so many children in the years to come. When you are older, come back to see us. I promise it will still be here. Whether you face disappointment, discouragement, or whatever, confront each challenge to get to the other side. Live the magic, Sarah, because you are the magic!" Then she handed me a marker to sign the mural in the corner. "We will never forget you." When she hugged me, I just couldn't pretend anymore and let all the tears built up inside me surface in wracking sobs. It was so hard to let go of her that day. *She believed in me.*

Two or three of my classmates came up to hug me, too, and I realized at that moment they liked me for me, not just for the pretend person I thought I was showing them. So I reasoned, those who really like me will see through my pretense to the real me. How could I have known at thirteen that hiding behind Rosa's bravado kept the darkest sadness and feeling of abandonment locked deep inside?

The caseworker took me to the nursing home to see Nana. She looked so frail, and the memory of seeing my mum lying in the ER burnt came flooding back. I am sure I must have cringed. Nana reached her hand out to me. Tears were flowing down her cheeks. Weakly, she began, "Oh, child, I realize now. I have been so unfair to you." Looking at the caseworker, she said, "Please take her back to my house. Hidden under my bed is a box Sarah needs to have. I need to know she gets it." Back to me, holding my hand, she continued, "About six months after Mary Margaret's funeral, I received a letter from your father. He said he deeply regretted leaving like he did and being so dreadful to you at the funeral. I was furious at him and almost tore up the letter. You do look more and more like your mum every day, Sarah. The exact reason your father left was why I wanted you to stay with me. Over the years, the letters continued almost every month, begging me to let him see you, or at least talk to you." Stunned, I withdrew my hand. *My father wanted to see me?*

Nana was still talking. I tried to focus. "William said he wanted to at least provide for you and usually sent money with the letters. Other than what I put in our secret box to spend on art school and art supplies, it is all still there in the box. I kept it there in case of an emergency. I know now how terribly wrong I was. There is no way I can make it up to you. Go to your father, Sarah. He loves you! Please try to forgive me. Losing your mum the way we did affected all of us. When you see your father, tell him I'm sorry."

Chapter 5

My world turned upside down once again that day. I think I looked at my caseworker wanting her to help me understand. She simply shook her head in disbelief. She drove me back to my grandmother's house, and I retrieved the box from under the bed. She and I sat on the sofa and opened the box to find thirty-two letters, three birthday cards, and a rubber-banded wad of bills. She got her notepad and wrote the inventory. We counted the money. There was seven hundred dollars! She found my father's phone number in one of the letters and wrote it on the pad. Finding two suitcases, she told me to start packing while she walked outside to call Daddy. Daddy? I seemed too old to think of him as "Daddy" anymore. All the hurt inside me had caused me not to think of him at all.

In light of what Nana told them and the evidence in the letters, Social Services agreed to turn me over to my dad. I decided "Dad" would work since the last years' worth of letters ended with "Love, Dad." He drove to Brighton to get me the moment they told him of their decision. I remember being so nervous to see him. All this time, I thought he didn't want me and had forgotten me. That was all untrue, but it wasn't easy to simply switch my feelings.

Feeling awkward the first time we saw each other was to be expected, I suppose. After all, I was a ten-year-old kid when he left, and now I was about to turn fourteen and enter high school. Finally, tears in his eyes, he held out his arms. "Sarah, you look even more like Maggie May, if that is possible. You're beautiful! I was so foolish, not just for running off like I did but not coming back to see you for myself. I don't know how I will ever make it up to you but I will certainly try if you'll let me." That was the moment I walked to my dad's waiting arms, into his embrace, and let his warmth flow into all those cold remote places of abandonment and hurt.

We stayed at Nana's for a few days to settle things with the house. Dad went to see Nana and, in the end, seeing how frail she was, chose to forgive her. After all, Mum's horrific death affected each of us. I took him by my old school to see the mural, and he met the principal, who smiled over at me and winked. He seemed to like my painting, and I have to admit that made me proud. Eventually, we packed up Dad's car with my suitcases, my bike, and my set of paints to drive to Southampton. I watched out the window as Brighton and the days of my youth faded away and looked forward with the hope that a better future lay ahead.

Dad seemed to want to know everything he had missed. I thought it would be awkward between us, but I could tell he was determined to make up for the last four years. I told him about Amelia and how I felt like she was my big sister, and that she came back each year she was in college. I shared about how the paint set came up and then art school. Knowing he had paid for art school, I thanked him because it had become such a part of me. Then there was Amelia's insistence I enroll in drama class and how I found Rosa Bonheur to toughen up my exterior. I saw him look away when I said I needed to pretend to be someone else to interact with people. The one thing we never talked about was that day at the hospital and the day of the funeral.

Dad told me about his job as a journalist. He mostly did local pieces, but every now and then, he had to travel for work. He then said he had recently met a lady, Eleanor, whom he occasionally had dinner with. He wanted me to meet her someday soon.

The first thing he did was find a local art school for me for the summer, and I am first to admit my Rosa public face was in full force with all the new people. He arranged a private high school for the fall, but the biggest surprise came on my birthday when I became fourteen. Dad handed me a present. When I opened the present, there was a book about Rosa Bonheur and her animals! Inside the book cover was an invitation to come with him on a five-day trip to Paris, and the biggest surprise of all was that there would be an exhibition of Rosa Bonheur's paintings going on at the Musée d'Orsay! I was jumping up and down with excitement when he smugly said, referring to Rosa's pets, "Just so I'm clear, I draw the line at having wild animals in the house for pets!"

I laughed and was giddy with excitement. We were to leave for Paris in two weeks right before I started my freshman year of high school. I couldn't wait to take the book to my room to study and learn more about this fascinating artist!

15

Chapter 6

That summer with Dad stands out as a highlight of my youth. Rosa Bonheur's book became a bit of an obsession learning about her contrarian antics. And the trip to France with Dad was filled with sightseeing, dinners in special places, and visits to the museums. I was eagerly waiting to see one of Rosa's paintings up close. When I finally did, I think I could have studied it for hours! I tried to envision the layers that would have been required to produce such real-looking three-dimensional animals.

But the end of the summer marked the end of the easygoing days with Dad. I was a freshman at a new school where, once again, I knew no one. I tried to hear Amelia in my head telling me to get out there, even if I had to pretend. All the talk was about soccer games, concerts, and slumber parties. I would watch the others seem to effortlessly fit in and feel that familiar pang of loneliness. I didn't know anything about soccer, and the guys on the team seemed arrogant and distant. Girls walked past me without a glance like I was invisible. At home, Eleanor started coming to the house more frequently. Maybe Dad thought having a teenage girl at home required some female influence. Or maybe he was starved for company his own age. No matter the reason, I had less of his company at night and on the weekends. Painting once again became my lifeline.

My electives at school were art and drama, but I never gave up learning more about Rosa's controversial behavior, her artistic technique, and how she became a genius at painting animals. Rosa went to the zoo and the circus constantly, took a class in anatomy, went to pastures in the countryside to draw, and dressed up like a man to go to the slaughterhouse! And then, unbelievably, she kept an assortment of wild animals as pets to live with them and understand their habits.

As much as I tried to follow in her footsteps, I shook my head in amazement at her brazen defiance of the customs of the day. Rosa lived one hundred years before me! She was also taught by her father, who was a classical painter in his own right. I somehow knew I had to find my own way. The slaughterhouse, keeping wild animals as pets, and a course in anatomy were out for me. Instead, I got a part-time job working on Saturdays at the zoo and on Sundays took the bus just outside of Southampton to a working farm to volunteer to help with the animals.

When it came to Eleanor, I know I misjudged her. She often reached out to me to bond. I'm sure it was frustrating to get little to no response from me. It just wasn't in me to have someone try to replace Mum. By Christmas of my freshman year, they were married, and Eleanor moved in permanently. Time after time, if there was a debate about something, my dad supported her over me. That root of abandonment that I tried so hard to put away reared its ugly head once again. When they expressed their joy that a baby was on the way at the beginning of the following summer, it seemed more than I could take. I asked if there was a summer abroad program or an internship I could do for the summer. It was actually Eleanor, probably happy not to have me underfoot, who found an apprenticeship I could do in London for the summer. I didn't realize it would be another changing point in my life, but I also didn't realize how my eagerness to leave made Dad and Eleanor feel.

I could hardly contain my excitement that I was working at an art gallery! They offered room and board at the curator's upstairs loft, but no pay. There were artists onsite doing restoration of classic paintings, and I would be there to assist them. It was fascinating, and at the gallery I was in my element, like a sponge soaking up knowledge. There I discovered other artists' styles that were different from Rosa's and unique in their own way. That apprenticeship taught me to study another artist's work and put my head and my brush into their thought process. If I could somehow determine how they could paint it, I could figure out how to paint it myself. I learned what was so important was to maintain the integrity of the original artist.

There was a young artist, Tara, who had just been hired by the gallery to begin their training program. Her easel was set up in one of the galleries working to replicate a classical painting from the 1700s. Tara noticed me watching and took me under her wing to explain her approach, dissecting in her mind the layers of foundation of paint necessary to provide depth. I am sure that is when I began my annoying habit of chewing on the tip of my brush when I study a scene. Tara would set up an easel for me next to her and challenge me to duplicate her current step and then quiz me on what the next step would be. Although Tara's painting actually looked close to the original, I could tell mine did not have the richness or the soul of the painting.

Toward the end of the summer, the curator came up to stand behind me, watching. "Sarah, the gallery would like to ask you back next summer if your father will allow it. We think you have promise. It would still be an apprentice position, but you would receive a small wage for your work." Tara gave me a thumbs-up! It was interesting that it was these two young women, Amelia and Tara, both older, who accepted me as I was and offered me the support and friendship I so desperately needed.

Back in high school as a sophomore, I stayed as busy as I could, primarily not to be at the house where Harry, no doubt named for the prince since my father was William, was a holy terror. Nothing felt right at home. I continued my job at the zoo on Saturdays and was promoted to feeding the monkeys and the lions. I studied how their mannerisms and facial expressions changed when they were hungry. I was unaware at the time how I would draw upon this experience at the zoo later in life.

Chapter 7

During the school year, I tried to merely exist and work on my painting until the following summer. I remember a group of classmates whispering about me one afternoon and heard the word *loner*. I know I seemed different...I felt different. By now, I understood Rosa purposefully dressed up like a man and cropped her hair short. I didn't go that far, but I did not emphasize my feminine side either. As for my hair, I let it grow long, usually carelessly tied up in a ponytail. There were a few times when a classmate would try to befriend me, but my shyness was so ingrained in me I just couldn't. I was told once I came across aloof and self-important. That night I cried myself to sleep knowing they did not know the real me. The problem was that I was confused and didn't know me either. Somehow pretending to be brave made me feel even more alone. It was as if for nine months I was a square peg trying to fit into a round opening, and then I would arrive at the gallery and the opening would magically adjust so I fit.

That second summer, Tara was promoted to the restoration department. She had taken a break from college and was finally earning a respectable living! The curator put me out in the gallery to try the replicating. He watched closely to see my progress, and I knew every afternoon of painting during the school year had paid off. I found it intriguing to watch Tara meticulously blend her oil colors to precisely match the area of whatever painting she was currently restoring. Other times she would come to watch me and offer ideas on techniques for me to attempt. We would often take our breaks at the same time or have lunch together in the cafeteria. It was still difficult to go into a cafeteria knowing what a kitchen explosion had done to my mum. That summer, I finally told Tara about what happened and tears rolled down her eyes. We developed a friendship, the first I'd had since Amelia. She invited me to her flat where we popped popcorn and watched sappy movies. I showed her my book about Rosa Bonheur and I remember her staring at me a little longer than usual. I wondered why, but I was so happy to have a friend I shrugged it off.

When the summer before my senior year came to an end, I was seventeen. The curator asked me to his office and to sit down. I thought he would discuss coming back the next summer, but that was not what was in store. "Sarah, I have spoken at length with your father about the talent and potential I see in you. I took the liberty of having your transcripts from school sent along with some examples of your work to an art school outside of Paris that takes boarding students. They mostly offer college courses, but if a student is particularly bright or talented, they will occasionally take a few high school seniors. You have been offered a scholarship there! Your father would like to discuss it with you first prior to accepting, but I think this would be a wonderful opportunity for you!" I know I was speechless and most likely in a state of shock!

So many mixed feelings were racing through my mind. *Would my father say yes? I would not see my classmates again, but I really didn't have any friends other than Tara, and she was in London. I would once again be among strangers. But most importantly, they wanted me and they thought I was good enough for a scholarship!* I promised to call Dad to get a final answer and went to tell Tara.

Tara jumped up! "Oh my gosh! Paris! I am so jealous. You deserve this, Sarah." Tara held me tight in congratulations, and I was thrilled to have someone to share this exciting news with.

I remembered that principal who believed in me when I was thirteen and told me to "live the magic." At that moment, nothing would stop me. I grabbed Rosa's well-worn book...Rosa and I were going to Paris!

I thanked the curator for all he had done for me these past summers, and he wished me much success. "Down the road, if you ever need work, Sarah, come see me." I never forgot that. I said goodbye to Tara and promised to write. That was when I regretted not being able to share this news with Amelia and called Social Services in Brighton to see if I could find her forwarding address, but with no success.

My father said yes to my going and then happily announced Eleanor was pregnant again. He had his new family, and I seemed like an outsider, so it was just as well I was leaving. When Eleanor took me shopping for new clothes to take to boarding school, it never occurred to me that she was doing it with affection, not duty. I was just too naïve to understand it was me who, like the classmates said, was aloof and the reason why I was alienated from the family. I just didn't know that or how to fix it.

Chapter 8

My dad was more nervous than I was on the train ride to Paris. He lectured me on the perils of a seventeen-year-old girl alone in such a cosmopolitan city with unconstrained morals and a mecca for free-spirited thinking. I was one of only six high school seniors, so everyone else would be older.

We found my dorm room and put my stuff on the empty bed. I had never had a roommate before, and the very idea was incredibly intimidating. Would she leave me alone? As if on cue, a perky not-so-slim brunette literally bounced into the room carrying a bag of pastries. "Oh my gosh! These French pastries are divine! Hi, I'm Beth. Have one!" She held the bag out to me and my dad. "I'm going to gain a hundred pounds!"

Beth made me laugh! It was such an unfamiliar feeling. I introduced myself, and she babbled on, "You know there's just six of us seniors, right? They are having an orientation for us at two o'clock. I just got here this morning. I'm from Sussex, so we're practically neighbors. I'm going to see who else is on our floor and find out where the boy's dorm is. Oops! Sorry, Sarah's dad!" As quick as that, Beth bounced out. Dad and I stared at each other in disbelief about the tornado that just came through the room!

Dad shook his head. "Sarah, this is nothing like anything you have ever experienced. Are you sure you will be all right? If you have any second thoughts, just call me and I'll come get you. Sweetheart, I want you to have this opportunity, but Eleanor and I will miss you terribly."

"That's just it, Dad. It is different. My roommate made me laugh! I want to laugh and try new things. Make friends. Look, Beth has already set up her half of the room. I need to do mine. Orientation should get us going in the right direction. I promise to call, okay? Don't worry." With a hug goodbye, my dad left, and I felt the most sensational sense of freedom and excitement about the adventure that was to come! I was in a school with students dedicated to art like me.

Just as I finished unpacking, Beth returned ready to report her discoveries. She found the cafeteria where we could get lunch before orientation. She had met the two other girls, who were also seniors, Yvette from Nice and Suzanne from Zurich. They were rooming together too. Beth couldn't get in the boys' dorm, but she at least got to find out there were two high school senior boys, James from Chicago and Peter from Glasgow. Beth chattered on about our international group, all of whom were strangers. I vividly remember a cold set of nerves rising in me to meet these students, especially the two boys. I had never had a date, much less a boyfriend!

Beth practically dragged me to the cafeteria to meet Suzanne and Yvette. What I realized at lunch was that other than Beth with her outgoing nature, the other two girls seemed as timid as me. What we had in common was our mutual love of art and our willingness to give up our senior year in high school for this experience. It was definitely not a sacrifice for me, but I didn't know about the others.

The four of us arrived at orientation together. James and Peter were already there. Monsieur Reynaud ushered us in. When we were seated, he introduced himself. *"Mes étudiants, je m'appelle* Monsieur Reynaud. I will be your counselor for this year. Welcome to L'École d'Artes! We have only recently begun this program to allow exceptionally talented high school seniors into our curriculum. The six of you were chosen from over one hundred applicants from all over Europe and the States. We take your youth and education, as well as your artistic talent, very seriously. Although your professor will conduct your classes in English this year, we insist you be fluent in French if you are accepted to enroll as a freshman next year. The six of you are expected to work together and help each other throughout the program. Try to let go of any personal hidden agenda you might have and consider yourselves beginning on an equal playing field. Now, allow me to introduce you to Professor Bernard. She is a gifted scholar and an acclaimed artist in her own right. Professor..."

Chapter 9

Professor Bernard appeared to be in her forties, medium build with short chin-length brown hair and dark spectacles she used when reading or writing. "Thank you, Monsieur Reynaud. Welcome to each of you. You have taken a grand step to study your senior year here with us, and we intend to give you an exceptional education as well as dig deep into your talent to determine if you have what it takes to be an *artiste de prestige*. You will be working together closely so let's get an idea of who you are, where you're from, what artist most inspires you, and what style of painting they represent."

Not so surprising, Beth raised her hand first. Unapologetically eager, with light-brown hair braided down her back, Beth spoke up. "I am Beth from Sussex, England. I have five brothers and sisters and I fall into the middle. Painting has always been a passion of mine and I love the work of Henri Matisse, a French visual artist from the nineteenth century. I believe you would call his style Fauvism."

Peter was next. Slim, dark hair neatly parted on the side, he looked very wholesome and clean-cut. "I am Peter from the port city of Glasgow, Scotland, known for its art nouveau architecture. Perhaps that is the influence that had me fascinated with Toulouse Lautrec and his Art Nouveau style. My father is also an artist, and I have apprenticed with him. At home, I live with my parents and brother who is two years younger than me. And in case you're interested, I did bring a kilt or two." That got a chuckle from the room.

Yvette raised her hand next. Very tall and slim, Yvette's blond hair was cut close to her head with a single narrow braid suspended from her hairline down one shoulder. There was a bright pink streak through the middle of the tufted front. "I am Yvette from Nice, in the south of France. My mother is divorced, and I live at home with her and my two younger sisters. I discovered the artist who most inspires me on a trip to Barcelona during a tour of the Salvador Dali Museum. He was a genius, in my opinion, and his style is Surrealism."

Although I knew perfectly well who my artist would be, I found myself holding back. Suzanne, a shoulder-length brunette with glasses and a petite body, began, "I am Suzanne from Zurich, Switzerland, and am an avid skier! I began painting at a young age because I wanted to convey some feeling or emotion I was experiencing at the time. I had a teacher in school who was very influential in helping me. Since I'm an only child living at home with my parents, I wasn't sure they would let me accept this position. As far as an artist's inspiration, I admire Paul Gaugin, who wanted art to represent emotions and ideas rather than the natural world. His style is Symbolism."

That left James and me. He glanced at me, and I nodded for him to go. An African American, James was impeccably dressed and had a smile that could warm hearts. "Hi, I'm James from Chicago, USA. Downtown where I grew up, there was street graffiti everywhere. I have to admit I might have participated a time or two. But when I pick up an easel, I think of the piece with all the versions of Marilyn Monroe's face that Andy Warhol did. I used to paint a canvas looking at a scene and wonder how he would paint it. At one of the local art shows, I started selling them. It was one of those patrons who encouraged me to apply here. Warhol's style is Pop Art."

It was my turn. *Just tell the necessities.* "I am Sarah. I grew up in Brighton, England, where I began going to art school in the summers while living with my grandmother. Before high school, I moved to Southampton to live with my dad and stepmom. From the early days of art school, the artist who made the most impression on me was Rosa Bonheur and her amazing paintings of animals. I interned at a gallery in London for two summers, and it was the curator who sent in my application. Rosa's unconventional lifestyle intrigues me, and her style would be Realism."

Professor Bernhard had listened carefully and made notes. She then said, "Well done. Good choices, each of you. You have just outlined our Art Intro class, which we will divide into six styles to study: Fauvism, Art Nouveau, Surrealism, Symbolism,

Pop Art, and Realism. As we move through each style, I will call upon you to demonstrate an example of what we study. What I do find most interesting is that five out of six of you selected male artists. Yet there are four females and two males in this class. Should we presume the females are doomed to be of lesser artistic importance?" She looked at me and added, "In many ways, Rosa Bonheur painstakingly paved the way for women artists. Sarah, for our first class, I would like you to prepare to explain to the class how she did this." *Wow! Rosa was there with me!*

Chapter 10

There I was in 1989, at seventeen years old, sharing a dream of finding an artistic path through art school in Paris like so many thousands before. Paris has drawn aspiring artists as a center of inspiration through revolutions, the founding of the Louvre Museum, the coveted collections of art (primarily Italian) by the French monarchy, and the bohemian artist colonies throughout the city.

It was here, with this group of five other art students granted a scholarship under the tutelage of Professor Bernhard, that I would find my voice both for my art as well as my individuality. That first assignment could not have been more perfect. How to explain Rosa Bonheur's role in paving the way for women artists? She had been my obsession for so long, and I now had the chance to share the impact of her story. I planned what I wanted to share with my class and warmed to my topic.

Maybe it was those drama classes, or maybe it was the passion I had about my topic, but I went into class ready to explain Rosa Bonheur's impact on women artists that still affects us today. I began by telling the other students how I found Rosa amidst the stacks of library books I brought home to study when asked to paint a mural for my school in eighth grade. They wanted an animal theme with an educational twist. My story went something like this:

"It intrigued me that as a small child, Rosa was already drawing pictures of chickens and roosters in the dirt. Then Rosa's mother came up with the idea for Rosa to learn her ABCs by drawing an animal whose name started with each letter of the alphabet. It was that idea that I took and engaged the help of other students to finish the alphabet animal mural.

"At age eleven, Rosa was living in Paris with her mother, younger brothers, and sister in dire poverty. Her mother tragically died that year as mine did when I was ten. Another thing we had in common. Her father, Raimond, was key to her story, as he idealistically believed men and women should be considered equal...a premise unheard of in the mid-1800s. When the school near them took her two brothers into their classroom, the priest running the school saw how bereft Rosa was in losing her brothers to play with. He offered to let her also attend class, and Raimond quickly accepted. Imagine, just to get an education as a female among the lower class was rare in their time. Raimond was a painter in his own right, and it turned out each of his children inherited that gift. In order to earn a living, Raimond opened an art school to teach Realism painting, seeking to paint the world exactly as it was, good or bad.

"Rosa became a pupil of his at age thirteen, and by age sixteen, she sold her first painting for one hundred francs, or the equivalent then to the average monthly wage of the time! Painting was her passion, in particular painting animals. She would study them for hours to determine how to portray them accurately, especially their eyes. Her pet rabbits were the inspiration for her *Rabbits Nibbling Carrots* that got selected for presentation at the Louvre Museum's annual Salon in 1840, which attested to her growing talent. She was nineteen. Within eight years, Rosa had six paintings presented at the Salon and had won her first gold medal!

"Critics, mostly male, tried to belittle her talent. However, when the French government commissioned her to do a painting to represent French farming, the result was *Plowing in the Nivernais*, which still hangs in the royal Palace of Fontainebleau. Her talent could no longer be denied. Rosa continued to defy the stigma that to be a fine artist meant you had to be male. In order to study horses and other animals thoroughly enough, she insisted on visiting the Paris slaughterhouse and horse fair where horses were bought and sold. Both places were off limits to women, but that didn't stop Rosa. She dressed up like a man and went anyway. It was those experiences that helped her create the massive painting, *The Horse Fair*, which was presented at the 1853 Salon and hangs today at the Metropolitan Museum of Art in New York City. Her work even caught the attention of Empress Eugenie, who personally visited Rosa and presented her with the highest award, the Legion d'Honneur, ever given to a woman prior to that time.

"Rosa Bonheur became known as the most famous female artist of her day, and she encouraged and paved the way for other female artists. She lived to see the first year ten female students were finally allowed into the premier art school in Paris, a giant step forward for female artists!"

I suddenly realized how long I had been speaking to the class, but no one had interrupted me. Professor Bernhard stood up and smiled. "Sarah, what an insightful presentation. Well done!" And to the class, she said, "I suppose you wonder why you don't hear of Rosa Bonheur more frequently. Rosa died in 1899. It was at the turn of the century that Impressionism came roaring into the art world with artists like Monet, Renoir, Manet, Pissarro, Degas, and Cezanne. Realism's popularity waned. However, that does not deny the talent and the influence on female artists brought to the art world by Rosa Bonheur."

Chapter 11

Beth did her presentation on Fauvism and Henri Matisse at the following class, and the other students one by one after that. I was amazed at how immersed each student was with their artist of choice and how that artist's influence showed in their work. I could understand why no one interrupted me after seeing each of the other presentations and the passion that lay behind them.

As seniors, we were not allowed to take life drawing classes with nude models yet, but Professor Bernhard allowed us hours in museums, studying statues of the human form. She also created an exercise where we would take one of our paintings and try to translate it into the other styles we were learning about. I found the class and the professor both fascinating and liberating. The six of us did everything together, and a strong friendship blossomed between us. I was perfectly content staying at the dorm during holidays when the others visited home, although I felt the need to tell my disappointed dad a made-up story about needing extra time for an art project. A visit back to Dad and Eleanor and their two children held no appeal to me. Usually James would also stay because of the high cost and distance to get to Chicago.

When we were at school on our own, one of our favorite activities was to go to Montmartre, the very center of the Paris art community. There was so much there lurking beneath the surface of artists and their easels drawing portraits of tourists for money. James and I would sit at our favorite outdoor café and watch for hours to pick up the dynamic unfolding between these starving artists and what they had to do to survive. In the end, what we learned made us work harder to succeed in order to earn a living from painting.

The end of our senior year was fast approaching. The year seemed to have sped by, and I knew for certain I had found my calling. That didn't stop the nerves for all of us when we found out there was to be a series of challenge paintings required and judged by the upper-class professors. We had to pass the series to be invited back with a full scholarship. Beth and I worked out an area in our dorm room to set up our easels and keep working after school hours. Even Beth's perpetual good humor was subdued with this daunting task. It took our full concentration. We had to produce six individual paintings in the medium of our choice to represent each of the six styles of painting we studied throughout the year. We could choose one to feature, and it would represent 50 percent of our score. The other five represented 10 percent each, but we had to have an overall score of 75 percent to maintain our position and scholarship!

Beth and I debated everything from subject matter to choice between acrylic or oil paints. I tried to focus on my times at the zoo, on the farm, and at the London gallery...but mostly tried to breathe in what Rosa would advise me to do. I studied the details in the paintings in her book, finding the layers creating the dimension of her animals. When I picked up a *National Geographic* magazine at the library showing the natural dependency between the zebras and wildebeest during the migration in Africa, and how they travel together, I decided to paint the migration as my feature. How ironic that I would be painting the actual migration live in Africa years later and that it would be my first painting to sell. It was that senior year painting that planted the seed of the artist I strived to become.

Our paintings were displayed in the banquet hall for the judging and for the upperclassmen to view. We were not allowed to be there when the judges presented their opinions and scores. The six of us waited in the classroom, periodically pacing, encouraging, and holding each other's hands. Professor Bernhard returned from the hall with six envelopes, which she passed out. In unison, we opened them, realizing how important this was to our future. Only four of us passed. Beth and Suzanne missed by just a few points, but there was no makeup. Their only option to return in the fall was to come back as a freshman paying full tuition. Yvette, Peter, James, and I consoled them the best we could while being individually filled with relief it wasn't us. I never saw Beth or Suzanne again after we said goodbye for the summer. To this day, I will never forget Beth and her joyful manner that was all-accepting and never allowed me to feel alone.

Chapter 12

I had a two-week break before going back to London to work at the gallery for the summer. The last time I had seen my dad was the day he brought me to L'École d'Artes. He met me at the train station to take me home for the two weeks. Looking at him, I thought he looked rather tired. Then, once we were home with two small children running and screaming everywhere, I could understand why. Eleanor was the one who picked up the change in me. She could see my more confident nature and went on about how mature I seemed. She was right. I had changed. I would never get over the death of my mum or my dad leaving me, but the time in Paris had given me an anchor and a family of sorts and, most importantly, a sense of achievement. I had gotten the highest score in my class with 96 percent. Professor Bernhard had pulled me aside that last day to tell me how proud she was and that she knew Rosa Bonheur was smiling down from heaven to see a new protégé. It made me more determined than ever to try to be the best artist I could.

Eleanor and I had several talks on that visit. She shared how surprisingly difficult it was having two young children at an older age. She asked about Paris, and I told her how serious the six of us were about learning and being the best we could at our art. She wanted to know if I had met any interesting boys and if I had a boyfriend. I thought about James and Peter and laughed a bit. I explained the six of us for the most part traveled as a pack and didn't have much time for outsiders. Then I told her we had lost two at the end, which meant I would room with Yvette for our freshman year.

Dad seemed very happy I had maintained my scholarship, since finances were a little tight for them at the moment with two young children to feed and educate. I have to admit I was too. I can't imagine the conversations Beth and Suzanne were having with their families. It gave me a sense of independence and I planned to take *The Migration* painting with me to London to show the curator. Funny but not so funny is, Dad never asked to see any of my paintings. Because of that, I never offered.

The two weeks eventually ended, and I was on my way back to the London Gallery. This summer, with the salary that I would receive, I was able to rent an apartment! It was a small third-floor walk-up flat with uneven floors, which didn't even matter because I had my own place! I bought a bike to get around and determined while I was here to get to know the city better.

There was a new director of the gallery when I arrived for work. His name was Mr. Templeton. I debated whether to follow the curator who not only brought me back but also got me into the L'École d 'Artes with a scholarship. Tara had moved galleries with him. She wrote to me there would be a place for me there as well. In the end, I decided to stay at the original gallery, but I made a pledge to myself to never forget the people who helped me forge into what I would become.

Mr. Templeton welcomed me back and asked how my first year in Paris went. I showed him my notice of the 96 percent score and went to retrieve my painting of *The Migration*. He put his glasses on and studied the painting and then looked back at me. "Sarah, here is what I propose. I have a category here at the gallery where I present 'Emerging Artists.' I have certain patrons who are always looking for the next amazing artist. Why don't I hang it in that gallery and let's just see where it goes?"

He put me again in Replication rather than Restoration because of my youth and inexperience. He assured me one more year in Paris should allow me to move up. At school, I had replicated so many paintings and styles that this was a breeze for me. But ten days later, my assignment changed. That morning, Mr. Templeton pulled up a chair next to me where I was working on a painting. He began, "Last night, the gallery hosted a dinner for our upper-tier patrons. It was held here with all the exhibits open for viewing. One of our patrons was particularly interested in *The Migration*. I told him it was painted by a student who was training in Paris and worked here in Replication during the summer. He asked me if I thought the painting could be translated or replicated onto a larger format."

Hearing him, the first thing I thought of was Rosa Bonheur painting *The Horse Fair* on an eight-by-sixteen foot canvas! *The Migration* was currently eighteen by twenty-eight inches. "I brought my pad with all the original sketches. How large is he thinking?"

Mr. Templeton replied, "He said he would like a three-by-five-foot piece. He realizes you would have to add a small amount of width from the original. He said if I allowed you to work on it here this summer during gallery time under my tutelage, he would pay you, the artist, three hundred pounds and the gallery a hundred and fifty pounds! What do you think, Sarah? Can you do it?"

My mind whirled! Three hundred pounds? My first sale! Rosa was sixteen when she sold her first painting for one hundred francs...I am about to turn eighteen. Close enough! I excitedly answered, "Yes, I would be happy to replicate it to his requested size. When do we begin?"

I smiled as Mr. Templeton stared at me with renewed interest. "This is powerful news, Sarah. This particular patron is an avid collector and has an eye for discovering new talent. Others learning of his buying a painting of yours will begin watching for your work. Finish the piece you are currently working on. I will order the three-by-five-foot canvas. Bring your sketches in, and I will pull out the art projector for you to get the proper size adjustment from projecting your images onto the canvas."

Ah, technology. It seemed a little...well, really a lot...like cheating. I determined to use the projector to mark a few pivot points for size, but nothing more. Yes, it would be replicated, but it would also be an original. And hopefully even better than the smaller version! Excitement bubbled up in me as I began the project. I took my time. True to myself, I put the projector away after placing a few charcoal marks to indicate the varying heights and widths of the zebras and wildebeest. I do believe Mr. Templeton thought I was being foolhardy, but he remained silent on the subject of the projector.

Chapter 13

I had found my footing in Paris, but that summer in London, I found my soul. An art collector liked my work and was willing to pay me for it. The gallery actually paid me to use their facility and supplies to paint it! Living independently, I began to discover my own rules of when to eat and when to sleep. I took my bike to Tara's gallery to see her work and had the opportunity to thank the curator, Mr. Phillips, who had helped me. Tara came to watch me paint and discuss my emerging technique. We frequently met for dinner and occasionally went to a show. I did the typical tourist activities on my own. The difference now was, I could be alone but not lonely. I was working hard on my French to take this experience back to Paris. I had heard from James and Yvette, and they were both also working at galleries.

On *The Migration*, I followed the same master plan as on the original, but this time, I wasn't trying to paint five other paintings in styles I wasn't used to at the same time. I could step back and consider what I called subtle updates, particularly in the details like the eyes and fur. I'm sure the tips of my brushes were well chewed upon as I pondered. People would occasionally stop by and watch and then perhaps make a comment. For the most part, my concentration blocked it out...until one day when a young woman stopped by to watch. The difference was, she was not just watching me paint but watching me. That got my attention, and I turned to look at her. There standing in front of me was Amelia! A sob tore out of me as all the pain of those four years after my mum died rushed back to me and how this one young woman got me through it. I ran to her, crying. "Amelia, I didn't know how to find you! I've wanted to thank you so often. I tried Social Services, and they wouldn't give me your address. Oh my god, it is so good to see you. How did you find me?"

Amelia was crying, too, and we couldn't stop hugging. "Everything was so crazy in my life when I graduated college. My parents were going through a divorce, and it was difficult at home, so I moved here to London to get a job. It has been five years! Look at you all grown-up! Sarah, you're beautiful. I tried to find you too. When I reached out to Social Services, they told me you went to live with your father once your grandmother went to the nursing home, but they wouldn't tell me where. I was hoping you would find happiness there, but I was worried about you."

"My dad remarried and has two small children. I survived high school by coming here to work during the summers as an intern. After my junior year, the curator helped me get a scholarship to an art school in Paris for my senior year!" Pointing at the original painting, I added, "This was my final assignment at school that enabled me to renew my scholarship and go back in the fall. One of the patrons here wants a larger-sized copy, and that's what I've been working on."

Amelia smiled and nodded. "It was the painting that drew my attention. I kept looking at it thinking it seemed familiar. Then it hit me! It reminds me of that painting you loved by Rosa Bonheur. When I saw you, I recognized the grown-up version of that little girl I loved like a sister."

"Yes! *The Horse Fair*! You remembered? I am painting because of you! But a lot of my style comes from Rosa's technique. It makes me so happy to have found you after all this time." We went to the café next door to catch up, and it was as though the five-year gap of time in our friendship disappeared into thin air. I introduced her to Tara, and these two women, about the same age, having had such an influence on my life, quickly became friends themselves. This year for my birthday, I turned eighteen with these two amazing friends by my side.

Chapter 14

Toward the end of the summer, I was putting the finishing touches on the larger version of *The Migration* when Mr. Templeton brought the buyer in to scrutinize the new painting. He was introduced simply as El Amir from Marrakech in Morocco. His demeanor disguised the fact that he was a young man. I found myself studying this man of visual contradictions as if assessing a subject for a new painting. He wore a collarless ivory shirt with loose black pants and a burgundy textured scarf held by thick black cording as his headdress. He had piercing eyes that for the moment were focused on my painting. There was the most unusual golden tint in what would be brown eyes, somewhat like panning for gold in a shallow rocky-bottom river and finding tiny golden nuggets. His darker complexion and short black sculpted beard emphasized those eyes.

Looking back on that first meeting, I knew then I would paint those eyes over and over, trying to portray them. He turned his attention to me and said, "There is a difference from the original." Looking at Mr. Templeton, he added, "I asked that it be copied."

Before Mr. Templeton could answer, I felt like I had to defend myself. "Sir, I apologize if the painting is not to your liking. I am an artist, not a copy machine."

El Amir laughed at my indignation, and that stern demeanor softened to reveal a twinkle in those golden eyes. "Sarah, is it? I never said I didn't like it. I can see the subtle added nuances that add both realism and dimension. Realism as an art form is unfortunately not practiced enough by modern artists. It is refreshing to see such talent from one so young. But, Sarah, the painting is incomplete."

I looked all over the painting, trying to understand what was missing. El Amir pointed to the bottom corner. "Your signature, my dear. I plan to be the envy of art collectors around the globe to

have an original Sarah Wilkinson!" I'm sure I was blushing pro-
fusely as I reached for the brush to add my signature.

He nodded with a smile. "That is something you'll want to
practice over and over until you get your recognizable personal
signature. I have to admit that I look forward to discovering what
you learn in Paris over the next school year! Perhaps you can do
another piece for me? When do you go back?"

I answered, "I finish the week at the gallery and then go home
for a week before returning to Paris. I promise I will paint something special for you over the school year. What is your favorite
animal?"

El Amir thought and then said, "I love the sport of falconry. I
own two falcons with long brown feathers and spotted chests that
I train to hunt. From the time each of them rests on the wooden
block, to having their hood removed and transferred to the gauntlet on my arm...all lead to its release to find his prey, return with
it, and ring the bell attached to his ankle."

It seemed a challenge of sort, which made me anxious to get
to work. To El Amir, I replied, "I have never painted birds before.
They've always seemed to be such delicate creatures, but a bird of
prey? That sounds exciting!" El Amir handed me an envelope with
my payment and one to Mr. Templeton, who said he would have
the painting packaged and shipped.

When I met Tara and Amelia that night to celebrate, I glee-
fully picked up the tab! During our evening, the two of them began
comparing boyfriend issues. Neither seemed so happy about them
at the moment, and I wondered again if a boyfriend was even in
the cards for me. I would never have guessed how that subject
would elude me for yet another year.

38

Chapter 15

The week back in Southampton was filled with preparations for college. The French class I fit in over the summer had significantly helped. I wasn't totally fluent, but I could get by. I was planning to continue French during the year as an elective. Eleanor offered to take me shopping again, which was sweet. To be honest, fashions in the sleepy little sea town of Southampton did not have the fashion twist that living in such a cosmopolitan town as Paris required. Yvette and I had corresponded about the upcoming year and possibly doing a little shopping before classes got into full swing. Last year, she had found a street with some soho-type resale shops that might be perfect for us. So I decided to ask Dad for a clothing allowance instead that I could use once I got there.

Plus, I had the money left from the sale of *The Migration*. Mr. Templeton had shipped the larger version to El Amir. He decided to keep the original for the time being and moved it over to the permanent collection. I said my farewells to Tara and Amelia with promises to write. I thought about whether to take my bike to Paris, but in the end, it made more sense to leave it with Tara.

I think Eleanor wanted to come with Dad and me to help me get set up in the dorm. Unfortunately, with two children under the age of four, it was impossible. The drive was pleasant, offering more time together than the train. It was mostly filled with parental platitudes about staying safe in the big bad city of Paris! I finally told Dad about *The Migration*. It was that painting, for the most part, that got my scholarship renewed. I then went on to tell him about making a larger version for a patron of the gallery and that I had sold my first painting. I think that was the first time he actually believed I might earn a living from painting!

When we got to L'École d'Artes, I found my dorm room on a different floor than last year. I felt a moment's pang of missing Beth's outgoing manner and apprehension about rooming with

Yvette. I had to do a double take when I saw her! Gone was the small braid and brazen buzz haircut, replaced by a head full of soft blond curls. I hardly recognized her and asked, "Yvette! What happened to that defiant exterior from last year?"

"Ah, *mon petite chou*, it was a stage I wanted to try. I like the occasional experiment, *n'est ce pas*? I was tired of these unruly curls and wanted a change. Then, over the summer, I got tired of people assuming they knew the kind of person I was because of the way I wore my hair!" I was amazed that I had fallen into the same trap in assuming who she was because of her hair. So who was she for real? I had been used to putting on a false face. Had she as well? For some reason, it made me curious to find out who the real Yvette was.

I said goodbye to my dad and began to unpack. Yvette was working on her side of the dorm room and I casually asked, "Do you suppose James and Peter will be at the Hut tonight?" I assumed the four of us would pick up our friendship where we left it. The Hut had become our hangout in the last semester.

Yvette sat on her bed folding clothes and said, "It will be different this year with twenty-eight of us freshmen." She was thoughtful for a few minutes and then added, "I read more about Rosa Bonheur over the summer knowing we would be room-mates. She didn't think too much of men, did she?"

Internally, I had rationalized her unconventional lifestyle, which I shared. "She grew up in a world that we can't even begin to understand as women. The education we are receiving today would have been impossible in her time. She had to dress up like a man to be allowed into certain places, and in many ways she had to think like a man to force her way to recognition as the talented artist she was. Maybe all that affected how she felt about men and women. Other than her father and brothers, I doubt she trusted men enough to open herself up to one. Although it must have been horribly frowned upon at the time, I find it very interesting that her long relationship with Nathalie Micas, her childhood friend, was fully supported by Nathalie's parents, who treated her like a second daughter. And after Nathalie died, Rosa's second nature was to support young aspiring female artists to offer them a chance at fame. That was how she met Anna Klumpke, who loved and idolized her. Who knows the influences that make us turn out the way we do? I know my mum's death and my dad's abandonment will never leave the core of me." I don't think I ever opened up that much to anyone before, and I looked over at Yvette to see how it was received.

Yvette gently smiled and looked at me with understanding eyes. "My father left Maman, my sisters, and me for a younger woman. She is a fashion designer in Milan, and they now have two small boys. I think I have used art as an escape. Maybe the way I wore my hair was a protest of what was going on in my life. It's also what fascinates me about the artistry of Salvador Dali. His art is an escape from reality but filled with symbolism and irony."

Neither of us had expected this deep conversation. We gained a stronger connection that first day of our freshman year and an understanding of how important art was to both of us. Our following embrace was natural and a testament to the beginning of an important friendship.

Chapter 16

Orientation the next day broke us into four groups. Our freshman class demographic had twenty-eight students representing nine countries which meant the classes would be taught in French. It was our responsibility to have our language skills honed enough to keep up. Secretly, I felt I had an advantage having a French roommate!

As freshmen, we would now be introduced to the Art of Life drawing class with live models, so no more sketching sculptures. Our other art classes would be intermingled with our standard college courses required to graduate. As a side project, outside of class, we were to select a subject to paint a series of a minimum of five paintings that would follow a certain subject matter and visualize it from various angles. The score on this project would represent 25 percent of our grade for the year. None of us had expected something of this magnitude while maintaining our other courses, so a feeling of apprehension ran throughout the auditorium.

Yvette and I went for a soda with James and Peter after the meeting to discuss various possibilities. The two boys were being ridiculously silly regarding the life drawing class, and we just shook our heads. Peter had brought his scooter from home so he would be able to move around in the city and offered a ride to any of us should we need one. There was going to be a mixer for our class Friday afternoon to have a chance to get to know each other a little. We all agreed we missed that outgoing nature of Beth's that would have had us making friends with the whole class in no time. We compared our schedules and found we were in a lot of the same classes. James was worried about his French being strong enough, so he and Yvette set up some time to work on it.

I left them and headed for the library to get ideas for my project. I wandered down aisle after aisle, thumbing through books with a variety of topics. There were several books on artist series, and I started to formulate how to look at the same subject in a variety of ways. Book after book, I kept searching until I reached the one that gave me the inspiration I was looking for...*The Art of Falconry* by Frederick II of Hohenstaufen, Holy Roman Empire, written in 1241. The original book was in the Vatican! I thought about my subjects. The falcons themselves were incredible! Then there was the Arab man with the golden eyes. There was the hunt and the prey. I could feel my fingers itching to start the sketches! The chills that went up my spine confirmed I made a good choice.

Back at the dorm, the note left on my bed said Yvette was working on a French lesson with James. Although the library had the six-volume *Falconry* edition translated into French, I thought I would start with the English version that had been combined into one book. I could study in English and then go back to the French volumes for reference and additional photos. As I began to read, I envisioned El Amir in the arid desert of Morocco with his falcons. As each chapter progressed, I alternated putting myself in the mind of El Amir as the handler and then moving to the experience of this magnificent bird with its perfect eyesight. The process I used was rich with emotions, which I then hoped to interpret onto canvas. The image that kept haunting me was those golden eyes reflecting the sight of the soaring falcon.

I woke up in the dark, feeling disoriented. I must have fallen asleep reading. Yvette had put my book on the side table and put the covers over me. She was sound asleep in her bed. I had no sense of what time it was, only that it felt good someone had actually looked after me. That made it easy to drift back to sleep.

Chapter 17

I woke up early and decided to go for a run. The campus was relatively flat with some beautifully wooded areas, which made for a pleasant start to the day. Classes began today, and mine were scheduled back-to-back until two o'clock. Afterward, I hoped to go to the shop Yvette recommended to find something to wear to the mixer coming up. For now, a run, a quick shower, ponytail in place, a bite to eat...and let the year begin!

Yvette was already gone by the time I got back to the room. I showered and threw on a pair of jeans and a tank top and went to find her in the cafeteria. Peter waved as I finished filling my tray. He was sitting with two cute girls, and I hated to interrupt. Yvette and James were off to the side so I joined them.

They made space at the table and James said, "Yvette told me you were reading a book on falconry!"

"Yes, the patron who bought one of my paintings is from Morocco and has two falcons. I was thinking he might like the series. Have you two thought about what you might do?"

Yvette started, "Living in Nice along the southern coast, everything is about the sea. I have thought about *les poissons* or fish. Possibly a study on their freedom in the sea to their getting caught by a fisherman to getting prepared in the kitchen to being served at the restaurant. I don't think I am locked into surrealism because of last year, but when I think of Dali, I keep coming back to the subject of bells. It sounds strange. I see the bells in lots of different forms all without their clappers. The series would be *Sound of Silence*. I think I just need to start sketching to see what might work best."

James laughed and added, "Why do I keep envisioning Chicago pizza? I am pretty sure I need to keep thinking. Hey, we better get going!"

Our schedule for the day looked the same: History of Literature at 9:00 a.m., Calculus at 10:00 a.m., Life Drawing at 11:00 a.m. Then, after a lunch break, Art of Pastels at 1:00 p.m. Yvette and I agreed to shop after the pastels class, but we had a feeling there was going to be a lot more homework than last year.

Through my high school years, I had been a good student and excelled in note-taking, so although the literary and calculus classes were hard, I followed along pretty well. I also loved the pastels class. I had never used chalks before and loved the way they could be blended with my fingers. The course that gave me trouble was life drawing. I wasn't sure what my problem was. The inanimate sculptures never seemed to be an issue. But here was someone living and breathing with expressions that changed. Our first subject was an older dark-complected woman with wrinkled skin and sad eyes. She was leaning back against a cubicle with a maroon light cover seemingly tossed across her body, covering one shoulder and breast and some of her hip area. There was just so much to take in—the intensity in her eyes, the sadness in her face, the texture of her skin, the drape of the fabric. It was overwhelming.

The professor walked over to my blank canvas and said, "*Quel est le problème, mademoiselle?*"

The only answer I could find was, "I am used to painting animals."

Reasonably, she answered, "Then you must think of her as an animal. Study your subject. Find the nuances. Translate them onto the canvas. The animals you paint live and breathe just like she does. I have seen your work, Sarah. You just need to practice." I tried to look objectively at the scene before me. I etched out the dimensions and produced an outline. I never expected to feel the urge to cover her up. Was it my overwhelming modesty stemming from my shy nature that was at the root of the issue? I knew I had to get past it. The animals I drew wore no clothes, but I had no problem painting their intimate areas.

Once class was over, I looked around at some of the realistic renderings of this woman. I put a cover over my work and, somewhat defeated, went to the pond to sit and think. The female body has been revered throughout the centuries, but I had never before seen a naked female in the flesh, and I had never even studied my own body. Maybe I needed to go back to the library and study the classic artists who had zero problems painting nudes.

Yvette glanced over at me a few times during pastels class as if to check up on me. This class, however, had my full attention, and I left the class pleased with what I had created. As planned, we took the Métro to the shopping area. Yvette and I laughed as we selected vintage resale items that we thought would be fun to reinvent. We mixed and matched colors and styles to create our own look and returned to the dorm pleased with our purchases.

The shopping as well as the pastels class had pulled me out of the dark place of inadequacy I felt during life drawing. Fortunately, I didn't have that class again until Friday. Back in the room, we were pulling clothes out of the bags when Yvette tentatively brought up the subject. "*Chérie*, have you never seen a naked man or woman before today?" Embarrassed to the core, I shook my head. "Ah, we French grow up surrounded by nakedness, so it becomes second nature. Would it help you if you used me as a subject here in the privacy of our room? Maybe it would help you get used to the idea."

For some reason, the idea made total sense to me, astounded at her uninhibited thoughts about it. "You would do that for me? How would we begin?"

"Okay, let's have fun with it. Get your sketchbook." Yvette left on her tall boots and red thong panty and put on the vintage hat she purchased. "Shall I get in a similar position as the woman from class for you to get the shapes? Do I need a drape?"

I began to sketch. "No drape. I like seeing how your body shifts and shadows at certain angles." The first sketch done, my fascination wanted more. "Would you turn over and lean up on your elbows? Yes! Bend your knees and cross your boots. There, perfect!" The curves were perfection, and the thong left little to the imagination. I had a gorgeous subject to move and bend at will, and I took full advantage. I sat her up and took a silk scarf to place around her neck to partially cover her breasts but maintain half exposure. The scarf wasn't lying right, and a frustrated Yvette told me to place it how I wanted it. Inadvertently, in moving the scarf, I touched her breasts, and she gave a sharp intake of breath. Quickly I backed away and apologized.

Yvette smiled at me and, rather huskily, said, "Perhaps I should sketch you. We can't get too much practice, can we?"

Thinking that was only fair, I turned my back and, under my robe, took off my tank top and jeans. Mortally embarrassed to display my big-girl panties, I felt I would be better off without them. With the robe loose in front, I turned around. "What position do you want me in?"

Her sketchbook in hand, Yvette asked me to lie on my side with my top knee rolled forward and then pulled the robe off my shoulder, exposing my breast and torso. Yvette stared at me and began to draw. She finished one sketch and then came over to rearrange my position. I wasn't expecting her to pull my hair out of my ponytail. It had gotten quite long. Before I knew it, the robe was removed, and she had my hair strategically placed. "Sarah, your body is quite beautiful and quite a difference from our classroom subject! Do you think this afternoon has helped you look at the body differently?" And as an afterthought, she added, "And by the way, you need to wear your hair down more often!"

Chapter 18

Looking back on that afternoon, it just seemed to unfold naturally. It was indescribably liberating to feel comfortable in my own skin, and a sense of confidence in myself was born that day. Rather than it being awkward between Yvette and me, we actually got closer. There was somehow a bond of trust between us. And most exciting was the smile Yvette sent across the classroom when she heard the professor praising my rendering of the current life drawing subject, knowing the difference she made.

The time for the mixer had arrived, and we were sorting through the clothes we got to get the right combination. Yvette insisted I wear my hair down and borrowed a curling iron to give it some waves. I had it partially pulled up in the front and the rest falling down my back. Makeup was another thing I wasn't used to, but with my roommate's prodding, I added a little blush, lipstick, and eyeshadow. She gave me an approving nod, and off we went to the party. Peter saw us right as we entered, and he came up to compliment us on how we looked. He then introduced us to the girls I saw him with at lunch.

The music was great, and someone spiked the punch which resulted in a surprisingly lively party! Everyone seemed intent on getting to know all the classmates, and soon everyone was on the dance floor dancing together. A couple of the boys seemed interested in me, but I managed to avoid them. Yvette came up to me with another cup of punch and laughed, saying, "I guess the next thing we need to work on is flirting!" I remember looking over at her at one point surrounded by four guys all listening intently to her every word. Naturally, I was envious at how at ease she always seemed.

That first week set the pace for the rest of the school year. Yvette and I didn't sketch each other again, but we had fallen into an easy camaraderie with little or no modesty. We helped each other on projects and bounced ideas off of each other. Peter offered to take me to Montmartre, and we sat there wondering if we should set up easels. In fact, Peter was proving to be a very talented painter. He had already secured a sponsor for his works back in Glasgow, and his father had been a great influence. He loved doing landscapes. It fascinated me to watch him bring a scene to life. The series he was doing was both thought-provoking and inspiring. He was painting a particular favorite landscape back in Scotland that would stay the same but vastly change depending upon the time of day or the season. To see the changing colors, shadows, blooming versus barren, was spellbinding. I think he felt the same way watching me with my falcons. I shared with him the passion I found because of Rosa Bonheur. Over the next weeks, my falcon series was coming along. I had managed to find some news photos of El Amir to help me capture his likeness. I thought the piece with the golden eyes, with a little more work, could be outstanding.

One day, seemingly out of the blue, Peter asked me if Yvette and I were a couple. He quickly added that if we were, he was not judging. He simply wanted to know if there might be a chance for him. Can I just say this completely caught me off guard! I didn't know how to respond. Sure, Yvette and I were close friends, but we weren't intimate. Or were we? Does intimacy have to require physical touch? We seemed to share everything else.

Peter must have felt like he struck a nerve because he refocused his attention on fixing something on the scooter. Knowing I somehow needed to answer his question, I responded, "Peter, Yvette and I are best friends, but we are not physically intimate as a couple."

"I didn't know, Sarah. You two are always together. I just wanted to explore whether you might have a place in your life for me. Will you go out with me this weekend?" When he talked low and fast like that, the Glasgow dialect of his Scottish heritage came through, and I had a hard time understanding him, although the melodic sound of it was actually quite pleasing to hear.

"Peter, we are good friends. I came here with you today, didn't I?"

He leaned over and kissed me on the cheek. "I would like to be more than friends, Sarah. Just think about it, will you? I'll be painting at the class studio Saturday afternoon. If you decide to come by, we can go out from there."

I walked back to the dorm by way of the pond to think about what Peter suggested. Here I was, eighteen and I had avoided all intimacy so far in my life. The only person who had seen me naked was Yvette, but that was for sketching, right? Did I desire more than that from her? For that matter, did I desire things to progress with Peter? I felt way too naïve on the subject to make any kind of rational decision. Maybe I should talk to Yvette about it. She was so much more street-smart than me. She had always said I could talk to her about anything.

So, deep in thought, I entered our room to find Yvette cross-legged on her bed in an oversized T-shirt, studying and chomping on an apple. It made me laugh. *How can she be so nonchalant when I am so serious about everything?* "Hi, what are you studying?"

Yvette looked exasperated swallowing her last bite. "This calculus chapter *me botter les fesses!*"

I laughed. "It's kicking your butt? Can I help?"

"*Oui, bien sur*! I would love that, or I am about to toss this book out the window!"

I took off my jacket and went to sit beside her to see what the issue was. Fortunately, it was a subject I was good at, and I was able to guide her through the calculations to get to the answer. I plopped down on my stomach on my bed and said, "So I have a problem as well."

"What is it, *chérie*? You were with Peter, right? Did anything happen?"

"He said he wanted to be more than friends and wondered if you and I were a couple!"

Rationally, she answered, "I can see how he might think that. How did it make you feel? Do you see yourself getting closer to Peter?"

I could feel a headache coming on. Shaking my head, I said, "Yvette I don't have any experience to draw from. I like Peter as a friend and enjoy spending time with him. Do I see kissing and all that other stuff with him? I don't think so."

Yvette laughed at my innocent remark. "By 'all that stuff,' do you mean sex?" When I nodded, she continued, "Do you find yourself attracted to me?"

"I honestly don't know. What I do know is that so far in my life, I have trusted women long before trusting any men. How would I know?" I knew at that moment I was trusting her.

"Sarah, attraction is a normal part of life. Which gender you are attracted to evolves from a lot of things, but certainly trust is a major one. Maybe you are at a stage where you need to experiment a little. I am not going to push you one way or the other. You have known from the beginning that I am open to experiment in many areas, including sexual attraction. Why don't you keep your mind open and sleep on it? The pendulum can swing both ways, you know."

I dared to ask because I needed to know. "Does that mean if I cared for you in a physical way, you would not be exclusive?"

"It is hard to contain a free spirit, *chérie*. I know I would be gentle and care for you, but I do not know that I could promise exclusivity. Maybe you just need to awaken the sexual side of you so you are able to distinguish a genuine attraction to a male or female. Think about it. There's no hurry. Now I have to get back to homework."

Chapter 19

I gathered my books and left for the library to digest what Yvette had said. By the time I returned to the dorm room, Yvette was in bed. I quickly changed into my shorty pajamas, turned out the light, and got into bed, lying on my side and facing the wall. Sleep was not coming easy for me, and I'm sure I must have let out a few sighs.

Just as I was dozing off, Yvette crawled into bed with me creating a spooning position with her arm casually draped over my middle. With all my hair up in a top knot, I could feel her breath on my neck. I soaked in the comforting feeling and snuggled back into her. Silent tears fell from my closed eyes, realizing how few genuine hugs I had received in my life before that night. I awoke at one point in the night after I had rolled over on my back. Our legs were intertwined, and her arm still held me. An overwhelming sense of peace came over me.

I never made it to see Peter that Saturday. Yvette and I spent the rest of the semester painting each other's portraits, taking long walks, and talking for hours. There was no urgency to press the physical, and Yvette seemed content showing me she loved me just as I showed her how I needed her. I convinced my dad to let me spend Christmas holidays in Nice with Yvette's mother and sisters, but he said in return I had to come home for a visit in the spring and then again for the first two weeks of summer.

Yvette's sisters were thrilled to have her home, and we swam and rode the family bikes with them. I think her mother, Patrice, could tell how close we had become, and she was very supportive. It was during that vacation, in their large claw tub that our relationship turned physical. Yvette was sitting behind me, with moisturizing bubbles surrounding us. She bathed me with a natural sponge that was soon replaced by her exploring hands. She toyed with my nipples, making them taut, then reached down between my legs. I gasped at such a new feeling and had my first orgasm in that tub. Once we dried off and moved to her bed, it was my turn to discover her. I remember stroking her, studying her body like it was a piece of art.

It was extremely arousing to be able to give her such pleasure. She explained the difference of what it would be like with a man and that we would find different but equal pleasure. I think she toyed with the idea of having a man with us, but I wasn't ready to share her yet. The more comfort I found with her, the more I understood I could never contain her free spirit. I knew in my heart she would always love me. However, once we were back at school, it wasn't long before she met an upperclassman, Jackson, and became physical with him.

I walked in on them one time in the spring, and they asked me to join them. I declined, but they seemed perfectly content to have me observe them. I lay on my bed watching them move as shadows. Yvette occasionally glanced over at me to make sure I was okay. I was not just okay, I was fascinated. Jackson was a good-looking man, and at first, his full erection was quite alarming with its size, and I was afraid he might hurt Yvette. Somehow she managed to adjust her hips to receive him, and she met each thrust of his, getting deeper and deeper with obvious and undeniable pleasure culminating in an intense mutual orgasm.

When they finished and Jackson rolled over to hold her, Yvette summoned me over to touch him, saying, "Next year, we will be allowed to paint nude males. We will see their private parts more like this rather than the way they are before they mate. I felt his chest, and his muscles rippled under my fingers. As my hand moved lower, Jackson started to become aroused again. Yvette smiled. "See what magic we wield?"

Jackson smiled, too, in a nonthreatening way. "Come on, Sarah. Take your clothes off and join us." And there it was, the night I lost my virginity to Jackson and Yvette together. It was like some magical secret we shared and never discussed. I had a few dates with Peter after but never got past kissing and some light petting. I look back on those days and wonder how my life took a turn toward more sensual openness because of Yvette and how different it would have been without her. Yet I felt no urge to go any further with Peter, or anyone else...for a while.

Yvette and I would room together another year before she decided to move in with Jackson. They were delighted and surprised to still be together after all that time, and I was pleased for both of them, that their love story continued to grow.

Chapter 20

As the school year came to a close, all of us were putting the last-minute details into our series of paintings. My series was a grouping of five three-foot square canvases: (1) the large hooded falcon resting on the block perched out in the desert at sunrise; (2) the Arab man in the long robe and *kaffiyeh* or headdress with the falcon, now proud and unhooded, on the gauntlet attached to his arm; (3) a two-part painting of the falcon high in the air searching for his prey with a close-up of his face with the sharpshooter eyes; (4) the falcon midair having just clutched a now limp rabbit; and (5) a portrait of El Amir from the waist up holding out his arm with the gauntlet and the soaring falcon reflected in his golden eyes.

Peter's Scottish landscape series got first place, and mine was runner up. Yvette and James still scored well, and we all four retained our scholarships. I was nervous for El Amir to see the falcon series, but I also couldn't wait! Summer was set for the two-week visit home in Southampton before leaving for London. As promised, Mr. Templeton offered to move me to the restoration department to see how I handled it. Yvette planned to visit me in London if her schedule around an in-depth art class allowed.

Fortunately, visits at home had become much more pleasant primarily because I had matured a lot. The toddlers were also growing and becoming cuter every day, and I had a blast teaching them to draw. I still remembered the story of Rosa Bonheur sketching designs in the dirt as a toddler. I wanted to give these two little ones an opportunity to see if they might feel the same passion as I do for art. Dad and Eleanor seemed to have gotten into a better routine and I could see they genuinely cared about each other. I finally accepted them as a couple and was grateful to see them happy.

While I was home, I got fitted for glasses to help with close-up eyesight. In restoration, every small detail counted, a major difference from the replicating I had been doing. Yvette had taught me a trick with my hair to put four large curlers in my top knot when I slept. I would wake up the next morning with a decent set of waves, so I started pulling the front of my hair up in a clip to get it off my face and let the rest fall in waves down my back. Looking in the mirror, I knew how much I had grown over the past year. I could see it in my face and how I held my body. I chuckled when I added the glasses at the more studious look I portrayed.

I looked forward with anticipation to being back in London for my fourth summer. Amelia had gotten engaged in the spring and was planning her wedding for the fall. Tara was still in restoration and offered to give me some pointers. There were two new interns working in replication for the summer, Sam in sculpture and Hailey in painting. Mr. Templeton asked that I help them whenever I could.

With my promotion, my salary allowed me to get a little nicer flat this summer. I wanted to save as much as I could, though. Rumors were flying around at the end of the school year about a world-renowned Australian artist creating an international scholarship program for college juniors and seniors. The course would be paid for, but you still had to cover your air and living expenses. I would learn more about the competition in the fall, but I intended to work hard for the opportunity and wanted to think positively and be prepared. I know Peter planned to compete for it as well. It would bring the best of the best emerging artists together from all over the world to study under Kenneth Patrick!

I brought my falconry series in for Mr. Templeton's assessment. He seemed to appreciate it and discussed with me how to price it, individually or as a set. I had never thought of breaking the series apart, so I tried to look again at each piece as a standalone work of art. I preferred them staying together but agreed they each had enough merit to stand on their own. He wanted to show them to El Amir first. That gave me a case of nerves, since this was the piece I had promised him, and he and his falcon were the subject matter! El Amir would be in London the following week, so we decided not to publicize them until he got the first look.

During that first week in London, I went to study Tara paint a few times. I needed to adopt a technique to apply when working myself mentally into another artist's mindset to restore a damaged area of an old master whether that damage was caused by age, natural disaster, or breakdown of the medium used. Tara taught me how to age the paint to comply with the rest of the painting.

Hailey had the same internship I had my first year at the gallery and was still in high school. Her job was to assist, learn, and replicate whenever possible. I remembered how generous Tara was to me and vowed to do the same for Hailey. Sam, however, had graduated to the second tier and was exclusively replicating sculpture full-time. He had an interesting way of molding his sculpture in a pliable clay and, when he finished, would use wax and plaster to cast it in bronze. During the heating process, the wax would melt, and the original sculpture was now gone, leaving the hardened bronze coating to create a one-of-a-kind sculpture. He would then fill the inside where the wax was with liquid metal, allowing it to cool, which gave it the weight of a true bronze statue. I thought Sam would be an interesting artist to watch this summer.

Chapter 21

My primary assignment of the summer was in the Old Master section of the gallery. My subject was an original Rachel Ruysch, which, if restored properly, had the potential to bring in hundreds of thousands of pounds to the gallery. It was a huge honor to be trusted with this painting, and I could not afford to make a mistake. Before I ever touched it, I wanted to study Rachel to understand her background and get into her psyche. As I learned about her, I knew with certainty Rachel Ruysch would be an artist like Rosa Bonheur, who inspired me greatly.

Born in 1664 in the northern Netherlands, Rachel arrived in history 158 years before Rosa and 304 years before me! I had to first wrap my mindset around that difference between what we as female artists faced growing up in our own time and location obsessing over the realistic depiction of our subject matter. For Rosa, it had been animals. For Rachel, it was still-life florals. I believe in my heart that my style was still unfolding as I experienced these influences that entered my path.

Similar to Rosa, Rachel was highly influenced by her father, a professor of anatomy and botany. Although an amateur painter in his own right, her father, Frederik, was extremely detailed in his precise depictions of the subjects he studied, from animal skeletons to insects to a variety of botany samples. Rachel derived huge pleasure from painting samples in his lab, particularly flowers. Most likely unheard of at the time, by age fifteen, Rachel was apprenticed to a well-established flower painter in Amsterdam. I thought of Rosa selling her first painting at sixteen and my own at seventeen. Rachel was allowed to learn the flower painter's technique, and by age eighteen, she was selling her own pieces with what she learned. In addition, she mastered the art of arranging florals in a unique way to produce a three-dimensional effect. The precision in her style of painting each of her flowers allowed her to show their beauty as well as their flaws. What I found particularly interesting was that for effect, sometimes she would add an actual bit of moss or a butterfly wing into her painting to provide texture to her subject on her canvas.

Unlike Rosa, who rebelled against men and found her partners in women, Rachel married and raised ten children! Even while living this family life, while most women of her day were confined to sewing or kitchen duty, she continued to excel in her painting. She particularly liked the dark forest flora, which at the time was a style called forest floors. Rachel would then add her insects or frogs or lizards for authenticity. While working at The Hague, Rachel Ruysch became the first female member of the Dutch artists' society, *Confrerie Pictura*. What an accomplishment for a woman of that era!

Rachel's ability to produce a picture-perfect flower was incredibly intimidating. But I learned how she created the large stroke base structure and then moved to fine brushes to layer in the detail. I practiced hours and hours on blank canvas to reconstruct her steps to tackle the flower and part of a grasshopper that had been damaged. The effect was remarkable, and the technique stayed with me in my paintings going forward. I was relieved to have Mr. Templeton by my side to approve of what I was about to do. With a little tweaking, the end result would be indiscernible to the untrained eye and difficult to detect for even the trained eye.

Tara came by and shared some of her own experiences fighting nerves when working on an old master. She nodded her approval as she watched my approach produce the necessary result. She was still there when El Amir arrived. He walked into the gallery and studied what I was working on. "How astonishing to have such brilliant colors laid down upon such a dark background!"

"I agree. Amsterdam has always been known for its vast array of flowers. The practice of painting the colorful flowers to stand out against a dark background was commonly used during that time. Look at her detail work! By the way, this is my friend, Tara. We met when she worked here while I interned." Then to Tara, I said, "This is El Amir from Morocco. He is a patron of the gallery and bought one of my paintings last summer."

Tara remembered *The Migration*. "That's right, the original is still here." Looking at El Amir, she added, "You must be the patron who commissioned the larger version."

El Amir replied, "I have hung it in a place of honor in my home. I must say I looked around the gallery prior to coming in here and I did not see any new works of yours, Sarah. I have to admit to being quite disappointed."

Mr. Templeton had walked in on that last statement and intervened. "You are in luck, sir. Sarah has outdone herself this year. We decided not to present it to the public until you had the chance to see it first. Sarah, shall I get them?"

El Amir noticed. "Them?"

I nodded at Mr. Templeton and asked Tara to help him. To El Amir, I said, "My major assignment this year was to do a five-piece series looking at a subject from different vantage points. My work came in second place. You might recognize the subject."

Tara set up five easels side by side. Mr. Templeton had the five canvases specifically marked by their order number and individually covered. He allowed me the honor of removing the covers. I have to admit I was happy Tara was there in case his reaction was not quite what I hoped it would be.

In sequence, I removed cover after cover, revealing the various paintings of the practice of falconry. When I unveiled the close-up of El Amir's face and upper body, I felt a tremor of unease that he might be offended by my taking the liberty to use his likeness without his permission. El Amir moved closer to examine each painting on its own and then moved away to observe them as a whole. Tara looked over at me in amazement with a subtle thumbs-up. El Amir's scrutiny seemed to last forever.

Finally, he spoke without taking his eyes off the series. "Sarah, any time an artist can evoke a feeling or emotion from his or her audience, that is a wonder in itself. I know this subject well and I feel as though I am living it! I can feel the hooded falcon's restlessness to get started by the strain and pull visible in the folds of the hood and the bristling in his feathers. The sharp focus in both of us as he waits for my signal to launch from the gauntlet creates the anticipation. The reflection you have added to the expression in my eyes is the way I *feel* watching him take flight.

You have outdone yourself, and I must have the entire set. I know exactly where I will hang them."

Mr. Templeton stepped in with his business voice. "I see you agree with my judgment on this series. We plan to offer the paintings for two hundred fifty pounds each or a thousand pounds for the series. There would also be a ten percent fee to the gallery."

Scrutinizing me for a long moment as if trying to judge my talent, El Amir then turned to Mr. Templeton. "So a thousand and a hundred pounds secures the set? Put it on my account and ship it, Mr. Templeton." He turned back to me and asked, "Sarah, where do you want your talent to go from here? Are you preparing for art to be your career and your passion? I see a future in you but I do not want to waste my time if you are not totally serious."

"I am extremely serious, sir. As a matter of fact, my next goal is to win a place at the Australian scholarship competition to train under Kenneth Patrick!"

El Amir looked closely at me and, with a challenge, said, "You win that scholarship in Australia and you will have a sponsor when you return. Good luck, Sarah!"

Chapter 22

It was several weeks before El Amir returned. I was just finishing the restoration of the Rachel Ruysch painting and had two weeks left before I returned home for a week and then back to Paris. Mr. Templeton congratulated me on an admirable restoration job and said he had gotten notice from a Ruysch collector that the painting was acceptable. My heart did a little bounce of relief!

The following day, El Amir strode in and dropped a folder on the table next to me. "I have looked into this competition to win a scholarship in Australia. You need to do this, Sarah. Kenneth Patrick is a gifted and renowned artist. It would be a privilege to learn his technique to add to your own. This pamphlet offers a long list of what is necessary for a student to qualify. You have a lot of them, but you need to spend this school year getting every single thing on this list perfected. I have total faith in you! You will be competing with young artists from around the world. If you don't make it your junior year, you still have one more year to try. But I think I know you well enough to know you will go all out to make it happen this year."

I told him I would study the list and get to work! El Amir then asked if I knew where Sam was working. For some reason, that piqued my curiosity. I fished a little. "Sam is quite a gifted sculptor. Have you seen his work?"

El Amir answered, "I have, indeed! He has been working on a piece for me and was hoping to have it finished by the time I got back here to London. Did you hear he received a scholarship to L'École d'Artes? Sam appears to be following in your footsteps." *How did I not know this?*

To El Amir, I responded, "With all of his talent, the school will be lucky to have him. I will have to show him around."

I had no way of knowing at the time Sam would play such an important role in my life. I have to admit I hadn't paid much notice to him over the summer other than to admire a work or two of his sculptures. Sam had kept to himself for the most part, or maybe I was obsessed with the Rachel Ruysch painting and any free time I had was occupied with Tara and Amelia. At the gallery, I had given a significant amount of time and support to Hailey, but what had I done for Sam? Embarrassed, I knew the answer was nothing. Yet here he'd won the opportunity in Paris! I had two weeks left. *Was there time to rectify my lack of support?*

At the end of the day, long after El Amir had left, I found Sam absorbed in a replication he was working on. I leaned against the wall, observing him, and then finally said in French, "*J'ai entendu dire que tu allais à L'Ecole d'Artes à Paris!*" (I heard you were going to L'Ecole d'Artes in Paris!)

Without any hesitation, Sam knew exactly what I was saying and responded with a wink, "*Je pensais te surprendre.*" (I thought I would surprise you.)

"You have definitely surprised me! How long have you known?" I was looking at Sam with fresh eyes. He was a year younger than me and he still had those boyish features...clean-shaven, brown eyes, short brown hair, medium height, and physically fit.

Sam began, "Unlike you, I am not starting until college. I found out I was accepted early during the summer, but I hadn't decided whether to accept yet, so I asked Mr. Templeton to keep it quiet. When I wasn't working, I took an intense French class and spent the rest of the time at the gym working out. All the hours of sitting was getting to me, so the gym was the perfect outlet."

I knew what he meant about all the sitting. "I have been riding my bike a lot, but I haven't taken it with me to Paris yet. Are you planning to join a gym there? If you do, I would love to sign up with you. Sam, I have not intentionally been aloof. I'm afraid it is part of my nature to concentrate on my work. It will be awesome to have a new friend there to hang out with!"

Sam said admiringly, "El Amir mentioned you would be trying out for the Kenneth Patrick scholarship in Australia. I'm happy to help any way I can." He thought for a moment and then added, "My uncle has an old car he isn't using and offered it to me to take to Paris.

It has a bike rack on the back, and I plan to take my bike. Would you like me to pick you up and drive us both to Paris? We could add your bike on the back."

"That would be great! I have to admit it seems a little awkward that my dad would still bring me. I don't have a way to get my bike back to Southampton, so maybe I will leave it with Tara again and buy a new one to take to school." I liked the idea of biking around campus.

Laughing, Sam replied, "Ha! That's right! You have a tidy little nest egg with the recent sale to El Amir."

"One thing on the Kenneth Patrick list is to have sold a minimum of three pieces. If you count the series as five paintings, I have actually sold six. However, they can't be to the same person or a friend or relative. Mr. Templeton told me he would try to get the original *Migration* sold in the gallery. We are trying to clarify if the sale of the Rachel Ruysch painting that I worked on all summer would count as one." It certainly felt to me like it should count!

Chapter 23

It is hard to believe Sam Barton and I spent that whole summer less than a hundred feet from each other and never got to know each other. Who would have guessed on that drive to Paris together that we would wind up as close friends? Well, actually more than close. I chuckle to think about what Rosa would think of me becoming friends with not only a male but also a competitive artist. Unlike Peter, who was also both of those things, Sam made me laugh. In some ways, he reminded me of Beth with his easygoing outward charm. I had never gotten over my innate shyness, so he helped fill in where I felt lacking. Somehow he never seemed to make me feel vulnerable or uncomfortable.

I swear Sam had dozens of unique facial expressions, so it was impossible for him to have a poker face. How could you not laugh when his eyebrows shot up, clearly saying in disbelief, "Are you serious right now?" Or when he wore his sulky face pretending I hurt his feelings. I think it is simply easy to say he was fun to be with. He got along great with Yvette and Jackson. We even went on a double date with them, and when they started making out, Sam made smoochy faces that made me shake my head in laughter and even made them laugh.

The best was when James took Sam to a little hole in the wall pizza place that featured his hometown deep dish Chicago pizza! Here we were in the culinary center of the world, but Sam was convinced he had never tasted anything so good, and he made it a ritual to get a pizza from there at least once a week. Naturally, James was up for it too. Unlike me, Sam slid comfortably into any situation that came up and easily made new friends. He was a good student and a fine artist. He excelled in a variety of mediums, but particularly sculpture. Charcoal and pastels were new to him, but he mastered them quickly. He loved the life drawing class, and I told him how hard it was for me and hesitantly shared how Yvette and I would practice. He pounced on that story, thinking we should do the same thing. After all, I had graduated to nude males this year and would obviously need practice!

Whether it was playing a game of spin the bottle, drinking a bottle of wine followed by a sensuous massage, or a pitiful story about how he needed practice drawing a nude female, Sam Barton certainly had a way of getting my clothes off me! Sam's roommate had left school with a medical issue, and Yvette was usually with Jackson, so we had plenty of time in either room to be alone.

We had fun and were adventurous, but there was no talk of love or romance. That didn't seem to matter. We were young and carefree yet cautious enough not to have a surprise outcome from our intimate endeavors.

I could tell Peter was not happy with the relationship I had formed with Sam. He was clearly also working on the list of requirements to apply for the Kenneth Patrick scholarship, but he no longer confided in me. I requested a meeting with my school counselor early in the year to show him the list and discuss our strategy. I was doing everything I could to be considered for my junior year. I got a lucky break when the project for the year was announced. It was "Spatial Translation." Basically, that meant I had to do a spectacular painting and then reproduce it on a much larger scale. With my experience enlarging *The Migration* and the knowledge I learned restoring the Rachel Ruysch painting, I was prepared to exceed expectations!

I thought of subject after subject and discarded them one by one. I could now do amazing flowers, but the flowers that were so popular with the Dutch artists were no longer in favor. Naturally, Rosa's animals came to mind, along with all the time I spent at the zoo and circus. The painting she did with the lions and their small cubs was particularly touching. Knowing how Sam felt about lions, I showed him her painting. He studied it for quite a while, thinking. "There is no question she did a masterful job creating a family scene with these powerful creatures. I myself hope to capture the ambiance of lions in the wild someday. But you can't just copy her. What about the zebras you painted into *The Migration*? You said the zebras were so unique. Could you create their own study?"

So back to the library I went to study zebras' ways of survival as well as their domesticity. I also could not help my curiosity about what Yvette, James, and especially Peter were doing for their projects. After I stashed all my library books, I went searching for Yvette at the studio where we all often painted when we weren't in class. She saw me and waved me over. There was a large corkboard with several blown-up photographs of the coastline along the Mediterranean in the south of France and others of the high-profile port of Antibes. "Sarah, come help me! I need to blend the richness of Antibes with the beauty of the coast. I've decided on watercolor, but it is a very unforgiving medium. I am hoping that will give me extra points. What have you decided to paint?"

I thought about all the books lying on my bed. "I still have a fascination with the zebras of Africa. They have such a diverse skill set that I am hoping to convey to canvas. I am also debating oil or acrylic...most likely acrylic." Studying her pictures, I offered, "Yvette, you have done several paintings with a cubist point of view. Would it be possible to intertwine the elite wealth displayed by the yachts with the serenity of the sea?" Yvette picked up her charcoal and began to draw.

"Something like this?" She magically created a rough drawing of a three-dimensional cube artistically arranged amidst the outline of the coast. Within the cube, it appeared there was a painting of its own representing the opulence, which is standard in Antibes.

I stood there in amazement. "Yes, I love it!"

Chapter 24

Next, I found James busy at work. Over the summer, he trained with an artist who practiced the primitive African style of Tinga Tinga. James explained its simplistic cartoon style loaded with incredible intricacies. This style was commonly used by African artists in bold primary colors to sell to tourists, but James was taking it to a higher level that would translate onto the larger canvas. In a small way, it reminded me of the animal mural I did in school. The study used a single tree with branches curving throughout the canvas. Tropical birds such as peacocks, toucans, flamingos, and even what might be a vulture were perched or flying overhead. The core of the birds' shapes was simple, yet the incredible talent was depicted by the detail presented within the shapes. What could pass as doodling filled in the shapes and the background with color and meticulous placement. It was brilliant!

Sam was busy working on his series like we did the year before. He had decided on a lion kill of an antelope in Africa. The series reflected the sequence of the predators involved during the course of one day, leaving the last scene just the terrain with dented grass where the antelope had fallen. He was clearly in his element with his subject.

Peter was the one being elusive, keeping his work private. We were both attempting to win a Kenneth Patrick scholarship, so in reality, we were direct competitors. I did receive good news that the KP committee running the contest had approved the sale of the Rachel Ruysch painting as one of my three required sales. Mr. Templeton had placed the original *Migration* in the sales gallery in hopes that it would sell, giving me the third, but so far it had not. If that sold, we would use the falcon series to El Amir as the third, which in reality would add five.

It was time for me to get busy! I was crossing things off the list. My grades were within the required grade-point average. My four references were from two of my counselors, Mr. Templeton and El Amir. El Amir had given me the required sponsorship. If you included my first summer at the London Gallery as an intern plus my subsequent summers, I far exceeded the number of professional work hours in the art industry minimum. My scholarship at L'École d'Artes was impressive, although Peter had that as well. Now my project had to be perfect!

I remember drawing dozens of sketches. At the time, I had no idea how important zebras would be to my future career as a result of this project, which catapulted them ahead of other subjects in my artist's mind. From Rosa Bonheur's perspective, I saw them as striking figures with natural beauty in their stripe formations that were never the same from zebra to zebra. I had learned about the relationship formed between the zebra and wildebeest during migration that required their sensory skills to survive. The wildebeest have a great sense of awareness of predators through their sense of hearing and smell. They also have a keen ability to find water. The zebra need this, but in their own right, they have excellent eyesight and an innate sense of navigation. They are also good fighters. And although they both live off the grassy plains, the zebra eat the long tips of grass, and the wildebeest eat the short grass. Some of those aspects were reflected in my painting *The Migration*. In this new painting, I was ignoring the wildebeest to focus on the zebra. I wanted to concentrate on their social instincts within a single herd or family group. The family would consist of one dominant male, several females (or mares), and their young foals. I wanted a painting that could translate to a large form that incorporated all of them when confronting danger in a predator.

First, I concentrated on the male. He was fierce and protective. Sketch after sketch, I tried to capture him aware of a predator close by, alert, then reared up with hooves poised to fight. He is facing the direction of the brush and a larger boulder where a cheetah is hunched down, watching where his next meal might come from. I tried one with two females flanking him, looking in the direction of the cheetah. Each of the females had bodies curved in different directions. Another series of sketches reflected a mare with her foal. The foal was very young, born recently. It was seated with legs folded looking to the side. What I wanted to capture was the mare's head and nose perfectly aligned with the foal's back of his neck curving into his back. The symmetry had to be perfect, and you had to feel the mare's protection of her foal, the stripes acting as camouflage.

The third visual that I wanted in the painting was the curve of a mare's head as she turned full circle back into her body. Since, unlike horses, the zebra have a short black mane forming a line from their ears down their back, the curve gave the image similar to a nautilus shell with its perfect curvature. Once I had my sketches ingrained in my mind, it was time to start painting. I did not plan to use a projector to get my enlarged scale correct. For that reason, I divided both canvases into three vertical spaces and planned to concentrate on one third at a time and do both sizes. I spent several weeks outlining the painting on both canvases.

During that time, all of us were focused. Whenever we weren't in class, we were working on our projects. Even Sam was distant as he tackled his ambitious series.

Christmas vacation came. Jackson, Sam, and James had all been invited to stay with Yvette's family and had readily accepted. Even though I was invited, I felt the strain within my family that they thought I continued to avoid them, so I made the decision to go home to Southampton that Christmas. I'm glad I did.

Chapter 25

The first thing that was unusual about that Christmas at home was that no one was at the train station to meet me. I was sure I had given Dad the correct time. When I called the house, Eleanor picked up. "Oh my gosh, Sarah, I am so sorry. Your dad has been in bed with a horrible cold and forgot to tell me. I don't have anyone to watch Harry and Lizzie. Would you mind taking a cab?" I assured her it was okay and that I would be there soon.

I arrived home, and before I could make it to the front door, Harry and Lizzie ran out the door to jump on me with excited squeals. Probably because it was so long between visits, they seemed to be growing at lightning speed! Eleanor gave me a hug and apologized again for not picking me up. When I asked about Dad, she shook her head with dismay. "Your dad seems to get worse every day, but he is being so stubborn! He insists it is a cold that he will get over soon and that doctors would turn it into something much bigger than it is." With that information, I went to check on him for myself.

I noticed right away Dad's cough had a raspy sound that did not sound like a normal cold. When he saw me, he quickly stuffed his tissue under the mattress and reached for another. Taking his hand brought a horrific flashback to the day in the ER when I reached for my mother's burned hand. I needed to focus. His hand wasn't burned, but it was burning up! I put my hand on his forehead, and there was no question he had a really high fever. Between the coughing spells, I could see how weak he was. "Dad, it's me, Sarah. You are burning up! Why haven't you gone to the doctor?"

With a low halting voice, he answered, "I don't want them to put me in the hospital."

"But, Dad, maybe they can give you some medication to get you better? I'm going to get a thermometer from Eleanor." He had a hard time holding his mouth closed between coughs, but the thermometer jumped up to 102 degrees anyway. Then I saw him tuck another tissue under the mattress. "Why are you doing that, Dad?" He tried to keep my hand from reaching under there. All that did was make me more determined. What I found made me look at him in horror, and he looked away, ashamed. I held handfuls of tissue with large spots of bright-red blood!

I marched out of the room to get Eleanor. "Are you aware of this?" I asked, holding up the tissue. "We need to get him to a hospital right away." Eleanor looked baffled at what to do, so I had no other choice but to take charge. "Eleanor, get one of the neighbors to watch the children. I will call for an ambulance." Eleanor looked over at Dad and saw the hesitation in his eyes, but when she looked again at the tissue, she sprang into action.

Once I called for an ambulance, I went back over to look at my dad. "Why would you wait so long? You are the only family I have left. What would I do without you?" Dad closed his eyes with understanding and regret. He pulled me closer. "There is an envelope over in the dresser...top drawer...your Christmas present. Just in case."

Shaking my head in denial, I found it and put it in my pocket, praying this was not as serious as it looked. Just as the paramedics showed up, Dad had a severe coughing attack with more blood. I overheard one of the paramedics talking about hemoptysis. I had no idea what that was, but I didn't like the sound of it. Eleanor took the children next door, and we told the ambulance driver we would be right behind them.

The whole way there, Eleanor was berating herself for not being stronger to force Dad to get checked out. I couldn't help reflecting that Nana never expected to raise a ten-year-old alone. Glancing at Eleanor, I knew she had her hands full with Harry and Lizzie. If something happened to Dad, would she really want to keep up with a college student? I had to stop thinking like that. He was going to get help at the hospital. Surely he would be all right.

We got to the ER waiting room, and it seemed forever before a doctor came out to report Dad's condition. When he did, I could immediately see he was angry with us. "Why on earth was this man not brought in for screening a week ago. I guarantee his symptoms have been active that long."

Eleanor was beside herself, but she took full responsibility. "Our daughter didn't arrive until today, and it was she who realized right away things weren't right. William was so adverse to getting doctors involved that he hid the blood from me." Breaking down, she added with a sob, "I should have known better!"

To Eleanor, the doctor said, "Your husband has chronic pneumonia. His coughing up the blood for a long period of time appears to have damaged the tissue in his lungs. We are testing right now to see if there is evidence of sepsis as a complication. I have to be honest, if there is, it could be life-threatening."

There it was...the severity of his illness and the lack of my importance. Eleanor pleaded, "Doctor, please make him better! We have two small children to raise. I need my husband!" I wasn't even an afterthought.

Chapter 26

That was the night I believed in my heart if I lost Dad, I had no family left. I would be on my own. It wouldn't do any good to blame Eleanor. Dad himself was just as responsible for the lack of concern for his own well-being. We waited vigilantly at the hospital for a miracle. Sepsis had indeed set in, and according to the doctor, the damage was irreparable. There was no miracle on the horizon, and fate had intervened far too soon to have to say our goodbyes. Eleanor spent over an hour with him. Harry and Lizzie were too small. Then it was my turn. I could tell he was trying to hold on for me. I sat next to his bed holding his hand and crying for all the missed opportunities. Finally I asked with tears in my eyes, "Dad, please kiss Mom for me?"

He closed his eyes, and his last words were "Maggie May..."

My dad died on New Year's Eve. As I passed the Christmas tree still filled with unopened presents for the children, I grieved for Harry and Lizzie. At least they still had a mother. I also grieved for another little girl who used to play at the beach with parents who adored her and felt a deep dark loneliness seep through my skin and take over my soul. Eleanor had her own grief, and I honestly could not bear another funeral, so I went back to school early. At the last minute, I threw the envelope in my suitcase to save for another time. When I said goodbye to Eleanor and the children, I'm not sure I ever expected to see them again.

My counselor came by the dorm to check on me and offer his condolences. He questioned whether I should stay at school, but in the end, the school director made the decision that I was probably better off there. Amelia and Tara both called to see if I wanted to take some time to be with them. There were also the encouraging notes from Mr. Templeton and El Amir. Yvette returned from the holidays with Jackson, Sam, and James, and they all tried to be supportive. I was just empty and had nothing to give back.

It was easier lying in my bed, trying to erase any feeling at all. I couldn't even pick up a paintbrush. I gather they were all worried about me because they began to tiptoe around me.

Ironically, when it came down to it, Peter was the one who broke through. School had been back in session for over a week, and I had not attended a class. Peter knocked on my door several times. When I didn't answer, he came in and saw me lying in bed with the blinds drawn. He came over and sat on the bed, holding me against his chest. "It's okay to hurt, lass. Think of all the challenges you have already made it through. I've admired the way you've always found a way to move forward. You'll find your way again." He could tell I was listening and continued, "It is you and me competing for the Kenneth Patrick scholarship, and I realize I have been a prick trying to prove I am more worthy than you. But I refuse to win because of you defaulting! So you need to get your beautiful bod moving so you can kick my butt to the curb!" That got a chuckle from me.

"What about your secretive project?" I asked rather petulantly.

"I guess I'll have to let you see it then, won't I? Now get up, open the blinds, take a shower, and get to work!"

Peter and I met with the counselor together. She confirmed what we already knew. Only one student per any school could win a scholarship. Since there were just the two of us competing at L'École d'Artes, we had the chance that one of us would get junior year and one of us senior year. We decided to work together and support each other that spring, knowing a decision would come in May. We wanted to be sure one of us got it for next year and the other the year after. We set up an area of our working studio to work on both our projects. Peter's specialty was landscapes, but he reached beyond to do his project on the great barrier reef with the viewer looking through glass above and below the water. I understood he was trying to capture the Australia theme. It was beautiful.

I think Sam was jealous that I didn't make time for him, and probably Yvette was as well. For now, I was focused on Australia. Peter mentioned a gift he got from his parents over Christmas. Like a lightning bolt, I remembered the envelope my dad gave me. I rummaged around until I found it. For some reason, I wanted to be alone when I opened it, knowing he wrote it during his last days. When I tore open the envelope, there was a letter and what looked like an airline ticket.

My Dearest Sarah,

I can't begin to tell you how proud I am of the beautiful and talented young woman you have become. I know I have not been the best father to you, and yet look at what you have already accomplished! This Christmas vacation, my deepest hope is to give you the love and support that you need. I am so thankful you chose to come home when I am sure you had other options.

As I thought about your growth as an artist, I simply knew you would win that scholarship to Australia, so I took the liberty to buy a round-trip ticket for you. Through the years, you have met each challenge you've encountered and refused to quit. It has been your attitude and diligent actions that have led you on this path of achievement. Great success does not come from just doing the easy stuff. It comes from being willing to enthusiastically work through those challenges. I think of you as a phoenix rising from the ashes. You have emerged from the tragedy of your youth to become smarter and more determined than ever to nurture that talent of yours.

You have a good life ahead of you and a talent that will be appreciated by many. I want you to know after your mother's accident, there was an insurance settlement. I have used some through the years, but I invested a little for you that you will receive next summer when you become nineteen. You will be able to access it through the trust department of Bank of England.

Go out there and make a powerful statement in your life, Sarah. Soar like the phoenix. Try not to look back with regret. Instead, build the future you deserve. I will always love you, my dearest daughter.

Dad

I must have read it again and again, letting its meaning sink in. *My dad loved and believed in me!* Peter might have snapped me out of my despondency, but Dad's letter gave me the momentum to move forward. A phoenix! A sense of overwhelming determination came over me, and I planned to use that ticket to Australia! My friends noticed the change and gave me the room I needed to work on my project. And in late January, I got the call from Mr. Templeton that *The Migration* had sold for £300...the same amount the large one sold for! That took care of my three sales. Peter still only had two sales, but his sponsor back in Scotland was working to get a third sold. He had split up his landscape series from last year, and two had already sold from the series. There were three more opportunities.

My first third of the painting was down to the final details in both sizes. It was of the dominant male zebra reared up in warning and threat to the perched cheetah high on the rock semi-covered in brush. Sam came by to watch for a while. Studying the painting, he said, "Sarah, how do you do this? I can see fear in the zebra's eyes, but the position of his hooves and flared nostrils shows his predator he means business. All the while, the cheetah is carefully checking which one in the herd is the weakest to soon become his next meal. He is so focused! Keep this up with the other two thirds, and you've got this!"

The second third had formed in the sketches and in my mind, so it moved along at a steady pace. There were two mares strategically positioned behind the male to protect two foals. A third female was a little farther back with one hoof drawn up on an injured leg. It would be hard for the cheetah to see the young foals, but the injured female was vulnerable. Once I had them on canvas, I went back to ensure the cheetah's eyes were focused on her. Yvette came by with an iced coffee and a hug of support. In a lowered voice, she said, "Peter's paintings are amazing, but there is something about the way you connect with these zebras that expresses itself on the canvas. Bravo, my friend!"

When I painted the two females, I wanted to get across concern yet fierce resolve to protect their foals. As I stopped to reflect, chewing on the tip of my brush, I could visualize Amelia sheltering me. At that moment, I knew I could never abandon Harry and Lizzie. They needed a big sister they could count on. I smiled, proud of the fact that I wouldn't let my own emotional weaknesses keep me from being there for them.

Chapter 27

A sort of seam had been created between the first two-thirds, so with a few brushstrokes of shrub, grass, and part of a mare's body, the two flowed easily together. The final third incorporated two of my sketches. First, the mare holding its head down to the new-born foal's nape of the neck in perfect alignment, which blended both of their stripes, creating a camouflage to make the foal invisible to the predator. Farther back, another mare used the turn of her head, giving me that beautiful curve of her short black mane while looking for danger behind them. I moved back and forth between the two paintings, making sure my proportions for the change in size were correct. I could thank Tara for teaching me that trick when I interned at the gallery as well as when I recreated *The Migration*. Stepping back with a critical eye, I could understand Sam's comments about the eyes. I could thank Rosa Bonheur for her obsession about eyes reflecting the mirror of the soul. So while I was feeling thankful, I didn't want to exclude Rachel Ruysch, so I added a few detailed background flowers and butterflies to soften the potential harshness of the painting.

I was finished! My application was in to the Australian art committee with a picture of my larger painting. Peter had his in as well. The deadline came, and we learned over four hundred applicants from all over the world had sent in applications. The committee would narrow the four hundred down to thirty who would get a personal visit from a member of the committee for an interview and to see their proposed painting in person.

While we were waiting with nerves on edge, we received the school's scores for our projects. Yvette, James, and Sam were all able to move their scholarships forward for next year. Peter and I scored at the top of the class with my score only a couple of points higher than his. On a good note, we both would retain our scholarship to come back if we did not make the cut for Australia. They were only planning to allow fifteen finalists in the class, so it was starting to feel like a long shot to even get the interview. The others were going out to a club to celebrate, so Peter and I decided to join them to let off some anxiety. Jackson was there with Yvette. James had brought his new girlfriend. Then there was me with Sam and Peter. I had a relationship with both of them but never considered either one more than a friend. After a few moments of awkwardness, I downed a shot of tequila that Jackson had ordered for the table! That seemed to tame the anxiety a bit. *Perhaps one more?*

The next morning, I awoke with a nasty tequila hangover only to find I was naked in Sam's bed. Immediately concerned we might not have used protection, I shook him awake. As if he could read my mind, he said, "Don't worry. Nothing happened. I haven't sunk to the point of having sex with a woman who is passed out... and good morning to you too!"

"Ouch...my poor head! Good morning to you too. How do you make it go away? And how did I get here?"

"Well, I admit Peter wasn't too pleased about me bringing you home, but you were sprawled over me at the time...what could a guy do?" There was that sheepish smile showing me he might have exaggerated a little. "Let's get you something to eat. Now that I recall, I don't think you ate any of your pizza." I agreed, knowing I had never acquired the same passion for Chicago deep dish pizza that James and the others loved so much. I was trying to decide what would taste good and soak up the tequila when Sam's phone rang.

"Hello." Sam looked over at me. "Hi Peter, yeah, she's here... What? Oh, that's not good. I'll tell her. Right. Goodbye."

To me, he said, "Get dressed, Sarah. The school director has been trying to reach you all morning! He wants to see you and Peter in his office as soon as possible."

"Oh my god, this is horrible! I smell like a distillery! I have to go take a quick shower and change. Then I will call him. I'll call Peter, too, to see if he can stall the meeting for an hour."

As I ran out the door, Sam threw me a bag of chips. "Here, at least eat these!"

Peter was waiting outside the director's door when I arrived, showered but about to throw up. Referring to the delay, he looked at me, shaking his head, and said, "You owe me, lass." My head was already pounding. That didn't help. Peter knocked on the door, and we went in to be seated. The director was holding a letter. Out of sight, I reached for Peter's hand. We knew how important this was to each of us. He glanced at me with a quick nod of support and squeezed my hand.

The director began, "As you know, there were over four hundred applicants for the Kenneth Patrick scholarship. You were two of them. They liked the concept behind the project of 'Spatial Translation' and seem excited to see what you each came up with. Very rarely can a school claim two of the finalists, but we are celebrating at L'École d'Artes today because you both made the top thirty, and we will have a committee member and art critic here to interview you on Monday! You both deserve it, and we have every faith in you to make it to the final selection."

Before we could help it, we both jumped up and hugged each other! The director shook our hands and said we were to each meet with our counselor to go over our projects and practice for our interviews. It was really happening! Peter and I were competing head to head for the scholarship. The counselor took us aside to advise us it was highly doubtful the committee would pick two students from the same school. The good news was that if we made it to the top thirty and did not get picked for this year's program, we had an excellent chance to make it the following year.

Chapter 28

Monday came quickly. A classroom was set up where the interviews would be conducted and our paintings could be displayed. We were scheduled an hour apart, and Peter went first. Trying to keep my nerves under control, I thought of both Rosa and Rachel having this kind of chance and how they would approach it. I truly believed neither woman would let this opportunity slip away. Then I thought about my dad and the waiting ticket, the belief my eighth-grade principal had in me to allow me to paint the mural, the years of support at the London gallery and the sponsorship at stake with El Amir. All of these thoughts provided me with the momentum I needed to go into that classroom ready to convince the committee member and art critic I would make a good addition to Kenneth Patrick's class.

When it was my turn, I fell into an easy rapport with my interviewer warming to my subject of all the influences that had brought me this far at such a young age. My passion for the subject gave me the confidence to show her the real me, no longer a pretend personality. Her next question asked how I believed Kenneth Patrick's class of technique would be of influence to me and what I was hoping to achieve. I had studied his work enough to answer, "I believe Kenneth Patrick has a unique way of creating an overall impression with the use of color. He brings life to colors that either work in harmony together or create a striking contrast that conveys how they look and feel. He can then set a tone to his use of color that is inspiring and I hope to learn. I can understand why 'Spatial Translation' would be a project of interest to him because his eye sees form and shape in his art that can define precision or defy it. He is a master, and I hope to absorb all he has to teach to make my own skill richer and multidimensional."

She nodded and smiled at my answer and made notes on her pad and then walked over to both of my paintings where the critic was assessing the accuracy of my proportions. My interviewer commented, "Kenneth looked at each submitted painting, and it was the expressions on these animals that got you a finalist spot." Shaking my hand, she added, "I have enjoyed spending time with you, Sarah. You are a remarkable young woman. Best of luck to you. We will be in touch soon." The critic had made his notes as well and then they both departed for the airport to go to their next interview.

Peter and I compared notes after the interview. I felt good about how mine went. Peter wasn't so sure. "The art critic kept measuring the proportions between my paintings and shook his head a couple of times making his notes. I admit they might not be perfect, but they were close. Watching him distracted me from what I had wanted to convey during the interview. Then she asked me what I expected from the experience with Kenneth, and I went on about learning new techniques. I somehow got the feeling she wanted me to be more specific."

Feeling like I had nailed that part, I simply said, "I spoke of his use of color and tone, along with form and shape, and how I wanted to add those talents to my skills."

Peter shook his head. "Right, I knew that. I think I might have blown it! What's done is done. I can't beat myself up about it. Let's go meet the gang. They should be waiting for us at the Hut."

From Peter's reaction to his interview, I had a feeling he wouldn't make the cut. Equally, I thought I might have a good chance. I tried to reign in my hope and excitement. At the Hut, all our friends asked questions and were filled with curiosity about the interviews. We were told we would hear within the week. The talk at the table moved to plans for the summer. Sam agreed to drop me at home and then head straight to London to work at the gallery. I had decided to take two weeks to get to know my siblings and to lend support to Eleanor before going back to London.

There was a special art class over the summer in Avignon that both Yvette and Jackson planned to take. Yvette wanted to save up some money to come visit Australia if I got the scholarship, and it was hard to contain our excitement about the possibility.

James had an amazing opportunity to intern in one of the major galleries in New York City, so he was really excited about that. Peter was waiting until he got news about Australia before determining his summer. Everyone would be back in Paris in the fall unless one of us went to Australia.

To keep my positive vibes going, I created an assortment of coloring book pages for Harry and Lizzie featuring kangaroos, koala bears, and crocodiles representing Australia in the event I would be there for the school year. I added some zebras from some of my sketches and then other animals like bunnies and chickens, dogs, and cats. Harry would be four years old and Lizzie two, but I was curious to see how they were faring without a father and looked forward to the two weeks I would be with them.

Chapter 29

As promised, by the end of the week, the announcements were made about who would attend the class in Australia. I made the list, and Peter was one of three runners-up, which meant he had a guaranteed spot for next year. In reality, we both made it, so the director was thrilled! Peter was the first to congratulate me and added, "You will learn all the stuff so I'll know what to expect. I'm happy for you, Sarah. You earned this!"

My response was sincere. "Peter, you were a big part of that after my dad passed. I'm not sure I would have pushed hard enough if you hadn't snapped me out of the depression I had fallen into."

The letter I received from the committee had a list of the names of the students selected and their home countries. It would be fascinating to meet these other artists from different backgrounds and cultures. I had loved that about L'École d'Artes. In addition, there was a separate letter asking me if I would consider coming in a month early to help two students with their English. There was a boy from Germany and a girl from Bali. Both were fluent in French, but since the course was to be taught in English, they needed help. To be honest, I wasn't sure how to go about teaching English, but room and board would be provided, and it would give me a chance to get to know the area a little before classes started. I accepted, knowing we would be able to begin by communicating in French.

My acceptance would shorten my time at the gallery in London, but the anticipation of getting over to Australia made me eager to get started. On the drive home from school with Sam, we talked about this opportunity, and I shared more about how well the interview had gone. Brighton wasn't that far out of the way, so Sam suggested we go see if the mural was still there after five years. By the time we got to the school, the students had been dismissed for the summer. Fortunately, there remained a small crew who kept the school open, so we were able to go inside. I found the mural still intact, and Sam stared at it in wonder. "Wow, Sarah! You were fourteen? This is great."

The principal must have sensed someone in the hallway, so she walked out to see us looking at the mural. "I see you have discovered our prized mural! It was painted five years ago by a very talented young student, Sarah Wilkinson."

Sam literally beamed. "I believe she means you, Sarah."

I turned to the principal with tears in my eyes. There she was, the woman who had such faith in me and offered me such encouragement before I left for Southampton. She stared at me with recognition and took me into her embrace. "Sarah, you came back! I thought you might someday. Two years ago, we got worried that wear and tear would damage the mural. We had the entire piece sealed to protect it. Now it can last for years as an inspiration to the young people who come to this school. Do you have a few moments to tell me about yourself? I do so hope you have pursued your art, dear."

We spent the next thirty minutes talking about the summers at the gallery, the scholarship to L'École d'Artes, my newest scholarship to study with Kenneth Patrick, and my continued love of painting animals that started with this very mural and the discovery of Rosa Bonheur. She gave me her address at the school and made me promise to write every now and then to keep her updated on my progress and current whereabouts.

Leaving the school with Sam, I had the sense that today was a priceless gift to be able to travel back in time, see where it had brought me, and catch a glimpse of what the future might hold. I was sincere when I thanked Sam for insisting we come. When he dropped me at home, I said goodbye and that I would see him in a couple of weeks. Sam had offered, when he found out I would be in London for a shorter time, to let me stay at his flat. Although it would save a little money, I declined. Things did not need to get more complicated with Sam than they already were.

The two weeks at home seemed to fly by. Eleanor appeared genuinely excited I had won the Australia opportunity. Although she still missed Dad terribly, she and the children had settled into a comfortable routine. Harry would start school in the fall, and

Eleanor was considering a part-time job. Dad had left her comfortable financially but she wanted to add something fulfilling. She told me she had been a reasonably good piano player, so while I was there, we found a used one to purchase for her to practice and possibly start giving piano lessons.

One night, I brought out the two zebra herd paintings to show Eleanor. I was planning to take them to London, but I was holding back. I told Eleanor, "Seeing the school mural that I did in eighth grade made me realize just how precious each stage of my journey is. I think I may always regret having sold both of my *Migration* paintings, and El Amir bought the entire falcon series. I think I should have at least taken photos and catalogued them. I love this zebra painting."

Eleanor studied them both. "Sarah, the precision in the replication is outstanding. Since they are the same, why don't you choose to keep one and take the other to the gallery? I would love to have one here at home to keep for you and show off your work. To think I could have an original Sarah Wilkinson painting hanging on my wall!"

Holding one against the wall and then the other, I asked, "Which would you prefer? The small or larger one?"

"Honestly, they are both beautiful. Which one do you think would show better at the gallery?" This was nice. Eleanor and I were having a conversation about my art, and it was comfortable and easy.

"If El Amir is an example of the other patrons, they would prefer the larger. I am fine with keeping the smaller." Then with a laugh, I added, "Who knows? We might need more room on the wall for more paintings to come!"

When the day came to take the train, the plan I discussed with Eleanor was in place. With me leaving for Australia a month early, it made the most sense to leave directly from London. Eleanor helped me pack a large suitcase with warmer weather clothing and all I would need for Australia separate from the bag I packed for London. She reminded me to contact the Bank of England on my birthday when I turned nineteen. Eleanor knew about the insurance. She was living off part of it. She had no idea how much Dad had put there but reasoned to let it be invested and grow meant whatever amount it was would be there in the case of an emergency. I should probably take a little with me to Australia.

One last time, I sat with Harry and the coloring page I made for him with the crocodile. He hadn't quite mastered keeping the crayon within the lines, but he loved making up his own ferocious crocodile noises! I hugged both him and Lizzie extra tight, realizing I would not see them for a year. I promised to write and send pictures of Australia.

The final hugs with Eleanor were bittersweet. My mum and dad were gone, but I had gained this amazing stepmother that I had only recently discovered. After Dad's death, I was so skeptical that she would want anything to do with me, and the reality could not be any further from the truth. I now knew Eleanor would be there for me and was rooting for me to succeed. One final hug and look at each of them, and I took the next step forward to my future.

Chapter 30

I would turn nineteen that summer, yet I felt much older. After all, this would be my fifth year working at the London gallery! The entire prospect of Australia looming ahead was both intimidating and exhilarating. A new country, another group of strangers, a new curriculum, and an artist/guide who was brilliant but known at times to be quite eccentric. And other than a possible visit from Yvette, I would be on my own for ten months.

Mr. Templeton greeted me warmly and said he had been anxiously awaiting my painting for this year. I retrieved the larger painting of the zebra herd, and when he studied it, I could tell he was pleased. "Sarah, my dear, I think there may be a time coming when you have enough paintings of this caliber to create your own exhibition! This is excellent, and I am sure El Amir will be pleased. Sam's series on the Africa kill also showed great ability. This school in Paris is doing a magnificent job cultivating both of your talents." Looking at what I now called *The Herd* a little closer, he added, "I think this summer we should move you to 'Artist in Residence,' working on your own originals. You might isolate certain elements within *The Herd* to create individual paintings."

I was intrigued with the idea and went to get my sketches that I used to work out the different scenes in the painting. When I showed him the variations I toyed with, he immediately felt he was onto a great concept. "Did you have a favorite part that you could not wait to put on canvas? Start with that."

I thought about the bucking male with the cheetah perched on the rock. I did love the mare with the curve of her mane, but I had to say the mare with the newborn foal bending her head down into the curvature of the foal's back was my favorite. When I told him, he nodded and said, "This summer, I would like you out in the gallery painting similar to the summer you painted the larger

Migration. However, this time, your picture will be featured at the front of the gallery. That way, visitors can see the paintings unfold. Hopefully, by the time you leave for Australia, we will have a mini collection of your zebras to complement the larger group painting." I was enchanted by the idea and couldn't wait to get started.

Sam was still working in the replication department, but now that Mr. Templeton had seen his paintings, he wanted him painting in addition to doing sculptures. He was waiting for me after my meeting with Mr. Templeton. "Hi, beautiful! You made it. It has been so boring without you!" Sam hooked an arm around me like I was his girlfriend. "What do you want to do tonight?"

"I'm supposed to see Amelia and Tara tonight. Amelia's husband, Zeke, will probably be there. You know you're welcome to join us."

"Sounds good...how about a midnight massage after?" He had said it with one of his mischievous facial expressions. *I swear, the boy makes me laugh, and a midnight massage did sound rather nice.*

"Deal!" As an afterthought, I asked, "Did you hear El Amir will be here tomorrow afternoon and wants to take the two of us to dinner?"

"Yeah. What's that all about?" Sam was trying to speculate what his intention might be. Then his mood shifted, and he looked more serious. "Sarah, you only have a month here in London before you leave for ten months. At some point, should we have a conversation about where we are with each other? It is a long time apart."

"Sam, you and I have the most amazing time together, but we have never spoken of being more than friends. You are a handsome guy! I expect you to go out there and have fun while I'm gone. Show off those abs of yours! If it leads to something more important, you are free to pursue whatever makes you happy. That's what I want for you. *But* I reserve the right to give my thumbs-up or down on any prey you go after!" That had both of us laughing; however, we both knew we would miss our easy camaraderie.

Later that evening, once again, I felt the sense that I was closing doors in order to open the door to the future. Seeing Amelia so happy with Zeke, I felt remarkably blessed to have her, and now her husband, and now to find out soon to include their child in my life. Tara had brought her new partner, a woman with very short hair and lots of tattoos. Goodness knows I would be the first to support whatever relationship gives someone joy and fulfillment. I thought about my early days with Yvette. They were perfect, but it didn't strike any chord in me to seek another female partner. Sam was incredible, but it felt like something was missing. Possibly that year difference in our age made him seem young to me. My thoughts wandered to Rachel Ruysch with her husband and ten children. I wondered how she managed to maneuver her career through all that.

Chapter 31

It was Mr. Templeton's decision to keep *The Herd* painting off the market so I could use it to isolate sections of it in new paintings. El Amir stopped by the gallery at the end of the day to pick Sam and me up for dinner. He stood in front of my zebras for a long time before saying, "You chose your subjects well. Such fascinating animals with each of their bodies a work of art in itself. I love the curve of the neck and the image it creates. The mare and her young foal blend so well it is difficult to comprehend where one ends and the other begins. Excellent! Your talent is growing each year, Sarah. Congratulations on winning a Kenneth Patrick scholarship!" He went back to studying the painting and added, "I will have a hard time knowing which of these renderings I must have and I look forward to seeing them unfold."

El Amir left to go check on what Sam was painting, and we agreed to meet at the entrance when the gallery closed. There's no question I owed El Amir a huge debt of gratitude. His support and patronage had already played an important part in the foundation of my career, but I had no idea he had just scratched the surface.

It did not take El Amir long before getting to the point of this dinner meeting. "I sincerely believe both of you are on an artistic path of great importance. The fascination you share for animals in the wild, whether in painting or sculpture, has been on my mind a great deal. I have no doubt the year ahead will be expanding that talent. I do not want to steal you away from the gallery next summer, but I have a proposal for you. The annual migration in East Africa occurs midsummer. The plains of the Serengeti will be teeming with all species of animals in motion, coinciding with the migration. I have arranged for the two of you to stay at a safari lodge for a month in Tanzania and for guides to take you on safari among the animals." Sam and I looked at each other in disbelief! *How was this happening?*

El Amir continued, "My only requirement is that you each produce two distinctive works of art for me while you are there. I will add them to my collection. Any additional work you do will create the start of a collection of work so that once you have a sufficient number, I will arrange for your first exhibition. Depending on the nature of your results, you will either be featured together or independently. How does that sound?"

I couldn't believe my ears! I jumped up and hugged El Amir to let him know I was so lucky to have caught his eye. All I could think was how incredibly jealous Rosa Bonheur would be! Sam was shaking his hand in grateful excitement. *Wow!* El Amir handed us each a brochure about the lodge we would be staying at and then piercingly looked at each of us. "Take this upcoming year seriously. Make me proud I saw remarkable talent in you at such a young age. I believe you will both go far."

Sam and I stopped at a market on the way back to his flat to buy a bottle of champagne to celebrate. We couldn't stop the excitement bubbling out of us, and we talked for hours, speculating on what such an experience would be like. At one point, I asked Sam, "Do you have any idea what El Amir does to have all this wealth and power to throw around? He seems really young in age but wise and so serious like a much older person."

"I wondered the same thing and asked Mr. Templeton. He told me El Amir's family came from big wealth back in Dubai when it underwent its transformation. I think there was also oil wealth on his mother's side. Several years ago, his father moved to North Africa and brought El Amir with him. His mother and sister stayed in Dubai with her family. Mr. Templeton said his father was somehow tied to the British military. He speculates that might be why he frequents London so often. No matter what, he seems to have taken a fancy to us and our work, and we have a chance to paint in Africa! And we get to do it together!"

We did not see El Amir again until just before I was to leave for Australia to meet the two students who needed help with their English. I was finishing the zebra series, which I limited to three because of the time constraints. El Amir seemed to like them and then surprised me once again. He brought Mr. Templeton into the room and began. "I would like to do two things with Sarah's work from this summer. First, I would like to buy the painting with the bucking male zebra and the waiting cheetah for you to pack and ship to me. Secondly, I would like to buy *The Herd* and donate it back to the gallery to be put on permanent display. You will then have the other two paintings to sell. When they do, which they will, you will be able to say the entire Sarah Wilkinson zebra *Herd* collection of paintings sold out."

That was unheard of for someone of my youth, and I could tell Mr. Templeton was both shocked and pleased. When he wrote up the invoice and showed me, I was shocked! I had turned nineteen the week before and gone to Bank of England's trust department as instructed in my dad's letter. The banker had showed me the ledger of Dad's initial deposit after my mum's death that had compounded and grown with interest. The account was just under £200,000! The trust department had been working on the account for close to nine years. They asked if I wanted to start withdrawing an allowance. I was tempted to say yes, but after looking at Mr. Templeton's invoice, I called the banker and told him to just continue doing what they had been. I actually added most of my new funds. We exchanged contact information, and he assured me the bank could respond quickly now that I was nineteen if I needed financial resources. I called to check on Eleanor and the children to be sure they had everything they needed and to tell them about the sale of *The Herd*. I told her what it sold for and to keep the one I left at home safe. Hopefully, someday it would be quite valuable.

I said my goodbyes to Amelia and Zeke as well as Tara. Saying goodbye to Sam was much harder. Our playfulness together couldn't deny that we had feelings for each other under the surface. The idea of being apart for so many months hit both of us hard. I tried to maintain our carefree banter and told him to take care of the gang back in Paris and to be sure Peter did what it took to get this chance next year. He told me to beware of kangaroo, crocodiles, and Aussies on walkabout! But when we held each other in a final hug, there was a reluctance to let go and we were content to hold the embrace for a few more seconds. After all, we had Tanzania to look forward to next summer!

Chapter 32

For now, though, the enormity of the adventure I was about to undertake that had eluded me hit me in full force as I boarded the plane. I was about to travel over ten thousand miles to Brisbane and then make my way to the bus station on my own to travel two and a half hours more by bus to Byron Bay in New South Wales using over a full day in travel!

I took time during the long flight to read more about my new mentor, Kenneth Patrick. Originally an American from California, in the late sixties, Kenneth Patrick was on the brink of being drafted into the war in Viet Nam. He was an avid surfer who loved to create painted scenes on his boards. People who had seen them began to ask at the local surf shop if they carried these marvelous painted surfboards. It wasn't long before the owner found Kenneth and worked out a deal for him to supply the painted boards to his shop. When Kenneth wasn't surfing, he was either painting or hanging out with the owner at the surf shop.

The new lottery had come out in 1969 with current draft numbers for all eligible young men. Kenneth got number 71. Not such a bad number, but the draft was especially deep that year, and it seemed inevitable Kenneth would be drafted. He was at the surf shop one afternoon talking to the owner about his dilemma when two surfers came in, having just returned from a surfing trip to Australia. They excitedly shared they had seen an incredible surfing film taken from inside the tube of a wave that was shot in Byron Bay, Australia. They went there to see if the waves were what the film promised. The surfers talked about the varying conditions and wave heights but mostly that they had never experienced surfing like what they found along the surrounding beaches of Byron Bay.

Within seventy-two hours, Kenneth Patrick secured a loan from the owner of the surf shop, booked a flight, and was on his way to Byron Bay. What he didn't know was, if his draft number was called and he didn't show up, whether he would ever be able to return to the US. When he finally made it to Byron Bay, Kenneth found a sleepy little beach town with lots of fish and chips and meat pies, a couple of pubs, two bakeries, and a beer garden. Plus five surf shops! There was already a growing population of surfers from both Australia and the US in residence. Kenneth looked around in each of the surf shops, looking for a raw board he could paint and then finish. One of the shops was particularly interesting to him. The owners were two surfers who were trying to reduce the size of the large surfboards that were so difficult to transport. They were using the waves in their backyard as their testing ground. Kenneth was inspired by their task and sought to form a partnership in creating vivid scenes to cover these smaller boards.

When the owners/designers saw the board that he created for himself, they were convinced they could create a memorable brand of surfboard. Kenneth was right there to help test the new prototypes. Even when one didn't meet their standards, he used them to create masterful designs. Those prototypes were sold in the shop as decorative items. Nothing could have shocked them more than when the decorative prototypes began to sell for more than their standard boards! They knew then that once their boards were perfected, they had to have an original Kenneth Patrick signature design. Others were attempting to copy the concept, which made it even more important for theirs to be exclusive and copyrighted.

Once the prototypes met their required needs, the three of them formed a formal partnership. Kenneth was clever enough to offer exclusive rights to the surfboard designs he did, but rights to all other designs on whatever medium remained with him. His instinct to include that clause in those early days was instrumental in paving the way for his future success.

Byron Bay was expanding and becoming known as an international surfing destination unequaled elsewhere. Surfers came from all over the globe to surf these waves, and rarely did they leave without ordering a Kenneth Patrick design surfboard. Kenneth and his two partners were making a good income, but things were about to change. Word of the Kenneth Patrick designs was spreading. Designers came to meet him from the fashion world, the textiles world, and any who thought his design might help market their product.

By the late seventies, Kenneth Patrick had become an Australian citizen and was well sought after as an artist. He had finalized an agreement to provide six new surfboard patterns a year to keep his one-third partnership, but he was then free to take on other assignments. He chose them carefully and added paintings on canvas to his repertoire. His use of bold colors and depth gave an almost three-dimensional look to his paintings. By the eighties, Kenneth Patrick was a household name.

This was the man I would study under. What a remarkable history! *Was I going to try my hand at surfing? How exciting!*

Chapter 33

By the time I made it to the bus in Brisbane and handed my two heavy bags to the driver to stow, all I wanted was to crawl into a bus seat and sleep all the way to Byron Bay. I totally forgot the boy from Germany was also supposed to be on the bus. I fell asleep immediately, relatively comfortable since thankfully the seat next to me was empty. It wasn't until the bustle of activity when the bus stopped in Ballina that I woke up. Some passengers were getting off, and others were boarding. The driver was switching out luggage. With a start, I realized the girl from Bali, Mara, was supposed to get on the bus here in Ballina. That meant the German boy, Hans, must already be on board!

I looked around, feeling horrible I hadn't thought of it earlier. There was a young man at the rear of the bus with his ball cap down over his face, obviously sleeping, oblivious to this new activity. Surely that must be him. It was then I saw the most beautiful young woman get on the bus, looking around. She was obviously not jet-lagged, and her dark brown hair was meticulously pulled to the side in twin braids adorned with a bright yellow flower. Her fitted yellow lace tunic flowed over black pants, accented by her bright fuchsia shoulder bag. All eyes were focused on her as she came down the aisle, yet she didn't seem to notice.

In total contrast, I looked like a throwback to hippie days in my gray baggy pants and off-white tee. My unruly hair had gotten longer, and at least I had tied a scarf around the knotted part that was pulled up. No makeup, narrow-rimmed glasses. Unbelievably, Mara walked right up to me and asked in French if I was Sarah and if she could sit with me. I moved my bag, and when she sat down, I pointed out the sleeping boy in the back and suggested he might be Hans from Hamburg.

The ride from Ballina to Byron did not take long. Mara was friendly but reserved. She mentioned it was her first time away from her home. Kenneth Patrick had rooms set up for us at a backpackers' inn. The fifteen of us would take over most of the inn with single rooms and adjoining bathrooms. Mara and I would share a bathroom, but I think both of us were pleased we would have our own room. The inn was just a few minutes' walk to the beach and had a pool and rooftop terrace.

When the bus stopped and passengers began to get off, I looked back to see Hans still sleeping. I walked back to nudge him awake, but I was not prepared when he stirred and took off his cap. Even with his blond-streaked hair tousled, I was sure I had never seen a more handsome guy. He was casually dressed in jeans and a T-shirt, but his muscles bulged through, leaving no question there was not an ounce of fat on his body. And his chiseled face looked like it could be the face of a Greek god, with eyes so blue they were almost transparent.

Startling me out of my embarrassing reverie, he smiled a most genuine smile and looked up at me and said in French, "*Tu dois être*, Sarah." (You must be Sarah.) I somehow mumbled out a yes and told him to hurry before the bus left with us still on board. All I could think was here with these two gorgeous humans is that Kenneth Patrick must have had looks on his list as a requirement and somehow my photo got misplaced!

I don't think Mara had ever seen a blond man before, since the men in Bali all had dark hair. She was very shy when I introduced them. What surprised me was how nonchalant Hans was with how he looked and the easy-going manner he portrayed. He made it easy for us to feel comfortable around him and not focus on his looks. Checking into the inn, we agreed to unpack and freshen up and then to meet at the rooftop terrace.

One of our teachers would be by tomorrow to check on us and go over the plan to work on Hans's and Mara's English. Alone in my room, as I unpacked, I contemplated the next month before the class started. I hoped the three of us would get along, similar to that first year at L'École d'Artes when the six of us became friends and looked out for each other.

Chapter 34

On the terrace, our introductory conversation was in French. It was easy for me, having spent so much time in France. However, even though both Mara and Hans could communicate in French, it was not their native languages. Communication was key. Now I just had to navigate them through French to get to English. The challenge was, I did not know a word of Balinese or German, so I had to understand them in French. When they fell back to their native language, I was at a loss to help them. We agreed anytime they didn't understand me, a simple *"je ne comprends pas"* would let me know they didn't understand.

That first evening, we walked to the beach and saw one surf shop after the other. I think perhaps the first English word Hans learned was *surf*. It turned out he was an avid water sports enthusiast. He loved to do anything in or on the water. It was his precision renderings of sailboats with their sails capturing the perfect wind that had caught Kenneth Patrick's attention. He literally could not wait to try surfing along this coast!

Mara had a knack for capturing a moment as it happened in a sketch and then transferring it to a painted canvas after. I was impressed with both of them and could only imagine this class of fifteen and what incredible talents we would be working with. For the moment, I had an annoying problem that was keeping me from focusing on teaching them English. Granted, my experience with the opposite sex had been limited to Yvette, Jackson, and Sam. The first two were so limited they hardly counted. But Sam? He was fun and safe and adventurous. I adored him as a friend, but had I ever felt anything like this attraction? Absolutely not. It was embarrassing!

There were times when Hans would just pinch my chin and grin. Or he would take off his T-shirt to display perfect abs to simply go for a swim. I was like a naïve schoolgirl starstruck. There was no way he didn't see it. He was probably used to breaking hearts back home. *Was he toying with me?*

From the days of simulating Rosa Bonheur to wow my art teachers, I liked knowing I maintained control of the situation. When I got close to Hans, I felt like an idiot. It was as if there was some magnetic field around him, and if I ever breached that border, I would be lost with no control over my senses. I didn't like it one bit. Would I just turn into a dribbling moron? I had to maintain my distance at all costs.

I now realize my actions just fed the combustion of what was about to unfold. The more I pulled away from him, the more intriguing I became to him. Mara saw it...how could she not? We had made it through most of the month, and both Hans and Mara were picking up English with Australian slang thrown in, which made us all laugh. There was a talented couple who once a week would *busk* or sing on the sidewalk, hoping to gather a crowd to watch for tips. It was terms like *busking* that soon became a normal part of our language. But actually their English was improving every day, and I knew the teachers would be pleased.

One afternoon, Hans heard there was a good surfing condition, so he left with a couple of guys from the surf shop to try his luck. Mara suggested we go set up our canvases on the beach to watch. The scene reminded me of those early days in Brighton painting among the sand dunes. Mara was capturing the surfers positioned inside the curve of a wave. My radar was on full alert, and I knew exactly which surfer was Hans, which totally irritated me. I sketched out the curve of the wave with the surfer rising toward the front of the wave. But I couldn't resist...in jest, unbeknownst to the surfer in the sketch, I added a huge shark with razor-sharp teeth breaking through the wave. Mara glanced over and gasped. "Sarah, that is a horrible image! Why did you add that? What has Hans done to make you dislike him so?" When I didn't reply and made one of the shark's teeth look even sharper, she continued, "That's not funny. It's not that you dislike him, is it? It's that you dislike the idea of liking him so much that you have to feign dislike. I'm right, aren't I?"

It was at that moment that the lifeguard began to blow his whistle and yell, "Shark!" The surfers were scrambling to shore. In shock, I pushed my canvas face down into the sand. I somehow felt I had conjured up the shark! Mara stood up in disbelief, searching for Hans. *Where was he? Oh my god! I didn't mean anything by it! What had I done?*

All I know was that I started running like my life depended on it. Hans had been distracted by the whistle and scream long enough to lose his balance on the wave. He fell from his board and was immediately engulfed in the wave being churned forward. Taking no heed of a potential shark, I ran into the sea to where he washed up. The wave had tossed him about, and he had taken in some seawater, but he seemed okay. I reached him and pulled him up, hugging him so tight some of the sea water came dribbling down my back. I didn't care. He was okay. The lifeguard guided us back to shore where Mara was waiting. He checked Hans over, and other than being slightly disoriented, he was fine. But he kept staring at me with a question in his eyes that asked me, "What just happened?"

I had breached his magnetic wall. There was no going back for me. I wanted this boy with my heart, my body, and my soul. There was an added intensity to the moment when he realized the depth of my feelings and decided to meet me halfway. He kissed me with a need that reached deep inside me to take possession of what he now knew was his.

Chapter 35

M ara handed me my glasses that must have fallen when I was running. Then she went back to where we were painting to get our supplies. While the enormity of what had just happened washed over me, a feeling of undeniable vulnerability seeped its way into my eyes as I stared up at him to somehow judge his reaction. He smiled, put his arm around me, and grabbed his shirt and board. "Come on. Let's get you out of those wet clothes." That made me smile back because he had said it in perfect English.

Hans dropped the board off at the surf shop. We had not spoken a word. When we got back to the inn, I wanted a moment to regain some grain of sanity, so I said I would shower. Hans literally shook me. "It is about damn time you figured this out, Sarah. You and I have an undeniable attraction. Don't waste time thinking of all the reasons not to pursue this. Why don't we explore what it would be like to be together? I don't think either one of us came here looking for romance, but it seems to have found us." Then to lighten the mood, he added with a twinkle in his eyes, "I think I am managing my English quite well. My English teacher should be quite proud!"

There were a thousand what-ifs that could be used to reason why a relationship with Hans would not work. But if there was one chance of it working out, wasn't it worth taking a risk and letting go of the fear?

While I dried my hair (which seemed to always take hours), Mara came back to her room with the paints and canvases. Holding up the sketch with the shark, she giggled and said, "You might want to get rid of this before a certain young German sees it."

I looked at it and shook my head. "I really didn't mean anything by it. It was a stupid joke to cover my frustration. Who would have ever thought there would be a real shark?" Wondering if I had become close enough to Mara to confide in her, I decided it couldn't hurt. "I have never experienced an attraction like this, and it is frightening to think this could be one way. I have a long history of not being very good at trusting. It just seems easier to avoid jumping into the fire."

I could tell Mara was thinking it through and probably glad she was not in the middle of a similar situation. "At home in Bali, we have a philosophy. 'Your future is determined by how you choose to approach it. If you give yourself a positive outlook moment after moment, day after day, to maintain high expectations, you will make your future the very best it can be.' Try it, Sarah. Go into it thinking about what can go right. Maybe instead of drawing sharks, you should be drawing rainbows?"

There was a loud knock on my door. I looked at Mara and got a nod of support. My hair was still slightly damp and I hadn't pulled it up yet, but I answered the door. There was Hans, blond hair tossed to the side, wearing khaki cargo shorts and a white linen shirt with a single button fastened at the waist, leaving his chest exposed. "What is taking you so long?"

Mara had slipped back to her room. "My hair. It has gotten so long it takes forever to dry."

Hans lifted a handful and rubbed it between his fingers. "It is like spun gold. Sarah, don't cut it. Your hair is beautiful. Why don't you get your brush and let me brush it for you?"

I had never had anyone do something so personal that wasn't sexual, but I got the brush. Hans sat on the side of my bed with his legs straddled to give me room to sit. He began to brush in long smooth strokes that had my eyes rolling back with delight. How could hair-brushing take on such an erotic turn? With one sweep of the brush, my hair moved to one side to expose my neck, which he proceeded to taste and nibble. He was in no hurry to make any demands. Right then, he was taking full advantage of getting me used to his touch. When he began to braid my hair, I wondered how he even knew how. With my neck exposed, it was if a primal instinct as a male took over to determine if the female is his mate. He kissed my neck, and simultaneously his fingertips stroked my arms. There was no way I could help the change in my breathing and my leaning back into him.

A fleeting thought crossed my mind that Sam would already have my clothes off, but Hans seemed to savor each moment of discovery, and my arousal was beyond anything I could have imagined. His touch was like liquid fire. I reached behind me to unbutton the single button of his shirt. I wanted desperately to feel his skin, not his shirt. He released me for a moment to remove his shirt and then with one motion lifted my tank top over my head. Moving his hands back around to my breasts, my chest rose into his hands, moving us both to the brink of madness and passion. I was no longer satisfied to have my back to him. I scooted off the bed and reached for his buckle to remove his shorts and then tossed mine aside to straddle him. Touching those perfect muscles, I could feel them clench and release as I felt him quiver. When I reached for him to guide him inside me, Hans pulled his head away to look at me to be sure this was what I wanted. My answer was a hard thrust into him, engulfing all of his hardness inside me. With that coupling, there was no question this was where I was supposed to be, and I rocked with him just to explore the wonder of it, in no hurry to finish.

We made love on my bed until the light of day was gone. Our bodies were moist with exertion, but such a contrast with his hard and tight and mine slim but soft and rounded. We had said no words, simply sighs and moans in the language of love. Hans was the first to recover his speech when he held me tight and fell back to his native language. He mumbled as he put his hand through my hair with the braid long gone. "*Ich liebe dich.*"

I did not know enough German to understand exactly what he meant, but my response was automatic. "I love you too." *Oh my god, he felt good!*

Chapter 36

That day in Byron Bay, Australia, was the beginning of my love affair with Hans Schuman. He was so much more than just handsome. We spent hours discussing our youth, families, and countries. He told me how his parents were the driving force behind his art. His grandfather had been a well-known artist in Germany, but somehow the artistic gene had skipped over his son to his grandson. Hans said he didn't think his father was resentful toward him, but that was most likely why he pushed Hans so hard. The owner of the gallery over in the artsy side of Hamburg had taken Hans under his wing, bought his first major painting, and helped him secure this opportunity with Kenneth Patrick.

Mara was with us a great deal of the time, and we loved hearing about her life in Bali. She still lived at home with her parents. It was one of her college professors who noticed her sketches and propelled her forward. I shared with them about El Amir and Mr. Templeton.

When it was time to attend our first class and the rest of the students arrived, we were astounded at the talent in our group of fifteen and knew without question this would be an important experience for us all. We represented eleven countries, which offered us a diverse cultural mix of personalities.

When Kenneth Patrick got on stage to introduce himself, Hans reached over to squeeze my hand in anticipation. He began, "I want to welcome each of you to Byron Bay and the Kenneth Patrick program. All of you were individually chosen for not only your talent but also your potential to achieve commercial success. When I was your age, my passion was painting and surfing. I had no idea those passions would combine to lead me to a certain amount of fame." That comment resulted in a chuckle throughout the room. "During this course, I will bring in specialists who will discuss textiles, decorative art, visual branding, fashion design, and decorative arts for you to experiment with where your talent might take you. In addition, the course will be divided into four categories—Design Principles, Design Requirements, Design Strategy, and Design Theory. Our hope is that you will graduate from this course able to enhance your talent to ensure its marketability."

Here I was with this small group of chosen students who had to be as excited as I was for this incredible opportunity! Kenneth Patrick was a legend, and we had a chance to learn not only the potential of our talent but also the means to protect the integrity of our work. Hans and I talked late into the night, wondering what part of our painting skills they would work with. Hans's passion was anything seaworthy, including graphic renderings of ships or boats of any size. He was a surfer but also an avid sailor. He was convinced that all my work in London at the gallery secured my future as a painter, but he seemed to still be questioning his own direction. He joked that he might start painting surfboards like Kenneth!

Throughout the fall, my feelings for Hans continued to grow, as did the intimacy we shared. His lovemaking made me feel safe and beautiful. In his embrace, I often felt as if our souls, not just our bodies, were connected as one. When I look back, the combination of the appeal of the Kenneth Patrick course with a fulfilled love life created one of the best times in my life. My friendship with Mara also blossomed during those months. Her talent was mesmerizing, and I always enjoyed watching her paint and learning from her technique. The month in Africa with Sam the following summer seemed a far-distant future.

As classes began, Kenneth Patrick scheduled a one-on-one meeting with each of us to determine what made our talent unique and why his committee had chosen us. Mara and I were anxious and intimidated by the upcoming meeting, but Hans was taking it in stride and sought to help us realize we needed to take advantage of the individual time we would have with him.

I remember walking in that room for my meeting nervous as a cat. Kenneth Patrick was casually sitting on the corner of the desk wearing board shorts and a button-down print shirt that had to be one of his designs. He was fit but stocky, probably in his late forties or early fifties, with brown wavy hair balding in the back.

He asked me to sit down and looked at his notes. "Sarah, is it?" I nodded and he continued, "I see you are particularly fond of painting animals and that your great influences have been Rosa Bonheur and Rachel Ruysch. Can you explain how their artistic styles have impacted your own style?"

When it came to Rosa and Rachel, they were subjects I could easily discuss. "Both artists practiced a realistic approach in presenting their subjects. Rosa Bonheur's love of animals and the ability to portray their soul through their eyes has been a lofty goal of mine, and I have warmed to the subject of animals, mostly wild in nature. Studying Rachel helped me conquer precision and detail in my work, and I believe the combination gives me a style that is unique."

Kenneth was paying close attention. "As a whole, realism is not considered the most current art style. It is the emotions you evoke in your paintings that make your style an exception. Do you feel limited by painting on canvas? Are you willing to try a different medium? You know, Sarah, there is art in every aspect of our lives. A sculpture that can be turned into a lamp, an ornamental embellishment can make a visual difference in a building, furniture, clothing, bedding, decorative accessories...the list goes on and on. Some artists are not able to stray from the comfort of the canvas. What I ask of you during this process is to keep your mind open enough to explore different ways to express your talent to provide that emotional response you are so good at. If you do that, you might find this course quite enlightening!"

I told him I would try my best to follow his lead and shook his hand, putting faith in his methods. Hans and Mara had similar meetings, and afterward we discussed how different this would be but agreed to give his process every effort.

Chapter 37

My letters to Yvette, Amelia, Tara, and of course, Sam, spoke of Kenneth Patrick and his openness to a variety of methods to explore our talent. I told them about Byron Bay and trying to surf (I could finally manage the smaller waves with Hans's instruction). I shared how interesting it was to be with students from all over the globe and, of course, shared my friendship with Hans and Mara. For some reason, I kept the romance with Hans to myself. *Was I still unsure if it could be real?*

Our classes presented us with multiple opportunities to try different mediums. Mara absolutely fell in love with painting on silk, whereas it made me crazy! The instructor would take a piece of stretched silk on a wood frame with the encouragement to lay it flat. To create a design, a special type of glue was used to make the outline. On silk, the paint would run but be stopped by the glue. While it was running, colors could be added to blend. Mara became quite good at melding different colors within the confines of the space she was working with. Unfortunately, I seemed to always manage to have a breach somewhere in the glue, which made the current color I was working with run somewhere it didn't belong, so it frustrated me. But to see Mara's pieces after they were baked and the glue removed (similar to the wax in Sam's sculptures) was incredible! Kenneth Patrick nodded his approval. They taught her how to roll and stitch the edges to make a beautiful scarf. She worked at getting her signature in the form of initials into the design. I could tell how desirable her scarves would become, but when she moved to making silk clothing, her designs took my breath away!

About two months into the course, Hans and I had tried our hand at many art forms, but for me, nothing seemed to feel close to the way Mara connected with her silk painting. Kenneth Patrick cautioned us to be patient. There would be much to explore. Lying in bed one night after a rather intense coupling that rocked my heart to the core, Hans was still holding me but seemed distracted. I rolled over and held him with my hand wandering over his body. "What is it, love? Where are those thoughts taking you?"

Hans gave a large sigh and said, "I am getting frustrated and wonder if I'm wasting my time here seeking some way to commercialize the little talent I have."

The first part of that sentence couldn't help but rub me the wrong way, and my reaction was somewhat defensive. Somewhat coolly, I said, "I certainly hope you don't think you are wasting your time here with me."

"No, of course not. Meeting you has been the best thing that ever happened to me. I watch Mara so involved with her silk painting, and I just hope there might be something like that for me." As if sensing I needed reassurance, he pulled me to him with caresses, leaving no question how he felt.

It was not long before Hans found his calling. The following week, Kenneth Patrick announced we would be leaving for a three-day road trip to Brisbane. We were going to study under a famous glassblower in his studio. Once we got there, our instructor introduced us to the glass furnace and the tools he used to form the blown glass. I was awestruck by the process but the 2,400-degree furnace was not something I was comfortable around. For Hans, he could not have been more interested! He watched as the instructor turned the blow tube in the molten glass simmering in the oven and brought it out, pliable enough to let it form as a tube smoothed by rolling it back and forth on a steel-top table. When Hans saw him blow through the long tube, making the glass expand with his breath, he knew he wanted to try it. Once the instructor heated the glass at the end of the tube further, he brought it back out to twist the glass in a vat with red-colored glass pieces that stuck to the molten hot glass. Back in the heat again, the colored pieces began to melt, and this time, when he pulled it out, the instructor used large tweezers to pull and tug the glass-like taffy, blending the red into the center, creating the most amazing shape. He smoothed the round piece on a spinning surface, and when the paperweight was finished, he tapped the tube to disconnect it from the glass. Hans literally was first in line to try the method. Three days was not nearly enough to satisfy his desire to learn more.

When Kenneth Patrick saw how Hans could work with the glass and add color and shape, he approved Hans to stay for an extra week to study, knowing when he returned there was a studio close by in Byron Bay he could continue to use. It seemed Hans had found his passion, and he was excited to stay the week. I returned to campus not so thrilled with no Hans and no passion of my own. I was one of only three who had not found something to challenge and excite us more than painting on canvas.

I could see now that Kenneth Patrick expected this to be an individual journey for each of us. Once we found that enthusiastic response in ourselves to try something new, he helped us stick with it, and we concentrated on perfecting that skill with our own individual instructor giving a customized experience. Mara and two other classmates worked with a brilliant silk painter under Kenneth Patrick's tutelage. Hans returned after his week in Brisbane with a sense of accomplishment that was hard to contain. I didn't know at the time that I would try working with glass in a different way but without the same ending.

Chapter 38

Kenneth seemed pleased with the direction his students were taking, but he knew I was growing impatient. He came up to me the next week to tell me he had a surprise for the class that he was convinced I would love. I could not imagine what it could be and had my doubts. The class size had dwindled with just three of us left. I sat in the classroom wondering if it was finally my day to find a way to challenge my art.

A petite Chinese woman came into the classroom, and Kenneth Patrick introduced her. She spoke broken English, so Kenneth was there to bridge any gaps in communication. Out of her bag she pulled an assortment of small glass bottles in varying shapes and four flat rectangular wooden boxes. Kenneth Patrick picked up one of the bottles and held it in the palm of his hand. "These small bottles date back to the Qing Dynasty in China beginning in the mid-1600s. They originally contained powdered tobacco that was imported from Portugal, but when tobacco was outlawed, snuff took over because they reasoned snuff was a medicinal remedy. The Chinese aristocracy would buy the snuff in these bottles that were comfortable to carry...therefore the small size. They quickly became known as snuff bottles. There were many ways to make the bottles more ornate and, therefore, more desirable. Hence, we find the development of Inner Painting."

I was paying close attention. *What would they do with these bottles?* The Chinese woman passed one of the bottles to each of us, then one of the boxes, along with paint and water. I have to admit I was intrigued. Kenneth continued, "With the popularity of snuff bottles, someone came up with the idea of painting a scene that showed through from the inside of the bottle. The challenge was, the paintings had to not only be extremely miniature but also backward!" The idea of changing the size did not concern me, although this would be major in reverse to make it so small. *But painting it backward?*

The woman proceeded to paint a lovely bird scene with bamboo shoots onto onion-skin paper. She let it air-dry. While it was drying, she introduced us to our box of special brushes that were bent at the tips to go through the neck of the bottle and paint on the wall. We gathered around as she took the onion-skin painting and turned it over, giving it a backward appearance. She mixed her paints, diluted them perfectly, and reached a brush down through the neck of the bottle with its sideways tip and began to paint. Concentration was crucial to make precise strokes. The result was a painting through the glass that was exquisite and a perfect replica of her painting on the onion-skin paper. I couldn't wait to try it!

Determination wasn't the only skill I needed to take on this task. The first time I pushed a bent-tip brush through the neck of a small bottle, I could not fathom how you would see the painting well enough to even paint it backward. The instructor, with an abundance of patience, came over and approved my small painting on the onion-skin paper. It was of a zebra mare and her two foals. She picked up the bottle and, looking at it from the front, began to stroke the paint backward. Ahh, I had to look at the painting unfold from the front as it should be, but I had to train my hand-and-eye coordination to get the brush to face me from the inside of the bottle and paint backward! I can definitely say it took getting used to it, but I loved the effect of the painting coming through the glass. Once I finished a design, I would use a different brush to create a wash of tint around the painting to create the background so none of the glass was transparent.

I began combing through antique stores and flea markets to find interesting bottles I could use other than snuff bottles. I found the small designs with intricate detail most pleasing, but I couldn't help my mind from wondering how else this medium could be used. The direction it would take came from a simple Christmas gift. The holiday was approaching, and we students would get a ten-day break. The only students leaving to go home were the two from Australia. The owners of the inn enlisted the help of those of us who stayed to put up the Christmas tree and decorate for the season. I wrapped stuffed animals for Harry and

Lizzy and the painted bottle with the two foals for Eleanor and sent them back to Southampton. Yvette was coming to visit for a week, and Denise, the girl from Australia who was going home, offered to let Yvette stay in her room.

When we went to class the last day before Christmas break, Kenneth Patrick gathered us all together. "This morning, I want to take a few moments to tell you how pleased I am with each of you and the progress you have made over the fall. You have been daring enough to stretch your talent to try a different medium, which might lead to a certain commercial success in your future. Remember, this new dimension you find here will never replace the undeniable talent you have as a traditional painter. What it will hopefully do is stretch your consciousness to explore what can be rather than fixate on what simply is. I want you to consider over the break how you create your own signature style and medium. Don't let anything hold you back. Collaborate with each other if you get an idea to try. I have faith in each of you to step outside traditional boundaries. For those of you away from home this Christmas, I would like to ask you to join my family for dinner Christmas Eve. Have a wonderful break!"

Chapter 39

Yvette was flying into Brisbane, so I planned to rent a car to go pick her up. Hans loved the idea of spending a few hours with the glassblower from our field trip, so we planned to go the day before and spend the night. Once we checked into our hotel that was walking distance to the studio, we decided to do a little window-shopping on the way. It was fascinating to me that once you get your eyes used to seeing something in a certain way, you notice things differently. Most of the windows we passed had the name of the shop and its logo painted on the glass...from the inside. When I went inside the shop and looked out the window, the name and design were backward. Nothing nearly as challenging as doing it through the inside of a bottle, but it had me thinking. We passed one window that was particularly thick. The type and design looked almost three-dimensional, but when I walked inside, the paint was flat like the other windows.

At the studio, the glassblower was in the process of making a paperweight. When he saw us, he summoned Hans over to hand him the iron pontil rod with the first mass of molten glass. Hans took the rod and began rolling the glass on the top of the stainless-steel marver table to cool it enough to hold its shape. Once it was ready, he lowered it into the container of crushed red glass and then lifted it. He gave the rod a quarter turn and lowered it into the purple crushed glass...another quarter turn and into the gold glass. Hans took the rod with the newly placed colors back over to the blowhole to melt the crushed glass, periodically taking it out of the heat to roll it on the metal surface to embed the colors. Once he was satisfied and the glass cool enough to maneuver, he took the metal shears and made several cuts in the pliable glob on the end of his rod. Using tongs, he twisted, tugged, and pinched the mass forming ribbons of colors. Now back to the furnace to add more transparent glass to encase the colorful center. He used cup-shaped molds with water spinning the rod constantly to form a rounded ball. He repeated the process until he had the right size and a perfectly smooth exterior. Over a soft landing spot, Hans tapped the rod, breaking the connection with the ball of glass, giving a flat edge that would be refined after it cooled in the oven. Hans was ecstatic!

I watched the entire process in awe to see the impact the depth of glass made on a subject. Over to the side, there was a woman surrounded by cylinders filled with various colors of glass canes that looked a little like drink stirrers. She was poised over a stationary torch melting the tip of a green cane, forming small pieces that would be leaves. Then she took a pink cane and proceeded to make petals. She had a wide assortment of miniature pieces that she then began to assemble using clear melted glass as the glue. I was fascinated with the concept of sculpting with glass.

Hans brought over a piece from the cooling oven that was a separate three-dimensional garden scene. It was beautiful! Hans said with excitement, "Come watch!" He set the still warm glass design down at the bottom of a metal mold. He then took his rod over to the furnace to gather a sizable amount of molten glass. He rolled it, working any bubbles out, and then came over and pressed the hot glass into the mold surrounding the design. A vacuum was created to pull the glass back out with the design attached. Once that was complete, he went through the process again to add more clear glass, shape it into the size he wanted, and smooth it out. He tapped the rod to release it, and I could not believe the masterful creation in front of me. The depth of the glass exaggerated all of the details of the design, making it seem that I was looking into a magical kingdom!

I couldn't help it. Before I knew it, I was sketching the mare and newborn foal with their heads perfectly aligned. I handed it to the artist making the detailed pieces, and she studied it carefully and smiled. "Would you like me to show you how this might be done?" I watched as she melted black glass and formed it to the shape of what would be the mare's mane. She made cuts from one side to give the texture of hair and then heated it again using tweezers to narrow and elongate the mane to perfection. Piece by small piece, I watched my scene unfold. When I saw the finished product encased in glass, I looked at Hans in disbelief. *What a day we shared!*

Chapter 40

At the hotel, Hans finished in the shower and stood against the doorframe with a towel loosely tied around his waist. The exhilaration of the day had spilled over, and the desire on his face that clenched his jaws was tangible as it swept over me and drew me to him. His eyes were glued to mine when he said huskily, "Working with the molten glass that is so fragile on the one hand and pliable to my touch on the other is how I feel with you." He unbuttoned the first button of my shirt and pressed his hand on my exposed neck. I felt his heat, and his hand was scorching, yet I was glued to it. "I love your fluid movements when I touch you that show me you are mine." Button after button was slowly released. My back arched and my breasts leaned into him, begging for more. All control was long gone, and I stayed mesmerized by the husky voice that continued to speak the most intimate of promises of what lay ahead for us that night. Every nerve ending in my body yearned for his touch, and to his credit, he was making every effort to accommodate.

After, with our bodies moist and intertwined, I asked, "The chemistry between us is so intense. Do you think it can possibly last?" It was the first time a permanent relationship had been mentioned, and I worried that I might have said the wrong thing.

Hans adjusted my head against his shoulder and said, "I hope so, Sarah. Once we leave Australia, we go in different directions. I plan to take the job as assistant manager at the gallery in Hamburg working under Geoffrey, my sponsor. I know El Amir is sending you to paint in Africa for a month. Our paths have connected during this time and in this place, but our lives will move on. I know my father is not going to let up on my pursuing an art career, and I have no idea what he is going to think about the glassblowing. I suppose we have to let our future unfold as it will." I thought about spending the month in Africa with Sam. I had never mentioned to Hans I wasn't going to Africa alone. *Why wasn't I telling him?* Sam and I were so carefree with each other, even with sex. After such an all-consuming relationship with Hans, I couldn't picture how it would be with just Sam and me in a foreign country. Maybe Hans was right, and we simply needed to follow our hearts and let them guide us.

The following morning, we had time to enjoy a nice breakfast and go back to the studio before picking up Yvette at the airport. Hans wanted to smooth the rough bottoms of the pieces he made where they had been connected to the tube. I was entranced to see the zebra scene as I had conceived it as a flat painting turned into a three-dimensional piece of art. I asked the artist if I could buy it, and she absolutely refused to take a penny. She gave it to me, and I knew it would be a special memento for many years to come. Hans polished it, along with his pieces, and then, with a spray of liquid nitrogen where he had heated, immediately cooled it down. We were shocked the instructor charged us for materials but nothing for the use of the studio or his expertise. We left incredibly grateful for our time there.

Yvette's plane arrived just as we got to the airport. I hadn't seen her since we left Paris for summer break and couldn't wait! She came through the gate holding her jacket that she would definitely not need here in December. Yvette looked very cosmopolitan in her Parisian clothes. What a long way she had come since our first year at L'École d'Artes as seniors in high school with her cropped hair and pink streak!

Even though months had gone by, we immediately fell back into our easy rapport. She teased me mercilessly about the supposed "glow" I had around my new boyfriend. Fortunately, Hans was a good sport about it and gave me a wink and agreed. "She is rather glowing, isn't she? I suppose I'll have to do my part to make sure she stays that way!"

On the drive back to Byron Bay, Yvette updated me on everyone. Peter was practically assured of coming to train with Kenneth Patrick next fall and was working hard to be ready for his interview. James had worked as a curator at a major museum in Chicago over the summer, but the gallery in New York City where he had interned was seriously trying to persuade him to return. He was taking extra courses at school to graduate early to work there full-time painting and teaching. Jackson would graduate this spring, and Yvette shared they were considering moving in together since they were practically living together anyway. And Sam was being Sam...he was having a blast dating a new girl every week, it seemed. All he could talk about was the upcoming Africa trip and that he couldn't wait to see actual lions in combat. That got a questioning glance from Hans. I rolled my eyes and explained, "Sam is the other artist going to Africa, and rest assured, I don't plan to be anywhere close enough to lions to become their next meal!"

Hans and I shared with Yvette stories about the methods Kenneth Patrick was introducing us to in order to expose us to expanding our talent. I told Yvette she would have a chance to meet him in person Christmas Eve when we went to his house for dinner. In the meantime, we all agreed to take full advantage of the warm weather and free time to surf and do all the water sports. Hans had even rented a sailboat for us to all go out on with a few of the other students.

Chapter 41

Mara was waiting for us at the inn. Her enjoyment of silk painting had progressed toward batik and color blocking with different fabrics, and she and two other girls were designing a small collection of clothing. When she met Yvette dressed so stylishly, Mara immediately wanted to quiz her on French fashion and possible styles that might translate into the design options they were exploring. Yvette fit right in, and we could tell this would be a memorable vacation.

The following morning, after Yvette had time to shake off some of the inevitable jet lag, we met for breakfast on the terrace. The plan was to give her a tour of Byron Bay and go for a swim. It was nice that it was just the two of us, and I brought one of my painted bottles and the zebra paperweight for her to see. She studied both of them, curious about the techniques to make them. I explained about the bent brushes and having to paint backward for the painting on the bottle, but I loved the three-dimensional effect of the paperweight. However, I admitted that the idea of working with fire was extremely intimidating.

Twisting and turning both samples in her hand, Yvette said, "Sarah, you have this incredible talent to paint on canvas with a dimension I have never seen elsewhere. Do you think this idea diverts you from simply improving your craft?"

She handed me back the paperweight, and I looked at it from a different perspective. "I'm not sure. What are you thinking?"

Yvette suggested, "Why don't we go find a glass shop after breakfast. Maybe it is time to experiment?"

Hans got an early morning start to surf, and Mara was working on the fashion project with her friends, so this was the perfect time for Yvette and me to venture out. I tucked the bottle and paperweight into my bag, and we proceeded to walk to the custom glass shop in an alley several blocks away. When we got there, the owner was cutting a deep bevel around the edge of a four-by-six-inch thick piece of glass. He looked up from his task to ask how he could help. Yvette told me to bring out my samples, and she explained, pointing her finger at me, "My friend is an amazing painter, and she loves the idea of creating a three-dimensional painting, but she is uncomfortable with hot glass. She would like to experiment with creating paint under glass to create an unusual and unique effect."

He looked carefully at both samples and then back at us. "Throughout the last century, resin has been an alternative to molten glass. But to be honest, it is considered a cheap, undesirable substitute. I have an idea. I have a bin in the back where I keep my cut scraps. You could get a variety of samples, and I could quickly smooth the edges for you."

I loved the idea, and we carefully went through the bin, selecting pieces. As we selected the various sizes and depths, he sanded the edges and found a box to stack them in. I had to admit my excitement about the project was growing, although I had no idea what it would produce. We took the box of glass back to the inn and set up a mini studio at one of the rooftop tables. I brought out my sketch pad and paints. Yvette was laying out the various pieces of glass while I tried to translate the visual image of the zebras through the glass.

Once I got an acceptable painting that I could replicate, I tried different depths of glass. As we suspected, the deeper the glass, the more natural dimension we got.

Yvette suddenly had an idea and diluted a little brown and green paint enough to make a wash. She took a thinner piece of glass similar in size to the one I just completed to create the faintest of color wash with the green representing the foreground and brown the background. Once both pieces of glass were dry, we placed them together, paint on paint. The background wash was soft behind the zebras and, with glass on either side catching the painting inside, gave the dimension we were seeking. Gathering our supplies, Yvette excitedly said, "Let's go back."

We walked to the glass shop to show the owner what we had created. He was able to fuse the two glass pieces together with the painting locked inside. He then asked how I wanted the piece cut. I looked at Yvette in question. What would it be used for? It really didn't look like a paperweight. Would it be framed? In the end, the owner suggested he try something. He cut the rather thick piece into a square and frosted the edge. Then he took two flat glass stones and fused them to the bottom to stabilize the piece, allowing it to stand and see through it. It was a pretty tabletop ornament, but there seemed to be no real intrinsic value to it.

The days before Christmas were filled with art, water sports, pubs, and live music. But most of all, new friendships began and blossomed. Christmas Eve arrived, and we all speculated about dinner with Kenneth Patrick. We knew he was married with two grown sons, who would be there. Yvette was particularly nervous about meeting such a legendary artist. We all assured her he was genuinely nice and that it would definitely be interesting.

Chapter 42

The Christmas dinner was delightful as Kenneth and his family opened their home to us. I introduced Yvette as a former classmate, and he immediately shook her hand with enthusiasm. "Ah, another student from L'École d'Artes! I admit I have a growing fondness for that school. I understand I might have another pupil from there next fall."

Yvette smiled. "Yes, Peter McKinney is applying again for next year. Sarah got the position this year. He is an outstanding artist from Scotland, and I know he is eager for the opportunity!"

"I am looking forward to meeting him." Kenneth paused, then added, "Now tell me, why did you not apply, Yvette?"

Yvette glanced at me, wondering what to say. "The rest of us knew that only one student from our school could be accepted each year. Sarah and Peter met all the qualifications. I haven't sold any of my paintings yet."

Kenneth studied her for a moment. "I see. Well, perhaps while you are here, you might do a painting for me. I would like to see your work." Transferring his attention to me, he said, "What is this I hear about your creating dimensional art within glass?"

Having no idea how he knew that, I answered, "I have been dabbling with art in glass. However, my sponsor back in England is sending me for a month to Africa to paint in the wild this summer, and I certainly won't have access to glass out on the plains!"

"Ah, moving creatures, eh? Let me give that some thought. Why don't you and I meet after the break to discuss how best to use the rest of your time here?" Kenneth smiled at Yvette and me as he moved on to his other guests.

Yvette excitedly whispered, "What was that all about? He wants me to do a painting? What should I do? And what do you think he will suggest for you?"

123

We walked out onto the patio full of speculations. I asked Yvette, "What if he invites you to come with Peter next fall? Would you do it and leave Jackson?"

Yvette turned pensive. "It would be an unbelievable opportunity, of course, but my mom and I don't have the money that would allow it. And besides, I don't even come close to meeting all the requirements, *n'est-ce pas*? Now let's forget about all this for now and rejoin the party!"

As we came back in, the look in Hans's eyes from across the room told me I had been missed. The heat they exuded seared into me and stopped me mid-step. Yvette turned to see where my focus had shifted to in time to see the spark of electricity between Hans and me. She whispered, "My god, Sarah. Look at you. I think you may be in love with this boy! Be rational, my friend. He lives in Germany. He knows you are going to Africa with Sam!"

It was as if a bucket of ice had been poured over me. Hans noticed and immediately began to walk toward me, determined to find out what happened. Yvette was right, I rationalized. Hans and I would leave Australia and go back to our separate lives. A single tear welled up in my eye just as Hans reached us. He took me by the arm and to Yvette he said, "Let's get out of here."

Mara saw us leaving and followed us to the car. She felt the tension on the ride home, and when they arrived back at rooftop terrace, she finally asked what happened. When Yvette and I didn't volunteer anything, Hans stared at me and asked, "Well?"

I had no idea how to express to Hans what happened and how Yvette's comment affected me, so I focused on the conversation with Kenneth Patrick to avoid the issue. "It turns out our mentor would like to see Yvette paint and has asked her to do a painting for him. He is also rethinking my projects for the spring to better pinpoint how to make the most of the time I will have in Africa."

Looking at me with a clenched jaw, Hans acknowledged, "So you leave for a month in Africa right after the spring term ends. Didn't you mention another artist, Sam, was going there with you?"

I wanted to downplay it and replied, "Yes, but first I plan to go home to Southampton for a couple of weeks to spend time with my family. Then El Amir has arranged the stay at a safari lodge for four weeks." What Yvette had said sank in further.

Mara asked, "Won't it be dangerous? Are you worried about all the animals?"

I chuckled and said, "I'll be fine. Sam will be there." As soon as I said the words out loud, I knew my mistake. I glanced at Yvette, who could see my dilemma, and she intervened, trying to be as nonchalant as possible.

"Sam is a classmate of ours at L'École d'Artes. He worked at the same gallery as Sarah, and his work also caught El Amir's attention. It is good she won't be alone." There was the clench of the jaw again.

Hans not so gently grabbed my hand and said, "We need to talk." He practically dragged me out, leaving Mara and Yvette staring at each other, helpless to temper the moment.

Chapter 43

Despite it being Christmas Eve, the Australian night was balmy, so we walked over to the beach. Hans stopped for a blanket, which we spread out on the sand near the sand dunes, giving us a view of the crystal-clear sky lit up with a brilliant array of stars, planets, and galaxies. I looked up at the sky, anticipating the inevitable conversation ahead.

Hans seemed to be gathering his thoughts, or maybe he was trying to sort out his own feelings. After a long sigh, he asked, "Why don't we start with you telling me what happened at dinner tonight? One moment we were totally connected, and the next you were cold as ice."

"Yvette saw the way we were looking at each other and simply reminded me that we are from two different countries, and after our stay here, we go back to two very different lives. The month in Africa happens right after we get back home. It just made me realize that, as intense as our feelings are here, they might dwindle once we get home."

There was the clenched jaw again. "Let me ask you, Sarah. You said you and Yvette were close. Were you ever intimate?"

That question shocked me. "For a short time, before she was with Jackson. Why would you ask me that?"

"Do you think it is possible that seeing us together might have rekindled her feelings for you and be jealous?"

"What an outrageous thing to say! We are close friends, but she is crazy about Jackson."

"Sarah, I've seen the way she watches you. I can recognize it because I do the same thing. Just think about the possibility. And while we are getting all this out between us, there is Sam. Exactly what is he to you? You are going to be isolated together on the plains of Africa for a month. Have you and Sam had a sexual relationship?"

Oh god, how was I going to answer that? Before I said it, I knew my answer was inadequate. "Hans, my relationship with Sam is nothing like what you and I have. I have known him for years. I hadn't even met you yet. Can you honestly tell me you have been celibate before me? No other women?"

"But I am not going off to Africa with a sexual partner."

I could feel the tears forming. I did not want to lose this man I had fallen so deeply for. *Dare I trust and squash that fear of abandonment that was always simmering under the surface. Was that why the arm's-length relationship with Sam felt safe?* With all the emotion I felt, I was almost afraid to ask, "Do you honestly think the relationship we are forming can move beyond the boundaries of Australia? I hate to think of life without you somehow in it."

Hans reached over to cradle me in his arms and wiped a tear from my cheek. "I love you, Sarah, with all my heart. The hurdles we might face after this time together are real. We have to trust each other and fight the odds. We'll find a way. Come here now. Let me show you how deep my feelings are for you." There, under the moonless sky with the sole glimmer of the stars, we made love slowly, with such an intensity that we were both sure could never be matched by another.

*****

With only a few days left of her visit, Yvette decided to forgo the painting. There was really no reason to pursue it since it was unrealistic to think she would actually be back. Instead, we spent the time taking long walks on the beach and talking about everything and nothing in particular. Once I explained the depth of my feeling for Hans, Yvette seemed fine to let the subject drop. I looked for any signs of the physical attraction Yvette and I had shared and which Hans had suspected, but all I found was a close friendship and genuine caring.

She spent hours with Mara discussing French fashions and sketching various patterns. The only shadow to those days was the edge of coolness that had settled in between Yvette and Hans. They were amicable, but there was no warmth to their friendship.

When it was time to take Yvette back to the Brisbane airport, Hans was working on a glass project, so Mara accompanied us. As Yvette and I said a tearful goodbye, realizing we would not see one another for a while, we swore to always be there for each other no matter what. Mara hugged Yvette, wished her well, and gave her a lovely, bright pareo with the sophisticated colors of the South of France. Clearly, a solid new friendship between them had formed.

Chapter 44

The meeting with Kenneth Patrick was a turning point for me. His assistant asked me to bring in pictures of *The Migration*, the falconry series, the *Herd*, and the individual paintings from the sections of the *Herd*. Kenneth took a great deal of time to scrutinize them carefully. When he finally looked up at me, he said, "Sarah, there is no question you have a great talent and can evoke the emotion from these animals. I have thought about our conversation the other night and about your upcoming time in Africa. I believe we mentioned moving creatures. What I would like to work on with you is moving elements.

I had to admit I was fascinated and curious about what he meant. "You want me to give up on the glass?"

He continued by asking, "I don't see glass as the answer. Is there a certain animal or something meaningful you might want to paint? Some unfinished thought you would like to complete?"

The list of animals I had painted was long, and I thought through them, but nothing seemed right. Then something in my dad's letter occurred to me. "A phoenix, sir. In a letter my dad wrote me before he passed, he said I was like a phoenix who rises from the ashes."

I could almost see the thoughts turning through Kenneth's mind. "Very symbolic. I like it. Do your research and then set up your easel in my personal studio. We will have you ready to excel in Africa by the time you leave here!"

After telling Hans and Mara what happened, they were both impressed. Mara was the first to react. "Sarah, he is singling you out to get his personal one-on-one tutelage. That's incredible!"

Hans brought up what I was most curious about. "What do you think he means by elements in motion?"

"I have no idea. At his dinner, we spoke of Africa and all the animals in motion...not pausing long enough for me to capture an image before beginning to paint them. Mara, I admire your ability to do that. I was thinking I would carry a camera to take my own pictures of scenes that I like as they unfold. El Amir said there was a dark room in the lodge to develop film. I can't help wondering what new perspective Kenneth plans to give me."

Mara rather shyly added, "I was just told that some of my sketches of the Parisian styles Yvette shared with me caught the attention of the fashion coordinator for Fashion Week in Sydney! My instructor said I have six weeks to bring them to life. If approved, Kenneth will fly me to Sydney to present them at one of the fashion shows."

Hans and I both jumped up. "What? Oh my gosh, you can do it! Do you have to sew too?"

Mara laughed at the thought. "Thank goodness, no. They are giving me a seamstress. I just have to paint and finish the fabric and then make the patterns."

Hans commented, "Kenneth must be stepping up the process for the second semester. He is sending me back to Brisbane to work with the glassblower for two weeks." That got my attention.

"You are leaving? When did you find out?" I wondered how long Hans had known without telling me. *Why do I think like that? Am I going to sabotage my own happiness?*

Hans answered, "Just this morning. Kenneth sent me a message that I am leaving tomorrow. But it is just for two weeks, and he wants me to experiment with the team glassblowing techniques that Dale Chihuly learned on the island of Murano. I'm excited to give it a try!"

"Wow!" Mara commented. "It sounds like we are all about to get remarkably busy." We all agreed, and as hard as it would be to say goodbye to Hans for two weeks, this was a great opportunity for him, and I knew I'd be busy with my phoenix project.

After he packed, we took a long walk on the beach talking about the time here with Kenneth Patrick, our hopes for our art projects, and how lucky we were that fate had intervened, allowing us to meet. We held hands and stopped to kiss frequently along the way, both convinced we had met our soul mate. The rest of the evening was spent eating at a small outdoor waterfront café and trying to fit two weeks of lovemaking into one night.

By the time Hans was on his way to Brisbane, I was surrounded by books learning about the phoenix.

Chapter 45

Though I'd gathered my materials, I was far from ready when Kenneth Patrick walked into the studio. He came right to the point. "Well, Sarah, have you decided where to begin?"

I shared my dilemma. "This is different from painting a regular animal. The phoenix is a symbol...a mythological sacred firebird dating back to the time of the ancient Greeks and Romans. Its image has been portrayed in thousands of ways. I wouldn't even know where to begin. I did find a rare bird that resides in China called the red phoenix, and I thought about painting it. It is quite colorful. But the phoenix my father compared me to was the mythological one, so I need to find a way to do it."

Kenneth reasoned, "You are correct that the phoenix has been portrayed mythologically in thousands of ways. What if you could imagine a real phoenix? How would you visualize it?"

I rubbed my eyes, trying to conjure up the various birds of prey, mentally discarding the falcon that I'd already painted, the hawk, and others. I allowed my mind's eye to take pieces of the various birds to make the phoenix. I got my sketchbook to see if it would work. Kenneth watched. I knew the wingspan would need to be impressive, so I drew the body and spread wings of an eagle with a little more ornamentation. On another page, I sketched the bottom half of a pheasant with its long feathered tail. For the face, I wanted something fierce, so I drew the head of a vulture with its crooked beak and piercing eyes.

Kenneth studied the images. "Together these images make for quite an impressive bird. How do you envision its background? What about its stance? What is this bird trying to convey?"

"The defiant spread of its wings represents overcoming the challenges and weakness it faces. The shutter of its eyes and slightly open beak will belie defiance with its residual fear. The smoldering fire is where it has emerged from yet still tries to draw it back. Freedom beckons in the colorful sunset sky above. All it has to do is fly." After I said all that, I knew without a doubt this would be the most challenging painting I had ever attempted.

Kenneth seemed to embrace the challenge. "Ah, Sarah, you have just added the moving elements. Both the fire and the sky pull at the phoenix, yet it is frozen. How can it break free of the fire and soar? Yes, my dear. I think you have found your project!"

It was such an intimidating challenge, but I began to immerse myself in the sketches. During my sleep at night, my mind would wander, seeking the expression to show fear in the phoenix's eyes. I would walk on the beach watching the various birds that so effortlessly spread their wings and flew. I was consumed with how to begin to paint once the sketches were formulated. Every now and then, Kenneth would suggest a tweak in a sketch, and it was amazing how its impression would change. Before I knew it, the two weeks had passed, and Hans was back in Byron Bay.

Hans and Mara were both equally absorbed in their projects. We were all dabbling throughout the fall semester so Kenneth could identify the strongest path for us to pursue during the rest of the course. It was the same for all of us, which just confirmed the expertise of Kenneth Patrick and this program. I couldn't wait to share the experience with Peter, since I now knew he had been selected for the coming fall.

Hans soon learned that Kenneth had reached out to his sponsor, Geoffrey, at the gallery in Hamburg to suggest an entire section of the gallery to be dedicated to the Hans Schuman glass collection! Geoffrey had agreed, and Hans was in the process of learning how to pack and ship something so fragile such a long distance. He would also need to return to Brisbane to do three more large pieces. He had moved from basic vases with ornate color to more abstract handkerchief-rimmed vases to large signature conversation piece bowls in a variety of novel shapes.

Mara was nervous as a cat. She had three more weeks to get her sample line ready for the show in Sydney, where Kenneth had arranged for her to interview with several key designers.

As for me, I had Kenneth's critical eye as he oversaw my painting. He taught me to sharpen and exaggerate certain points to make the elements of my painting come alive. The day I was working on the smoldering embers, he showed me how to make strategic flames flare to entice and pull at the phoenix. You could almost hear the crackle of the fire! The key to this painting was to capture the phoenix at the pivotable point where it is not totally free of the fire but is reaching for the freedom of the sky. I was totally entranced.

Hans and I found a mutual respect for each other's talent that added a new dimension to our relationship. When he wasn't in Brisbane, we spent every night together greedy for each of these last few months. There was only once, after Hans received a letter from home, that his mood turned sullen and standoffish. I asked what the matter was, and he shrugged it off, not wanting to talk about it, which made me more curious. Finally, he explained that a childhood friend was very ill. I think he was debating whether he should go back but made it very clear that was the end of the discussion.

His moodiness continued for several days until thankfully the surf shop raised the green flag, meaning the waves were perfect for surfing. Hans, along with all the serious surfers, went to grab his board and hit the surf. I went along to watch, knowing these waves were far beyond my ability. He rode wave after wave, hoping for that perfect barrel shape that would allow him to tube ride well inside the breaking wave. After what seemed like forever, he got lucky. He mastered the ride inside the tube and was jubilant! I was thankful for that ride because afterward, his mood considerably improved, and our love-making that night had a new magnitude to it...perhaps because we both knew our days together were numbered.

Chapter 46

Our time with Kenneth Patrick was also coming to an end. I finished my painting, and when I saw Kenneth's final reaction, I knew I would never sell it. Another one for the Eleanor home collection. Now I just needed to come up with its name. I had been thinking about it for weeks. The phoenix was still in turmoil, not totally free of the flames. In my imagination, I wondered what Rosa Bonheur would think about this painting with these new techniques and decided she might be quite pleased.

Kenneth and I were discussing the upcoming Africa trip, and he astutely said, "Sarah, my hope is that someday you paint the next part of the phoenix's story when it can emerge from the ashes. You have a masterpiece here, my dear. Have you decided what to call it?"

It was not until that moment that the name came to me. "*Phoenix Paradox.*" Kenneth nodded and asked if I needed help shipping it home. "I think I'd rather carry it, sir. I don't want to take a chance with shipping.

Mara's fashions had gotten rave reviews, and Hans was ecstatic over his glassworks to be featured at the gallery. The time had finally come for this group of fifteen to reconvene with our mentor and friend, Kenneth Patrick. We all felt like we could call him a friend, and there was no one in the room who didn't feel like their art had immensely improved during the time here under his tutelage.

Kenneth Patrick took the stage for our last class session. "Look at the fifteen of you! I could not be more proud. Some might think my methods are odd, but I have found this system usually works. We spent most of the fall distracting you with many ways to use your talent. Hopefully, once you discovered the right path, you found that when you are not fighting your own efforts, you have this incredible positive energy that you can draw from in its entirety to bring about spectacular results! That is what you each have done. And when you find enjoyment in working through the challenges, now you create a work of great value.

"As you leave, I want you to take one piece of advice with you. I want you to push yourselves. Go beyond wishing, hoping, planning, or even talking about what could be. Motivate yourselves to take the time, be determined, and do what it takes to get it done. Create an upward spiral for the development of your art and discover all the beautiful possibilities. And when you find one, be amazed and delight in it! On that positive note, I want to wish you all much success going forward and a safe journey home. If you ever need to reach out to me for anything, consider me your friend and don't hesitate to call on me."

The class stood up, and there were handshakes and hugs all around, along with the exchange of contact information. I felt I had made a friend for life in Mara. And to think here is where I found the love of my life! We ended our time here with a tremendous sense of accomplishment!

*****

There was desperation in the way Hans and I held each other that night. It seemed we couldn't get close enough, and it was hard to hold back the tears. Who knew when we would see each other again. I had heard from El Amir. The gallery wanted me back after Africa to start working in earnest on an exhibition. Hans was to start at the gallery in Hamburg by setting up his glass collection. His father had uncovered the resources at home for Hans to continue his glass production. Hans was hopeful he had his father's support for the glasswork he had grown to love.

Mara took an earlier bus to the airport for her scheduled flight back to Bali. Neither Mara nor I could stop the flood of tears, and even Hans had tears welling. The three of us had been so close for all these months there was sure to be a void once we separated.

Hans and I loaded our bags onto the bus to take us to the Brisbane airport. *Phoenix Paradox* was safely under my arm. We held hands and leaned into each other during the entire ride.

My flight left first. I could hardly breathe with the sobs lodged in my throat. I got it that a new door was opening, but surely this one didn't have to close. The words of love spoken between us attached themselves to my heart...and I vowed to myself they would stay until we saw each other again.

When the door to my plane closed, it was as if it was the door to a prison cell. I could no longer go back, and loneliness overcame me for the long flight back to England.

Chapter 47

After more than twenty-four hours via bus, plane, and train... and a ten-hour time difference, my bone-weary, jet-lagged body was exhausted. The arrival home was surreal too. Eleanor, Harry, and Lizzy were all a year older! It was hard to fathom that I hadn't seen them in so long. It was like I had traveled in time, and nothing was familiar. Harry and Lizzy barely recognized me, and I definitely had some catching up to do. Eleanor looked great! She was obviously taking care of herself, so it made me wonder if she had a new male friend. I found myself hoping so.

Fortunately, she recognized how tired and out of sync I was. Eleanor offered me a bowl of lamb stew and some bread. Seeing the wrapped-up painting, she asked, "Is this one of your pieces from Australia?"

"Yes, it's extra special to me and I have decided to keep it here on the wall if you like it. But if it's okay, after I eat, I would love to sleep for a while. Can we open it later?" Thinking to myself, *a very long while!*

*****

I woke up hungry, and it seemed to be late into the night. The house was quiet; I must have slept through dinner and the rest of the evening. Putting on my robe, I quietly made my way to the kitchen to see what was in the refrigerator. I smiled when I saw the plate with a chicken sandwich and salad. A little note was attached, saying, "Thought you might be hungry. See you in the morning. E"

I had to admit it was good to see the three of them. The children were growing up so fast! I took the plate back to my room so I wouldn't wake anyone. Sitting on my bed eating, it sank in—I was leaving for Africa in two weeks! Yikes! I got out my pad to make a to-do list. First thing tomorrow, I needed to touch base with Sam and El Amir to see if there were any updates about our stay. I looked at my folder labeled "AFRICA."

Sam and I would be flying on El Amir's plane to the international airport at Dar es Salaam. From there we transfer to the small airstrip near the safari lodge in the eastern part of Tanzania, set amidst a 350,000-acre protected wilderness in the Serengeti. This was no ordinary lodge! There were twelve well-appointed tents forming a circle with the hospitality lodge at one end. Sam and I would each have our own tent. Each had an outdoor *sala* where we could set up our equipment. They also had a netted bed with a small seating area, a small fridge, and an actual screened-in bathroom! That was a relief since I was not looking forward to traipsing around the wilderness at night to find an outhouse.

Reading the brochure, I learned there were options for a game safari, walking safaris, and even a balloon ride over the Serengeti! Wow! I looked at the list of what to bring and decided to begin shopping tomorrow...or, looking at the clock, later today. What an amazing experience we were about to have. I could feel the weight of leaving Hans lift a little and the excitement of what was to come take over.

I put the folder aside and rested for a couple of hours until I heard the pattering of Harry's and Lizzie's little feet. Throwing on some jeans and a T-shirt, I went out to greet them properly. They were eating some porridge and scones. They both squealed in delight when I joined them, realizing how long it had been since I had enjoyed an English scone with fresh preserves. Eleanor made us both some tea and sat down at the table with me while the kids went to play in the yard.

After I thanked her for my midnight snack, she asked about the time in Australia. "It was incredible, really. At first, I wasn't sure about Kenneth Patrick and his methods, but in the end, it was clear he knew exactly what he was doing. He taught me the use of vivid colors and sharp angles to not just add depth to a painting but to give it movement. Shall I show you?" When Eleanor nodded, I went to get *Phoenix Paradox*. I opened it and, looking at it again with fresh eyes, I was proud of how far it came.

"Oh my gosh, Sarah, it is breathtaking! I feel its struggle. I am certainly no art expert, but my guess is that this will be highly sought after."

"Possibly. In Dad's last letter, he referred to me as a phoenix. I think I want to keep it and hang it here with the other."

Eleanor rested her chin on her hands and sighed. A look of worry on her face, she said, "I want to talk to you about that. I didn't want to bother you in Australia, but we might be moving. I met a very nice man, a widower, actually, from the States. His name is Walter. He called soon after you left to request piano lessons for his daughter. He began to stay during her lessons, and soon it progressed to having coffee together after the lessons. His daughter, Sandy, who's nine, gets along well with Harry and Lizzie. A couple of months ago, he asked me to marry him and move to Jacksonville, Florida. His home is near the beach. Sarah, Harry and Lizzie need a father, and Sandy needs a mother." She continued to speak, but I couldn't hear. My heart screamed, *What about me? I needed a father and a mother!* I tried to focus on what she was saying.

"Sweetheart, I know this is sudden. I don't want to hurt you, and there will always be a place for you wherever we go. But the reality is, you've been gone for a year and are about to leave for another month. It is not as if we are deserting you." Eleanor looked at me, distraught, not knowing what to do. She knew I was shocked. "I waited until you came home to give him my answer, but, Sarah, I love him. I very much want to marry him and have your blessing. And, if you would consider it, I would like you to stand up with me as my maid of honor."

What she was saying rang true. She didn't just marry him while I was gone and leave. She waited. Eleanor had supported me these past years, and now it was my turn to reciprocate. Trying to shake off the numbness and summon a smile, I answered, "Eleanor, you deserve happiness. It's just that you'll be so far away." That made Eleanor chuckle.

"Hmmm, and Australia and East Africa are just around the block? We will just have to be diligent about staying in touch and making time to get together. What about the paintings? I hate to have them so far away."

At that moment, although I knew Eleanor's intentions were good, I realized any chance of having a family life with the three of them was over. "Don't worry about the paintings. I will find a place to keep them. When do you think the wedding will be?"

"I would like to wait until you get back from Africa. Possibly that first week after your return. That way we can move by the end of the summer so Harry and Lizzie can start school in Jacksonville." I nodded and assured her I would be there. The thought crossed my mind, *maybe Hans is my new family.* I allowed a glimmer of hope to run through me to soothe the empty feeling in my soul.

Chapter 48

The next two weeks flew by filled with shopping for Africa, spending time with Harry and Lizzie, and starting to pack up my room since the house would go on the market right after the wedding. I had to start thinking about where I was going to live... most likely London. That made sense with the gallery as well as Amelia and Tara there. I tried to call Hans a couple of times, but his phone went to voice mail. He was probably busy coordinating the glass exhibition.

I spoke with El Amir to get the final arrangements to meet his plane in London. He explained Sam and I would make a stop in Morocco to pick him up. El Amir would travel with us to make sure we got settled in and help us set up our studios. I hadn't spoken with Sam yet, but he did leave a message that he was excited about the adventure and would meet me at the airport.

My clothes were laid out on the bed and ready to be packed into my suitcase. I was looking at it all and shaking my head when Eleanor walked by my room. "Not much color, is there?" she asked with a grin as she entered. I had to admit I was thinking the same thing. All the basics, including the hiking boots, were khaki or beige! But the reality was that white or black would show dust and dirt so quickly. It wasn't likely we would have access to a liberal use of a laundry. For that reason, everything I took had to be multiuse. I did love the khaki pants with the zip-off legs that converted them to shorts and the beige parka that folded up into a tiny bag.

I held up a set of six bandanas in different colors. "This is all I came up with to tie around my neck or hair to add color. I have the long camouflage skirt and olive-green tank top in case we go to one of the other lodges in the area." I showed her my assortment of visors, ball caps, and hat with an adjustable chinstrap. "The sun will be intense, so I got powerful sunscreen. Since we will be there for the migration, there is no doubt the flying insects will be a nuisance, so I got plenty of the most potent bug repellent I could find. This is certainly not like packing for Australia!"

Eleanor leaned against the doorframe, taking in the scene. "Who would have thought the little girl from Brighton would be experiencing such a life? Your talent and hard work have carved an unprecedented path for you! Paris, Australia, and now Africa. Yours is not an ordinary life. There's so much going for you that my advice is to make good use of the opportunities that come your way. Take time to consider what truly matters and do what you need to in order to make it happen. Use the passion and commitment that have gotten you this far and make it count. Live your life with purpose, Sarah, and you will make a good life for yourself."

I cherished the wisdom Eleanor offered and realized her words would resonate in me for a long time. The embrace we shared that afternoon spoke volumes of how far our relationship had come. The time with Harry and Lizzie affected me as well. I hadn't spent much time around children, and it made me speculate how I would be as a mother and whether children were in the future for Hans and me.

My longing for Hans was nonstop. I was surprised I hadn't heard from him, but I assumed he was as busy as I was. Then the day before I left for London, I did get a letter from him.

Dearest Sarah,

I apologize for not calling. From the moment I returned home, I faced some major decisions while trying to set up the glass exhibition at the gallery. Hopefully, this letter arrives before your departure for Africa. I think about you every day. We have a great deal to talk about when you get back. Stay safe and have a wonderful adventure!

With love,
Hans

I clutched the letter to my heart, as if it allowed me to touch him. It then found its way into the side zipper pocket of my backpack, along with several special photos of our time in Australia, so I could easily reach for them.

*****

Before I knew it, I had said my goodbyes and was on the train to London to meet Sam at El Amir's plane. The train ride gave me time to reflect on Sam and the month ahead. It had been eleven months since I last saw him before leaving early for Australia. Sam had just turned eighteen when he began at the London gallery the summer before he went to L'École d'Artes. That was two years ago. He would be twenty, and I would turn twenty-one while we were in Africa. I wondered if he had changed much during the last year. I know I had. The intense love affair with Hans made me somehow feel older and more settled down. Yet here I was venturing out to the plains of Africa to live among wild animals!

The transfer from the train station to the airport went smoothly enough considering I had the duffel bag, backpack, shoulder bag, and the two paintings to maneuver. After finding out about Eleanor's pending wedding, I decided to have El Amir hold the paintings for me until I returned from Africa. I would somehow figure out what to do with them after that. I made my way to the airfield dedicated to private planes. By the time I got there, I was exhausted.

Sam saw me and ran toward me to take the duffel. He reached for the paintings, too, and after a moment's hesitation, I let him take them, suddenly feeling a great deal lighter! "Sarah, you made it! I was wondering what happened to you."

"Obviously, carrying all this took me longer than I expected. Thanks for rescuing me! Wait! Look at you. My gosh, I hardly recognize you. Where is that adorable boy I was in school with?"

"Sarah, I could say the same thing. You look radiant! Yvette told me you are madly in love with a boy from the class. You have totally broken my heart!" The last he said with a sheepish grin, and I knew our easy rapport from before was restored.

I smiled at how great it was to see him again. The simple friendship that was so close. I owed him an explanation and wanted to be sure he realized there would be no more sex between us. "Honestly, I never saw it coming. I wasn't even sure I liked him at first, but when I saw him surfing and the alarm was called for a shark in the midst, I just started running. It is hard to explain. From the beginning, there was something like a magnetic pull."

"Well, darlin', you're stuck with me for a month, so I guess we need to make the best of it! Seriously, Sarah, I hope to meet him someday. You deserve all the happiness in the world."

We stowed the duffel and the paintings before boarding El Amir's opulent aircraft. Sam looked at me with raised eyebrows and said, "Guess we found the right sponsor!" Once we got in the air, the flight attendant asked what we would like to drink and told us our meal would be served shortly.

Neither Sam nor I could believe this was really happening. I sat back with the most amazing smile, wondering what Rosa and Rachel would think of this opportunity. Those two artists had been part of my life for so long I somehow wanted to make them proud to see their legacy rise to new heights. My heart told me I was destined for this. All the heartbreak and loss had led me here. Was it possible for the phoenix to finally soar?

Chapter 49

Sam asked a little more about Hans, but he was mostly interested in Kenneth Patrick and how he had influenced my painting. I pulled out the wrapped *Phoenix Paradox* and opened it for
Sam to see. He took it and set it on the seat opposite us to study.
I admit it gave me a tingle of excitement to see it again. Finally,
after what seemed like a long silence, Sam shared his reaction.
"Sarah, you know I am one of your biggest fans and admire the
emotion you always seem to evoke in your paintings. But this...
there is a new sharpness to the painting. You can feel the bird
pulling to escape the fire. I love the added edge. This is what
Kenneth Patrick taught you?"

"Yes, he had us moving in so many directions during the first
semester that I often wondered what he was trying to achieve. For
a while, I thought I was going to make paperweights! But somehow, after the Christmas break, things seemed to come together
for each of us. When he found out about this upcoming experience in Africa, the thought of moving creatures led him to moving elements, and that is where we focused for the entire second
semester. My father referred to me as a phoenix in the last letter
he wrote to me. Kenneth helped me portray its struggle."

"Was he teaching the same thing to each of you?" Sam
wanted to know.

"No, that is what was so brilliant. He somehow found a passion in each of us and did amazing things to get our work to the
highest level. Mara learned to transfer her incredible paintings
to fabric and eventually started to design fashions that were displayed in Sydney during Fashion Week. Hans became fascinated
with glassblowing and developed some intricate ways to add color
inside his designs. Those pieces will become the start of a dedicated glass exhibition at his gallery in Hamburg."

Sam marveled at Kenneth's process and eventually began to tell me about his year in Paris. It was his year to do a series. "My inspiration was the group of individual paintings you created from *The Herd*. I concentrated on lions, knowing I would soon be in Africa. It was received well, and I left them with Mr. Templeton to display at the gallery while we are gone."

Our conversation flowed from subject to subject. I told him more about Mara and how exotically beautiful she was. He mentioned some of the girls he had dated but that no one enticed him to get more serious. We speculated why El Amir was coming with us. The truth, which we were about to find out, would leave us in awe of this man of so many dimensions!

The plane stopped in Marrakesh on schedule. We got off briefly to stretch our legs while the plane refueled and what we thought would be El Amir's luggage get stowed. Instead, after one small suitcase, box after box was loaded into the cargo compartment. El Amir finally appeared and examined the placement of the boxes. A few were rearranged to make room for one more. Once he was satisfied, El Amir turned his attention to us. He greeted us with pats on the back and a genuine smile. "Let's get on board and let me take a look at you both!"

We buckled up and soon we were in the air on the way to Tanzania! El Amir looked both of us over, and a smile broke through his serious face. "You are becoming adults in front of my eyes! It is hard to believe I discovered you both when you were just seventeen. Now look at you. I must say I am impatient to discover what you have learned this year. Sam, Mr. Templeton tells me your lion series is quite impressive. I will be in London later this month and will be sure to see it. And what about you, Sarah?"

I pulled *Phoenix Paradox* back out for El Amir to see. "I only carried one painting back from Australia with me, but I think it portrays the flow of movement Kenneth Patrick taught me. Actually, I brought it and the small painting of *The Herd* with me to ask you a favor." I told him about Eleanor getting married and moving to the States. "Would you mind taking care of them until I can find a place of my own after I get back?"

El Amir assured me, "Of course I will, Sarah." All the while, he continued to study *Phoenix Paradox* with a trained eye, and I could tell it affected him. His attention to the painting gave me a chance to ponder this mysterious man and what his background and motives were. He was opening doors for Sam and me that were beyond comprehension. *How would we ever be able to repay such an enormous debt?*

Chapter 50

Once the flight attendant cleared away the dishes from dinner, El Amir indicated he needed our full attention. Once he had it, we listened, astonished to hear the true reason we were here.

He began, "You are most likely unaware that I chose you both for more than just your talent. It is the fascination you both have with animals in the wild. You see, it was not long ago that East Africa was faced with uncontrollable poaching and hunting. Elephants were slaughtered for their ivory tusks. Hunters displayed their kills as heads on a trophy wall. Cheetah and leopard skins were turned into coats. The animal population, particularly in Tanzania, was dwindling, which put the delicate ecosystem of the Serengeti in serious danger. In addition, the government faced rampant wildfires that brought in invasive foreign vegetation. The depleted plains were no longer a flourishing wilderness.

"A younger, more aggressive group gained majority in the parliament determined to restore the area but found the task enormous and daunting, requiring an unthinkable amount of resources. One man among them, Chima, decided to take their problem outside of Africa. Chima was a fine ambassador, and he requested a meeting with me. When I heard the reason for the meeting, I asked that it be held in Tanzania so I could see the problem for myself. What I heard and saw during the three days I was there convinced me I could not walk away without helping. Through my influential network and several of my family members back in Dubai, we campaigned to form a fund to restore and protect the ecosystem of the Serengeti.

"The safari lodge where you'll be staying is situated adjacent to the path of the great migration. You will see it up close. Sarah, seeing your painting of the migration inspired by Rosa Bonheur, which you could only imagine through books and magazines, motivated me to nurture your talent so that one day you could paint the real migration. And, Sam, the way you portray lions, whether in sculpture or painting, illuminates how important that species is to the wildlife here."

Sam and I listened to El Amir, totally entranced by what he was saying. We had no idea how delicate the balance of nature was here. "How can we help?" I asked as Sam nodded in agreement.

El Amir smiled. "I somehow knew I could count on you. I will spend the next few days in parliament meetings to oversee the group managing such a huge undertaking. Think of me as a sort of director on the board. They have allowed for your accommodation and your protection. My request of you is to get involved. Be an advocate of this land, of these animals, and of its people. Immerse yourselves into the community. Help determine people's needs and weaknesses but also their strengths and abilities. You saw the boxes. They are filled with medical supplies, necessary vaccinations and medications, cleaning supplies, and things like simple bars of soap. I assure you, if you allow yourselves to breathe in this magnificent land, your one month here will leave you yearning for more."

I looked out the window as the sun fell below the horizon, lighting up the sky in brilliant colors, resulting in the most spectacular sunset I had ever seen. Emotion overcame me that I had the chance to make a difference to these people, the animals, and the land. What a feeling! The only thing missing was Hans by my side to share it. But my focus needed to remain on the here and now, and I looked over to see Sam gazing at me with a knowing smile.

Chapter 51

Night had fallen by the time we reached the tiny airstrip of Sasakwa in the Grumeti Reserve. Our arrival was surreal, as the landing area was lit up by a row of safari land cruisers on either side of the runway with their headlights on. Once out of the range of the headlights, a look upward to the sky promised many evenings of magnificent stargazing! Because of our late arrival, we would spend our first night in the lodge before moving to our tents tomorrow in the daylight.

My first thought entering the lodge was that its layout was quite simple. A comfortable living area around a two-sided stone fireplace and a casual dining area were the main features of the open area, although a closer look found a small library in the corner. I wandered over and picked up a book that caught my attention, *A Typical Day on Safari*. El Amir checked us in and motioned us over to a small table where a platter of grilled meat and root vegetables were waiting.

While we ate, El Amir explained our agenda for the next day, including that days start early here in camp. The three of us would meet for breakfast at six thirty in the lobby. Sam and I were to bring our bags and after breakfast we'd be shown to our individual adjacent tents. I glanced over at Sam and, for a fleeting moment, wished we would be sharing a tent. *Would I be lonely? Would I be afraid?*

El Amir assured us we would be assigned two rangers to teach us what was necessary to stay safe and enjoy the full experience. El Amir had an early meeting with the manager of the funding effort, and then he would join us to visit the surrounding villages and meet the people. The following day, there would be a morning safari in one of the land cruisers before El Amir was scheduled to depart that afternoon.

Even as tired as I was, sleep eluded me. I even let out a chuckle while lying there, trying to sleep, that I could have ever thought being here in a tent camp in Tanzania would be anything remotely like working in a zoo in Southampton! I strained to listen to the distant sounds of the animals, wondering how much louder they would seem once I moved to my tent. By the time daylight broke, I breathed a giant sigh of relief and quickly dressed in my khakis and T-shirt. Hair back in my familiar ponytail, I brought my bags to the lobby.

Sam was already there having a cup of coffee and asked, "How did you sleep?"

"Not a wink! You?"

"Nope."

I took a sip of my coffee. "I can't imagine tonight, alone in the tent. Did you hear the sounds?"

"They were faint, but I imagine they will sound a great deal louder from the tent. At least we are next door to each other!" Sam gave me that look that said we could easily be in the same tent.

"Hey, don't try one of you pranks to scare me! I'll be skittish enough." Then, looking around, I added, "I can't wait to see where we will be living for the next month." Just as we were getting up from the table, two African rangers came over to us to shake hands. They both wore olive button-down shirts with a Serengeti National Park patch over dark khaki pants. Each of them wore a tan bucket hat.

The taller ranger seemed to be in charge. "*Jambo!* My name is Tibu. This is Mosha. We are here to get you set up in your tents and give you some guidelines of our life here at camp."

Sam and I both took the cue, realizing *jambo* must mean hello or good morning, so we both answered, "*Jambo!*" I grabbed my backpack, but I was shocked when Mosha effortlessly managed to carry both Sam's and my bags. Since we had arrived in the dark, I had no idea what to expect other than what the brochure El Amir had sent me showed. I walked outside to rustic plains that stretched in all directions as far as the eyes could see. The dozen tents formed the semblance of a circle with the lodge on one end. It reminded me of movies I had seen about America's wild west with the covered wagons forming a circle at night for protection.

However, these tents were nothing like any tent I had ever seen. Encased in canvas, the structures were permanent with added features that made them seem more like a home. The step-up wooden deck led to a double-flap entry that completely rolled up and tied back to be open or could release and secure to close. Inside, two battery-operated lanterns hung from the ceiling that was tall enough to comfortably stand. There was a full-size cot with a plush mattress and bedding with additional room for a desk and chair and small seating area. Tibu pointed out the flap to a separate small canvas shower while he explained how valuable water is. We would be allowed five gallons a day for a shower plus a pitcher of fresh water for drinking. Each morning, Mosha would bring by a carafe of coffee and sound the wake-up bell for them to make their way to the lodge for breakfast. If they were on an early safari, they would be served the local rusks early, and later have a full breakfast midmorning.

Tibu advised us not to go out at night and showed us the primitive chamber pot in the corner with a privacy drape if we could not wait until morning. He did explain we could keep some light snacks in the tent here by the lodge if they were sealed. However, if we were on a walking safari with portables tents, we were not to have any food inside the tent.

Here on the safari property, there would be a guard on duty twenty-four hours a day. If we planned to visit a nearby village or lodge, we should have a guard escort us. Sam and I were both taking it all in, bubbling with a mix of anticipation and excitement. Tibu finished by saying he would be available for questions if needed and pointed out the ranger post about fifty yards to the north.

Sam left for his tent. I stepped out onto the wooden deck and was relieved to know I could see him on his deck only about twenty yards away. We had thirty minutes to unpack before El Amir would come for us, so I hurriedly settled in finding a small dresser and various baskets to hold my belongings. *Wow! What an adventure this would be!*

Chapter 52

I am not sure what I expected to see in the villages we visited. But the profound impact of that afternoon compelled me to make a difference while I was here. I am sure Sam felt the same way. Village after village, we found people whose sole purpose was survival. Things that we took for granted like electricity, running water, toys, books, and so many things we use every day were totally foreign to them. Yet they greeted us with smiles and a welcoming spirit that was heartwarming.

El Amir explained that the fund to restore the land and protect the animals was also there to help the communities learn valuable ways to not only survive but thrive. We learned everyone had a job to do whether tending to the garden, hunting, gathering wood to make a fire to cook the food, doing laundry, getting fresh water to drink...and so much more. We met a young boy shepherding a group of goats to a watering hole, ever mindful of predators that might lie in wait. Back in the villages, walls or *bomas* were created with rings of acacia thorns to protect their livestock and themselves.

El Amir took us to one of the new rudimentary schools that had been created by the fund's management. I found myself looking at those beautiful children wanting them to grow up to have a better life than their parents had known before. Sam was curious about the lack of farming tools and what an impact irrigation, proper pruning, and even plowing could make.

We found out the supplies El Amir brought would make an incredible difference to the villages that needed them most. He planned to do more. We thought we were here merely to paint wildlife but found out during the afternoon our role was much loftier. We were to serve as liaisons between the fund's management team and the community. It seems most of the village people were highly suspect of change. Our job was to use our art to fundraise, engage the villagers, and create a bridge of trust so they would work alongside the managers to tackle their massive undertaking.

There was so much to take in and learn. I could not have felt further removed from Australia and Hans than I did when I got back to my tent. The only animals I had seen were goats and chickens. *Where were the African animals in the wild I had come to see and paint?*

Mosha had left a basin of warm water so I could wash my face and hands. Once I finished, I curled my legs under me to sit on the cushioned chair on my deck. Then I heard it. The most melodic sound...more like a song. I focused my attention on where the sound was coming from. As if he could sense my curiosity, the most beautiful bird I've ever seen flew out of the nearby acacia tree and perched close to me on the railing of my deck. I wanted to run to get my sketchbook, but if I moved, I knew I would scare him away. So I chose to watch him in wonder, trying to memorize his colors. He was a relatively small bird to be covered in such a colorful pattern. I studied him, and occasionally he turned for me to get a view from a different angle. There was the palest of yellows that moved across his eyes and blended to the tawniest of golden-brown on the top of his head and wings. His breast was deep magenta edged with ink blue, and his lower body and tail were the most iridescent aquamarine. The combination of colors with his soulful melody almost made me cry with its splendor. When he finally flew away, I ran for my pad and roll of colored pencils to try to recreate the wonder of that bird. If only I could add sound.

Wistful as I thought such a thing, the memory of Kenneth Patrick came rushing back to me. "Moving elements, Sarah." *Wouldn't sound be one of those elements? Why couldn't I record sounds of the scenes that I paint?*

I couldn't wait to share my idea with Sam and El Amir! My dilemma was that I had nothing to record with. Later, before dinner in the lodge, I told El Amir about the bird and its music but also that I had no recorder. He winked and said he would be right back.

Sam came over and sat down. "Where is El Amir going?"

I told him about the bird and his song, along with my crazy idea of adding sound to my work. Sam loved the idea and reflected, "Often, when I am doing a powerful sculpture of two lions fighting, I hear their roars in my mind. What a brilliant idea! Tomorrow should be amazing out on safari. When I was back at the tent, I made a list of all we should have with us." We began to go through the list. Both of us had invested in good cameras and were counting on translating our photos to canvas or, in Sam's case, sculpture.

El Amir returned with a small pocket recorder and a small bag of batteries. "Here, Sarah. Use this. It is not the most sensitive of recorders, but perhaps it will accomplish what you envision. When I took it, I thought of another use for the recorder. What if it was your words used to describe what the viewer sees in the painting? Or words that evoke inspiration to support the replenishment of the Serengeti?"

I took the recorder with the promise that I would try an assortment of ways to intersperse paintings with sound. The recorder in my hands, I felt the familiar shiver that went down my spine when something felt right. Like Sam, I couldn't wait for tomorrow's safari, but I also wanted to go back to see the children. There was work to do, and I feared one month would go far too quickly.

Chapter 53

I was awakened before dawn by the ring of a small bell outside my tent and Mosha's voice saying, "*Jambo*, miss. Your basin of water is here with hot coffee. Fresh rusks are in the lodge. We leave in forty-five minutes." Jumping up out of bed, I was surprised by the chill in the air considering how warm it got midday. Not sure what to expect, I doused myself in sunscreen and insect repellent and then threw on my parka over my jeans and T-shirt. I was ready for the day!

The platter of rusks waiting in the lobby was an interesting early-morning staple that I wondered if I would grow to love. They were crunchy bars filled with almonds and raisins in a cookie dough, but not overly sweet. *Hmmm. Maybe I'll take an extra in my pack.*

Sam's eagerness to get started was evident, since he was already at the door with his backpack ready. El Amir was enjoying the last of his expresso when I joined him. I could tell he was excited too. He explained, "This lodge is perfectly located to get an up-close view of the wildebeest and zebra migrating through the Western Serengeti and on the southern banks of the Grumeti River. What was not in your painting were the antelopes that move with them. Tibu is extremely knowledgeable about the migration and their habits. Today should be spectacular! The weather is clear, so the viewing will be excellent." I found myself as eager as Sam to get going.

Tibu arrived with Mosha at his side. El Amir had arranged for today to be just the three of us, explaining that future gaming activities would include other guests. Tibu confirmed our sunscreen and insect repellent were sufficient and told us the parkas would not be needed for long as soon as the sun started climbing up in the sky. He explained how the Land Cruiser, adapted for prime open viewing, was viewed by the animals as an inanimate object even while moving, allowing us to get close. He questioned whether we had any food with us. When I pulled out the rusk from my pocket, he cautioned, "You are in the predator's backyard. You do not want any fresh food to tempt them to make you their next meal!" I immediately ate the rusk making sure there were no crumbs left anywhere. Our binoculars and cameras ready, we were off for our first game drive!

The ultimate goal for Sam and me was to understand the delicate balance of nature here in Tanzania so our tours would not be the same as those who came for a three or four-day safari. Tibu was the perfect guide to lead us, as his knowledge about the land and its animals was extensive. When I had studied to paint my *Migration* piece at L'École d'Artes, I mistakenly thought the migration happened only once a year here in the Serengeti.

Tibu clarified, "The great migration of well over a million animals is the largest herd movement of animals on the planet and is constantly moving all year long! They follow an age-old circular route guided by survival instinct, constantly searching for nutritious grass and water. The large columns of wildebeest and zebras are joined by antelopes, gazelles, and a host of other animals. But along the route, there is constant danger. Hungry predators, crossing rivers infested with dangerous crocodiles, and injuries...all take their toll. Hundreds of thousands are lost along the way, but miraculously, during the calving season in January and February, a similar number of newborns replenish the herd, keeping the numbers relatively stable."

Mosha had turned off the dirt road out into the open plains. Sam asked Tibu, "Do we always go out in the early mornings?"

Tibu answered, "It is the best time for viewing, so it is best for the tourists. The sighting of animals is guaranteed. They are hungry and looking for food. Later in the day, they are full and hot, so they are lazy and harder to spot." Mosha maneuvered the cruiser toward a tree and slowed down to get close to a seated male lion. Tibu smiled. "Often you will see a young male alone. The female lions have gone to hunt and will call the male when they have downed their prey so he can come get his share."

Sam, obsessed by lions, anyway, loved this new fact and joked, "Ah, to have your woman get your food and call you to the table!" I rolled my eyes at him and shook my head. El Amir merely chuckled. We took our photos and moved on past giraffes and a moving line of young and old elephants with trunks and tails intertwined.

The highlight came shortly after. We could hear the thunder of their hooves before we could see them. I grabbed my binoculars, straining to see. Mosha found a spot to observe far enough away to not be in the path yet close enough for the magnitude of the sight before us to take our breath. It was a reverent moment, and I could simply watch in awe as they moved through the tall grass. I asked Tibu, "Am I correct that the zebras graze off the tall parts of the grass and the wildebeest take the short grass?"

"You are close. The zebras and wildebeest eat the tall grass but different parts of the stalk. When they are finished, it exposes the short grass, which the gazelles and others eat. It is the perfect example of nature's harmony. That is one of the many reasons the grass fields need to flourish."

Mosha started the engine and headed back to camp for the large breakfast that awaited us. Our first game drive had been a huge success, and I could tell El Amir was pleased with our reaction and the choice of Tibu to teach us. After breakfast at the lodge, El Amir left us with a few words of wisdom. "Remember, you have been given a great opportunity but also a great responsibility. There are many people in this world who would love to have the chance you have right now. Very few would understand how to use it. You both have enormous power in your talent. Don't ever take it for granted. Make it meaningful in the way you give back. I look forward to hearing all about it when you return to London." To me, he added, "Sarah, I will keep your paintings safe. Make a difference." Then, out of character, El Amir hugged me and patted Sam on the back as he said goodbye and went to the car for Mosha to drive him to the airstrip.

Chapter 54

Tibu came to tell us we had about an hour of free time before we went back to the village we visited the day before for the afternoon. Sam asked if he could talk to Tibu for a while, so I wandered over to the small library to find a book to read. I thought about pulling out my paint supplies but thought better of the idea. This was all so overwhelming that I wanted to absorb it a little more before putting my brush to canvas. I picked up a book. It was a story about a young African girl and the struggle she faced growing up female. I couldn't help thinking about the challenges both Rosa Bonheur and Rachel Ruysch faced as women in a male-dominated society and was curious about this young girl. Just as I was getting into the story, Sam stopped by and knocked on the wood frame of my tent.

He was excited and came inside, plopping himself on my bed. "You are never going to believe what we are doing for sunset!"

"I have no idea. Another game run?"

"There is a young male lion nearby who has taken a fancy to a certain lioness, and he's trying to take over the pride she is in! The current dominant male is not liking this idea. There have already been a few fierce fights. Tibu says they usually get into it early in the evening, so we are going to the dry scrub area where the pride is concentrated at the moment. There is also a lioness with a new-born who is keeping it sheltered and away from the pride until it is old enough for them to return. She and the small cub have been sighted a few times. Tonight will hopefully give me a lot to work with. I will see you in a little while. I need to make sure I have enough film for my camera!"

I wasn't sure how I felt about being in the midst of a lion fight. That would be later. For now, Tibu planned to drop me at the village school for the afternoon. Sam was going on an environmental awareness walk with two park rangers. He hoped over the next few weeks to learn as much as possible about the programs the Grumeti Fund was supporting.

Tibu explained that the children took a break from school during the hottest time of the day, between 1:00 and 3:00 p.m., after receiving a healthy lunch. For some of them, it was their only meal of the day. I would have some time with their teacher, Amari, during the break. Amari immediately struck me with her jovial spirit and impressive command of the English language. She was one of the lucky females from the area to have completed her secondary education. Her father had been a ranger working in the National Park in Johannesburg where Amari went to school. He was hired by the Grumeti Fund managers to oversee the rangers here in the Serengeti and was adamant Amari find a way to help.

She loved teaching primary school, but when I asked her about the challenges she faced, her cheerful expression disappeared. "The odds that I work with are not easy, especially for the girls. Over three-quarters of the girls here never make it through a secondary education. Most of them are married by the time they reach eighteen. There is little to no birth control so many are pregnant or mothers when they marry. There is a group that I have been working with that is dedicated to counseling young girls and giving them the empowerment to improve themselves."

She made me understand what El Amir meant when he spoke of the opportunity Sam and I had been given. The plight of these young girls clearly put the tragic circumstances of my youth into perspective. I was determined to help and asked if I could meet with the group she belonged to.

Amari quickly agreed. However, that was far from her only difficulty. "The government has determined that children must learn English as a second language. I am struggling with a way to make their learning fun. There is no standard teaching method for us." I listened to her various ideas and couldn't help wondering if some version of the animal mural I did in eighth grade could work for them. These children live with animals every day, so that subject might not be as meaningful as it was to my class. I told Amari about the mural, and she smiled, pointing to the vacant wall with nothing but an open window.

"What if we still used the alphabet idea but focused on words they were more likely to use on a regular basis?" Amari and I began to brainstorm, thinking along the lines of T for *tent*, G for *grass*, and R for *river*—words that were part of their world. The stumbling block was, none of these children had ever picked up a paintbrush, much less painted a realistic image.

We agreed to think about it overnight and meet the following day. I also planned to join her at the next meeting of the group counseling the young girls. But for now, looking at my watch, it was time to meet Sam to go find the lions!

Chapter 55

I found Mosha outside waiting to drive me back to camp. He was the more quiet one. When Tibu was present, he commanded center stage. However, it was clear Mosha was passionate about the work they were doing and the animals they loved and respected.

Sam was pacing in front of the lodge with Tibu, casually standing by the door. I knew I was only a few minutes late but I apologized, knowing how important this was to Sam. They climbed in, and there was no chance to share what I had learned during the afternoon before Tibu began his talk about the lions.

"There is much to be learned about lions and their behavior. For tonight, our focus is on one particular pride. There are eight females, a mother and seven adult sisters of varying ages. It is common for female lions to join the pride of their mother, although occasionally sisters will wander off to form prides of their own. The three males in this pride are the protectors and key to breeding to keep the reproductive rate of the pride high. However, they are now older and have become vulnerable.

"This new male coalition has four brothers vying for these females, so they have a strong chance of overcoming the home coalition to take over the pride. If they do, the cubs are the largest hindrance to their reproduction cycle. Mothers of surviving clubs will not mate again until their offspring are at least eighteen months old but will mate within days if their cubs are lost.

"The first thing the incoming males instinctively do is kill all the young cubs, which results in getting the females on the same breeding cycle. The females try to defend the cubs often by creating competition between the invading nomad male coalition. The female with the newborn cub is in hiding and instinctively knows her offspring is in danger. We will not do anything to draw attention to her and her cub."

The ferocious sound of the roars was an undeniable sign a fight was about to take place. Tibu continued, "The sound of a lion's roar can be heard over five kilometers away! They are extremely territorial. This particular pride has been in their current location for years." Tibu lowered his voice, and Mosha slowed the land cruiser to barely moving. Tibu indicated we must be silent now.

There, coming out of the brush, were three older cubs running away from imminent danger. Tibu and Mosha, speaking in barely audible Swahili, were obviously debating whether to follow the cubs or go ahead to where the pride was obviously defending itself. Knowing Sam's desire to see a fight, Tibu decided to move forward to find the males.

Mosha spotted one of the older males crouched down in a defensive stance. His roar was more like heaves resonating from deep inside his body, each movement being photographed by Sam, who was mesmerized. About thirty kilometers away were the four brothers forming a line ready to attack. Three of the females had moved to a better vantage point to watch the impending duel. The sight of the females provoked the raiding males to attack.

For me, there were parts of the fight to the death that were hard to watch. Sam studied every bite, every claw breaking skin, and the desperation of the defending males. Night was falling and the fight continued. Tibu finally pointed to the one fallen male and the other two wandering off with lowered heads.

The young brothers had been victorious. On the way back to camp, Tibu agreed that this was a rare sight to see, and the adaptation of the new pride would be very interesting to watch. Sam wanted to be part of it. I was more interested in the migration and how I could impact the community.

It had been a long day, and I was exhausted. There was no denying, however, the day has been exhilarating! Dinner was waiting for us at the lodge. Sam and I shared a carafe of wine and a three-course meal around the campfire. Butternut soup was followed by a delicious vegetable curry and then banana pudding for dessert. I could barely keep my eyes open, but Sam and I finally had time to share the day's events and discuss the plans for the next day.

We would go in two different directions. Tibu would take Sam and some of the other guests back to see how the new pride was reacting and try to find the cubs that had fled and the lioness with the newborn. Mosha would accompany me to the river with my paints and recorder, and later in the afternoon I planned to spend more time with Amari. My hope was to time it to meet the children.

As I fell asleep, I longed to tell Hans all that we had seen and learned in just two days. Our time in Australia together already seemed light-years ago.

Chapter 56

Sam was gone before daybreak. Since I was not leaving camp until eight o'clock, I helped myself to a light buffet of cereal and assorted meats and cheeses. There were packages of mixed nuts to take as a snack.

Mosha parked the cruiser downwind of the riverbank. The amount of species coming here for water was staggering! He attached a tarp to the pop-up roof with two poles creating a covered outside area. Mosha's rifle was close by, and my instruction was to immediately get in the truck upon Mosha's command.

I started to unpack my paint supplies, but honestly, the scene before me was so dynamic that I felt there was no way to capture one individual scene. Instead, I used the camera to try to isolate different scenes. Giraffes were feeding off the leaves of a cluster of acacia trees to the western side of the river. There was a flock of beautiful pink flamingos in the shallow flats area where Mosha said the saltwater was brackish, so they fed off algae and small crustaceans. There was a family of elephants very close on the bank of the river getting their fill of water. They seemed playful and were filling their trucks and splashing each other.

Mosha pointed to the other side of the river to vertical sprays of water jetting into the air. Those were hippos. And there were gazelles, sleek and quick, running about everywhere. The scene was all-consuming, and it was hard to know where to look next!

Suddenly, Mosha took hold of my arm and motioned me into the cruiser. He quickly dismantled the poles and tarp. Far ahead of us, coming out from the protection of the tall grass, were the three lion cubs that had fled the pride the night before. Mosha jumped into the driver's seat with me standing up with my camera ready. The cubs were no doubt hungry, thirsty, and scared. We moved slowly, getting closer. The cubs were too small to take down larger prey, but a young gazelle would be a likely candidate for a meal. However, the cavorting elephants blocked their way to the river for water. The cubs were crouched at the edge of the line of grass seeming to assess their plan.

Obviously intimidated by the elephants, the cubs backed into the grass, moving to the north to an area away from them. Mosha maneuvered our vehicle so we were right in their path coming toward us. My breath caught in my throat when I was sure one of them was looking straight at me. But it was just a glance, and they moved past us within a few feet. Once they did, Mosha turned us around to follow. Sam was not going to believe the photos I was taking! We followed them as they edged closer to the river's edge to drink, my camera capturing frame after frame.

It was not long before their hunger took over. Mosha told me they were probably used to the older females of the pride doing the hunting. Once they were hungry enough, their survival skills would instinctively push them to kill. There were three of them. They easily overcame a small gazelle who had separated from its herd. Survival was key here on the plains. Now that they had succeeded in their first kill, they knew what to do and would go on to try to survive long enough to grow to adulthood and find a pride to join.

At the lodge, Sam had just set his plate down on the table, but when he saw me, with total abandon and without thinking, he ran up to me and swung me around off my feet, laughing. "This is the most incredible experience I could ever imagine!" He set me down and stared at me in pure happiness and then reached down to kiss me on the lips. Taken completely by surprise, I was equally on a high from the morning and kissed him back. He felt it and drew me closer. *What! It's just our emotions running high,* I reasoned. *What am I doing?*

Chapter 57

Mortally embarrassed, I turned, convinced I was beet red, and busied myself with lunch. By the time I got back to the table, I had convinced myself that it was a silly overzealous reaction to our morning, so I went first. "You are not going to believe what I got to see! Aside from all the species gathered by the river to get water, guess who decided to show up?" Sam was still looking at me, a little flustered, so I went on. "The three cubs from last night! They were thirsty and hungry...probably scared too. We followed them and watched them get around a family of elephants, get their water, and hunt for their first kill—a defenseless young gazelle that was no match for the three of them. I was sad for the gazelle, mortified by the attack, and awed by the entire thing. Crazy! I took a ton of pictures for you!"

"We were keeping our eyes out for the cubs but never saw them. My morning was equally spectacular! The new males were doing a bit of courtship for the females, who were reluctant at first. The three older cubs got away just in time. The males killed all the younger cubs at first light. We combed the area, looking for the lioness with the newborn, and found her trying her best not to draw attention. She was clearly shaking with fear and not able to expose herself to hunt for food for herself and her cub. I immediately wanted to bring scraps back for her, but Tibu said, "No human interference. Nature has to take its course so the strongest survive."

I couldn't help but wonder at the scope of everything here that the Grumeti managers were attempting. I told Sam I planned to go back to the school to meet with Amari to somehow recreate the eighth grade mural I did. When I explained the challenge of the children not being able to paint, Sam suggested, "You know how you told me about all the comic book pages you made to

Harry and Lizzy? Why don't you let them see you painting and formulate an outline so they can fill it in?"

That started me thinking how I could arrange my time to be more present when the children were actually there. I couldn't wait to explore the ideas with Amari! I also wanted to hear more about the fund-sponsored group that counseled the young women. By the time Sam and I left for our separate afternoon activities, I had almost forgotten the impulsive kiss. *Almost.*

Sam had met some of the rangers the day before on the conservation walk. This afternoon, he planned to visit two of the anti-poaching observation posts. All I could think was, *how could we leave these experiences unchanged?* They would be with us our entire lives.

Amari was waiting for me. She had made a list of multiple ABC words for me to review. I told her Sam's idea, and she loved it. We decided I would be at the school for two hours late morning while the children were there. I would first make an outline of the mural with the images of the words incorporated into the scene. Then I would start painting, allowing the children to watch me and hopefully join in. The goal was to have the mural completed by the time I went back to London.

I left, assuring Amari I would meet her the next day at the Girls' Empowerment Project group meeting. Riding back to camp, I was filled with a sense of what El Amir's parting words meant. I planned to make a difference to these children, the young girls, and the conservation of this land. I had an eerie feeling that from the moment I discovered Rosa Bonheur and her animals there was a path laid out for me to follow. I was certain that path had led me here at this time, to this place, and these people. It was like a magical secret swelling inside, leading me to a world of possibilities. A pure sense of gratitude and peace settled over me that I could be here and have an impact, even if a small one.

Chapter 58

Seeing Sam back at the lodge, I searched his face for any sign of regret or remorse about the impetuous kiss but found none. His easy smile and enthusiastic attitude about our roles here was encouraging that the moment could just slip by unnoticed. Our days were so filled that once the sun set, Sam and I fell into an easy routine of sitting around the campfire, talking about the progress of the day.

The young girls involved in the empowerment group were a mixture of grateful, inspired, and, yes, suspicious personalities. Knowing their plight coming from rural Tanzania, the task of generating the funds necessary within the Grumeti Fund to sponsor this community partnership was daunting. The goal was to create an outstanding series of initiatives for the girls starting with eighty scholarships to be used for secondary school, vocational studies, or university. That hit home with me, remembering what it meant for the curator from the gallery to secure the scholarship at L'École d'Artes for me and then again winning the scholarship to study with Kenneth Patrick.

Aside from that lofty goal, there was also a mentorship program and basic classes in life skills. One of the upcoming empowerment fundraiser events would be held in the fall. The Grumeti Girls' Run would allow women from around the world, at a lofty price, to be able to participate in a three-day, sixty-three-kilometer run across the plains of Tanzania. There would be times they would be running parallel to the herds of wildebeest, zebras, and other species tagging along! The women would have an amazing itinerary and a great deal of interaction with the girls. I would be gone, but I searched my mind how I could help them get the word out.

I didn't have my normal library to go research what to do, but I did have one thing at this stage—my own library of knowledge. I thought about the importance of when the French government reached out to Rosa to convey the plight of the farmers in a commissioned painting. I needed a multipurpose painting of a grand magnitude that I could finish during my time here and still finish the mural for the school.

Sam and I brainstormed for hours. Tibu continued to teach us about the circular pattern of the migration and their continuous search for food and water. Sam was obsessed with keeping the growth and nourishment of the grassy areas ahead of the migration healthy, and he continued to monitor the new lion pride with a pictorial narration.

We still did early morning game runs with the current guests, many of whom were captivated by our efforts. I decided I had to paint the migration again but this time in the background. In the foreground would be a line of female runners, both black and white, interspersed with armed rangers. The painting would be an endorsement for the event to help increase participation and, therefore, funding.

On days I didn't work at the school, encouraging the children to paint with me, I set up my easel and paints in a corner of the lobby, which encouraged guests to come by and inquire about the run. The managers of the fund provided flyers for the event, which guests could pick up. It was incredible to see that often when a guest would learn about the event but not be able to participate, they would make a large donation to the fund. It was humbling to witness the simple impact of letting them understand the importance of this conservation mission.

Sam was particularly interested in portraying the dangers that lay in wait for the migration. The crossing of the rivers, particularly the Grumeti in the southwest and the Mara in the north, was packed with hazards! From the jaws of hungry crocodiles to losing their footing and getting caught in the current to injuries that slowed them down, leaving them vulnerable to the major predators...all of it was part of the process needed to maintain the balance of the ecosystem.

There was one day at the school, when I was painting, a little boy came over to paint with me. He was probably around nine years old and was particularly good at mixing colors and keeping the paint within the lines. Amari was watching us, smiling. When

I was about to leave for the day, we looked at the mural that was nearing completion. She hugged me and called me *dada* or sister. Tears welled up in my eyes knowing I had made a good friend.

The days behind us got longer, and the days ahead got shorter. In the midst of finishing both projects, I became more and more eager to see Hans again. It felt like an eternity since I had been in his arms. There had not been any more kisses between Sam and me. However, our time together and the amazing things we experienced had formed a bond between us that was undeniable. I hoped Hans would understand.

Chapter 59

The day finally came for us to say a tearful goodbye to Tibu, Mosha, Amari, and all the others who had made such an impact on me, and Sam as well. We were like family now and hoped to be able to come back someday. The children from school came to say goodbye, and there were lots of sincere embraces.

I was bringing *The Migration Girl's Run* painting back to London with me, but the Grumeti managers had taken photographs and were now using its image in their brochures. My hope was that it would continue to be used to create awareness for the cause I now so believed in. Sam and I said a final farewell to this vast wilderness, vowing to return. Then it was time to board El Amir's plane for the long journey home.

We had been so far removed from life as we knew it the subject of *what next* was our main topic of conversation. I wanted to get caught up on Eleanor's plans about the wedding and when they would be moving. I also needed to find a place to live. It made sense to locate in London. The gallery, Tara, and Amelia were all there. Sam said if I moved there, he would also. It was then he brought up the subject of Hans.

"Sarah, I know you have feelings for Hans, but you have to realize after all this time that we are good together." I started to answer, but he interrupted me. "Listen, I backed off after that kiss, but, Sarah, you kissed me back. I know you have feelings for me too. Do you have any idea how hard it was for me every night lying alone in that tent, knowing you were right next door? I know you need to get things right in your mind about Hans. Sort that out and know that I am here for you and would like us to be together."

"You never said anything." I was sure the confusion in my voice was clear.

"I didn't want to take a chance of ruining our time in Africa. I loved it there, Sarah. If I can swing it, I might go back permanently." *Sam gone? No! Why am I upset? I love Hans.*

The urge to see Hans as quickly as possible overcame me. It had been two months since we parted in Australia. The only communication we had was that one letter where he said we needed to talk. Well, he was right, and the sooner the better.

The day after our plane landed in London, I spoke to Eleanor and learned the wedding would not be for two and a half weeks. I threw caution to the wind and, on a whim, booked a train ticket to Hamburg to see if I could rekindle the love story between Hans and me!

The note with his address was in my hand. I took care to wear Hans's favorite outfit—black leather jeans and an off-the-shoulder raspberry knit top. And of course, I didn't forget the fragrance he gave me! I was so excited and nervous too. My experience in Africa had been exhilarating, living among the wild animals. It was productive as well. The children were responding well to the ABC mural at the school, and my painting with the resulting donations had greatly pleased El Amir. I needed to quickly resolve any question I had about Sam, and I hoped Hans would be as thrilled as me to see each other!

I knocked on his apartment door, and a young woman answered. She was blonde, rather frail-looking with the face of an angel. She looked at me and asked, "May I help you?"

Looking at the apartment number again to confirm, I answered, "I'm looking for Hans Schuman. Does he live here?"

"Why, yes, he should be home soon. I'm Camille, his wife."

Shock and disbelief held me spellbound while screams of silent protests penetrated my soul. Camille was watching me and finally asked, "Would you like to come in for a cup of tea? Hans should be home anytime..."

"N-no...just tell him Sarah from Australia was in town and wanted to say hello. I can't stay."

She nodded and closed the door to the future I had dreamed of with Hans. *Hans was married?* I walked out of the building, unsure where to turn. The feeling of hurt and betrayal paralyzed me. Somehow, in the raw mix of emotions, there was also anger. I knew two things: first, Hans would try to find me, and second, I was determined not to be found.

Chapter 60

Walking with no destination in mind, the gloomy sky overhead mirrored my mood, and no threat of rain fazed the melancholy growing inside me. *Focus!* I couldn't stay in Hamburg. *Where should I go?* Home in Southampton would be the first place he would look, and I was due there in two weeks for the wedding. No, I would not go until the last minute and would leave right after. The London gallery where I worked all those summers? No, he would look there too. Yvette and James were about to return to L'École d'Artes in Paris. It was too late for me to sign up. It would have been my senior year, but with the year I studied in Australia, I lost my scholarship to the Parisian art school.

Sam was debating whether to go back to Paris, stay in London, or return to Africa. He was not my answer. There were just too many mixed emotions right now where he was concerned. I didn't want anything to do with Hans or Sam!

As I drew near the end of the list of where I could go, I called my best friend Yvette only to get her answer machine...most likely she was in class. Why couldn't the earth simply swallow me up? That would settle my disappearance. *Where can I go to be miserable and alone?*

The rain began softly, but I never noticed. Perhaps some inner pull of direction began to lead me back to the train station. By the time the downpour began, the station was within sight. Inside I sat down on a bench and mindlessly looked at the departure board. *Where would Hans never find me?* I have no idea how long I sat there, drenched, looking at the screen, when eventually Yvette called me back. All that I could say to her was, "I'm back from Africa. Hans is married. Her name is Camille."

Yvette's shock echoed mine. "Why don't you come back to school?"

I shook my head, resigned. "It's too late. I think I am finished with school. I am twenty years old and can earn a living, but all I want right now is to disappear."

After a pause, Yvette said, "I think I have an idea. Do you remember the time you came home with me to Nice and spent Christmas with my mother and two sisters? At the time, she was renting out the guesthouse in the back. The tenant left a few weeks ago, and as far as I know, it is still vacant. I know Maman would love to have you! Let me call her and confirm, and I will call you right back."

Between the call back from Yvette confirming I could stay at her house and the train for Nice flashing it was about to board, the decision was made. I jumped up to get to the ticket booth and got the last train ticket to Nice. I was heading to the South of France.

Looking out the window, questions overtook my mind. Was it too greedy to seek happiness? Did I not deserve the charmed life I often read about? Every time I thought I had finally found happiness, something happened to knock me down. It was not as though I was a stranger to loss. But this? Hans had made his way into my very soul, and I would have sworn it was genuine. Now, all that was left was a void with an emptiness that made me question whether it was worth moving forward. *How could I ever trust again?* Nothing felt right. Just days ago, I felt worthy, like I was somewhat important, but thinking about his letter, that he wanted to talk to me...yeah, too much of a coward to say it in a letter. "Hi, Sarah, I'm married. So sorry." *What if I had known before I left for Africa? Would things have turned out differently with Sam?*

Chapter 61

It had been close to three years since I was in Nice visiting Yvette's family over Christmas when we were roommates. Arriving at the train station, I looked at the notes I made during our conversation. I could take the bus, or it was about a twenty-minute walk to the neighborhood of Cimiez where her family house was. I had only the one small bag, so I decided to walk, allowing my mind to speculate over what I was doing here and what I would do between now and the wedding.

Yvette's sisters, Sadie and Antoinette, had left for the university in Marseille, which left Yvette's mother, Patrice, at home alone. I wandered through the tree-lined streets, wondering if Patrice would try to force me into small talk when all I wanted was to get inside the little cottage and crawl under the covers. I really didn't want to talk to anyone.

At the driveway, I stopped for a moment to look at this stunning French home from an artist's perspective. It would make a beautiful painting. The neutral beige façade was topped with an angular multi-sloped roof in a deep blue slate, but the trim around the windows and the arched front gate were the softest shade of sage green. The brown wooden door and stone steps joined an abundance of greenery and colorful wildflowers to create an amazing oasis. Patrice had created her own little slice of paradise right here in the South of France. It was time to take a deep breath, say hello, and find my new home for the next week and a half.

Patrice came to the door after I used the brass knocker. Her warm welcome seemed to be guarded enough to gauge my mood... Yvette must have warned her. It seemed better that I just come out with it. "Patrice, you are so kind to let me stay here. As I am sure Yvette told you, I received some rather shocking news, and I am in need of a little solitude right now. Your cottage sounds like it will be perfect. It might take me a couple of days to wire some funds I have in London, but I absolutely insist on paying rent."

"Sarah, my dear girl, I am happy to have you and I am here if you want company. We all face disappointments in life, but they don't have to defeat you. Even when things are most difficult, there is no reason to give up. You just need a little time to restore your footing to give you the power to deal with whatever life brings. Take your time here, surrounded by the scenery that inspired so many artists like Matisse and Chagall. You'll find your way, I'm sure of it. When I found out you were coming, I took the liberty to stock the cottage with a few things I thought you might like. There is a lovely outdoor market a few blocks from here by the Hôtel Regina. You will find the neighborhood is welcoming but not intrusive. Why don't I show you your new home?"

We walked out the back through the pool area with the well-manicured gardens, and I commented, "You must really enjoy gardening. The grounds are stunning."

"I suppose it is my own version of an artistic talent. I enjoy the mix of the colors and textures similar to the way Yvette looks at her painting. Yet this is living nature that needs to be tended to and nurtured to thrive." She paused before she asked, "Yvette mentioned you wanted to keep your presence here quiet. Surely you will let your family know where you are?"

With a sigh, I answered, "My mum and dad are gone, but I will call my stepmother and let her know I'm here. She is getting married in two weeks, and I need to be back in Southampton by then."

We started walking over to the far corner where a dome-shaped trellis covered in climbing blue wisteria marked the entrance to the tiny cottage courtyard surrounded by a white picket fence. Irregular flagstone pavers created the floor with just enough space between them to be framed with a perfectly trimmed grass border. There was a small white wrought iron table and two chairs as well as a lounge chair tucked back by the lemon tree. The entire scene was private and created the perfect aromatic solace I sought. If the inside was even close, I knew this was certainly the place to consider this change of course in my life.

Although the cottage was small, it gave the illusion of spaciousness with its vaulted ceilings and skylights. The inside consisted of a comfortable-looking living room, an L-shaped kitchen with brick floors, white cabinets, and a checkerboard backsplash. The largest room was the all-white bedroom. The furniture was simple—two side tables and a ladder-back chair. But the queen bed with the white lace comforter and white sheer drapes flowing at the windows created the perfect environment.

Patrice watched my reaction and seemed pleased. She showed me where the groceries were and left me to get settled. Alone, I began to explore my new home. There was an assortment of books on the bookcase, and I actually managed a smile when I realized there was a noticeable absence of romance novels. The corner cabinet was filled with canvas, sketch pads, charcoals and paints, along with a note from Yvette.

Dearest Sarah,

It breaks my heart that you are suffering. After meeting Hans, I would think better of him. Perhaps there has been a misunderstanding? Nevertheless, I remember you telling me about Amelia, who helped you as a little girl when your mother died in that horrific accident. Wasn't she the one who guided you toward painting? That gave me the inspiration to provide some supplies to get you started. You are in the perfect place to paint. Explore your emotions. Find a way to translate them to canvas...you are certainly in an area where the scenery begs to be painted. Haven't you remained friends with Amelia? Call her, Sarah. It might help. All the gang up here send our love and wish you well.

Yvette

Chapter 62

It suited me to stay in my solitude the rest of the day into the evening, brooding. Patrice had left the perfect combination of a fresh baguette, some Camembert cheese, assorted cold cuts, and a bottle of local wine. I was in France, after all. Anytime there was food involved, it was a delicacy. It took a second glass of wine to make the call to Eleanor. I felt the least I could do is tell her where I disappeared to and give her a heads-up that Hans might try to contact me there.

She answered on the second ring. Once she discovered it was me, I wasn't prepared for the sentiment in her voice. "Sarah, I heard you suddenly left for Germany. You are in France now? Why didn't you come home? Harry and Lizzie miss you terribly. So do I. I was hoping to have time with you before the wedding. We leave for Jacksonville soon."

I sighed and began, "I know. I went there on an impulse to see Hans, but it appears he is married, and his wife answered the door. He might try to find me, and I just feel sick inside and don't want to talk to him."

"Oh, Sarah, how awful for you. I'm so sorry. But you are still coming to the wedding, aren't you?"

"Yes, of course. But I might not get there until just before. I promise to stay a few days after the wedding. Eleanor, I would really appreciate it if you'd keep my location to yourself. Tell Harry and Lizzie I miss them and will make them some new coloring books."

Eleanor asked, "What would you like me to send you?"

"It is not as though I have any plans. Could you just pack up some basics? That would be really helpful. And, Eleanor, if Hans does reach out to you, I don't want to know, okay? I will call again once I get the package." I thanked her again, said I would see her soon, and hung up.

179

Sitting on the sofa with my legs curled under me, I finally allowed the questions to surface. *How could Hans have seemed so sincere about me all those months without telling me about a wife? None of it made sense. How could he have taken my heart and just cast it away? What did he expect from me? For that matter, who was Camille? He never mentioned a girlfriend, let alone a wife.*

*****

Over the next days, I walked down to the seashore each morning and wandered aimlessly along the Promenade des Anglaise boardwalk, searching for answers. It seemed everywhere I looked there were couples sharing a loving gaze, holding hands, or stealing a kiss. There were times I imagined Hans and me as the couple and looked a little harder to see if the feelings expressed were genuine. Every now and then, as I walked, I could almost feel Hans stroking my hair or casually throwing a possessive arm around me. That would lead to the unwanted memories of how he used to love my long hair and made brushing it such a sensual experience. *Had that all been fake? Should I not have gone to Africa?* There were so many questions.

It was during one of those moments that anger intervened, and I walked into the nearest hair salon and asked them to cut my waist-length hair to my shoulders. The beautician tried to discourage such a bold move. "*Oh la la!* Your hair is so beautiful. How could you cut it? Women would give anything for your head of hair!"

"Good, then donate it. Now please cut it, or I will have to go somewhere else." She did a cut straight across, taking each handful and laying it out straight on the plastic she had put on the counter. As I sat there watching the piles of hair grow in front of me, I was determined to cut the cord of feelings I had toward Hans, the man who deceived me and lied to my face while he maneuvered his way into my heart.

The beautician trimmed the edges ready to proceed to blow-dry and style, but shaking my head, I took the brush from her, asked for a rubber band, and put it up into a ponytail. Leaving the salon, I could hear them whispering about me and the hair I left behind.

The shorter hair lightened my step during the daily walks, but the restless nights still raged with longing for his kisses, the feel of his muscular body next to me, and the intimacies of our lovemaking. As hard as I fought to make them stop, they continued to weave into my dreams, leaving me in tears to wake up to reality.

Is it fate or destiny when something or someone crosses your path, and it changes your life direction? My mind wandered back to where it began with the acceptance of the Australian scholarship under Kenneth Patrick. Art students from around the world had entered with only fifteen selected. I could not have been more excited that I was one of the lucky fifteen! Then given my fluency in French, I was selected to teach two of the students English. And when my drawing of a shark manifested into a real shark while Hans was surfing, how could I not have thought that Hans was in my path for a reason?

But why did he ever start a relationship with me? How could he not have told me he was married or even if he was about to marry? I could not fathom such betrayal.

To ease my thoughts to a better place, I focused on memories about Africa and the Serengeti. I felt like I was making a difference there! Had that experience somehow prepared me to cope with this heartbreak? I definitely needed someone to talk to! Could Patrice be that person?

Chapter 63

There was a struggle between my desire for solitude and the need for a sounding board. Patrice was working in her garden as I left for a walk the following day. I knew she wanted to help, but for now, a single wave was all I could give her.

However, when I returned from the boardwalk, Patrice was waiting for me with the package from Eleanor. She handed it to me and said, "This must be the package from home you're waiting for. It's from your stepmother, right? Are you two close?"

I knew Patrice was trying to start a conversation. Maybe this was the time to open up to her. "We have gotten closer since my dad died, but now she is about to get remarried and move to the States." I took the package inside to open, finding an abundance of clothing and accessories. I put the clothes in drawers, the shoes in the closet, and the toiletries in the bathroom. It was when I got to the bottom of the box that I saw a book that caused a lump to form in my throat so large I could hardly breathe.

It was the book Dad had given me about Rosa Bonheur and her animals. I slowly turned the pages, remembering what an inspiration she had been to me in my youth, which was filled with times of terrible sadness but also moments of victory. *Perhaps it was time to reflect on the journey that led me to Hans but is now in need of a new direction.*

I found Patrice in her kitchen pouring a cup of coffee. Rosa's book was tucked under my arm. I quietly said, "Eleanor included this book in my package. She knew how important it was to me. It has stirred up many memories of my youth that were not easy. I was wondering if you might have a little time to talk?"

Patrice poured another cup of coffee for me and suggested we go into the living room and get comfortable. She said, "I have nowhere else I have to be. Whatever has happened to cause you this pain has happened. There is nothing you can do about that.

What you can change is what you do from here. I am a good listener, Sarah. I somehow think you need someone to talk this through with to determine what your next steps might be."

I gazed out the window, wondering where to begin. I had felt this same numbness before. To Patrice, I began, "The sudden death of my mum and abandonment by my dad when I was ten years old crushed me, and the numbness that set in to subdue the agony is similar to what I feel now. It seems each time there is something great that happens in my life, fortune turns on me to seemingly push me to despair. I'm sure Yvette told you about the opportunity I had receiving the scholarship with Kenneth Patrick in Australia. When she visited over Christmas, she met Hans Schuman. He captured my heart far beyond mere chemistry. He completed me in ways I can't even explain. Yvette saw it. She even warned me about feeling so intensely about him given we were from different countries with different plans for our futures. But I have never felt such closeness to and raw need for anyone like that. And for him to have lied about being married? I can't see how he would do that."

Patrice poured us another cup of coffee. She seemed to use the distraction to gather her thoughts about how to respond. I could hear the concern in her voice when she said, "*Ma petite, quelle tragédie!* To have such a loss at that young age. I can't imagine how that affected you as you grew up. So you feel like Hans abandoned you, like both of your parents, right?"

"I thought I had found my lifetime partner. Eleanor and the children will be leaving soon. Maybe I am destined to be alone." Feeling pitiful, I reached for a tissue from the box Patrice had on the table, dabbing at the tears escaping my eyes. "I love my painting, and the time in Africa made a huge impression on me, but they don't come close to the sense of completion I felt when Hans and I were together."

Patrice gently asked, "Don't you think you should talk with Hans to try to get some clarity about his marriage?"

"No," I said, my underlying anger, hurt, and sense of betrayal too raw. "He is gone from my life, and it is time for me to face the truth. Maybe it is just an illusion that someone else, or something else, can determine one's happiness."

Patrice nodded her head in agreement. "My husband left me for a younger, more beautiful woman and now has a child of their own. I have tried to maintain a belief that happiness and true joy have to come from within yourself and flow from whatever you're doing, wherever you are."

We explored that idea a little longer, and then Patrice offered to pack up a container of lamb stew over rice for me to take back to the cottage. I readily accepted, and by the time I heated it up and sat on my sofa, I was mentally exhausted. It was true Patrice was a good listener, and it was clear she wasn't judging me. I had to admit that even after those times of inconsolable sadness, I'd also experienced times of joy and accomplishment. I thought about the faces of those children in Tanzania and their looks of wonder as I *magically* created the alphabet of pictures on the wall. Was it Amelia who told me once that life will always have its challenges, but it is up to you whether you let them defeat you? And wasn't that in essence what Patrice was saying? *Hmmm.* For the first time since I got here, I slept soundly.

Chapter 64

Rising early the next morning, I walked down to the marina where the aromas were an intoxicating blend of salty sea, fresh-caught fish, and baked delicacies from the onsite bakery. On a whim, I decided to pick up a whole fish and chose a *loup de mer* or Mediterranean sea bass. It was straight off the boat and looked delicious! In the bakery, I picked up a fresh baguette and couldn't resist a couple of pieces of the *tarte au citron* (lemon tart).

When I returned to the house, Patrice was out in the garden assessing a new area to plant. She saw my bags and couldn't resist the question. "Sarah, what have you gotten?"

"Patrice, you have been so kind to me, I wanted to make you a special dinner with a whole fish. I hope you like *loop de mer*. Maybe we could have some fresh vegetables from the garden? Oh, and I got dessert!"

"What a lovely idea." Patrice went to retrieve her basket, clippers, and gloves to gather the vegetables. I followed her to a far section of the yard where she was growing a wide assortment of root vegetables, tomatoes, bib lettuce, and cucumbers. I must have shown more enthusiasm than I had in days to consider such a gourmet dinner with such fresh ingredients...fish caught this morning, bread freshly baked, along with salad and vegetables freshly picked from the garden.

Patrice added a head of lettuce, a ripe tomato, and cucumber to the basket first. Next, she carefully chose a collection of color-ful beets, parsnips, rainbow carrots, and potatoes. What a vibrant display full of fresh color and fragrance!

While we prepared dinner, I shared with her how lucky I was with Social Services to have Amelia for those first few years. I told Patrice about the paint set and the eighth-grade ABC animal mural that was inspired by Rosa Bonheur. Patrice was easy to talk to, and I could tell the last two days had been a turning point for me.

Patrice and I sat down to a beautiful dinner, and I realized how helpful this had been, sharing this time with her. I said, "Patrice, dinner looks amazing! There is no way I can thank you enough for allowing me to be here and for being such a good listener. Yvette and her sisters are very lucky to have you."

She reached a hand over to mine and squeezed it for a moment. "It seems to me that in order to come to terms with how you deal with Hans, you have to face these deep-lying feelings that are part of the very core of you. I have faith in you, Sarah. You can do this."

I felt like she was right, but I was ready for a change of subject. I asked, "Tomorrow, if you don't mind, would it be possible for me to help you in the garden? I love dabbling with mixes of color, and to do so with living plants might prove very rewarding. I have never gardened before and would love to try."

Patrice seemed to like the idea since she quickly agreed. From that delicious fish dinner forward, I found myself enjoying her company and conversation. Patrice taught me the basic skill, as well as the art, of gardening. My time there in Nice with her was limited, but we made the most of it. She often joined me on my walks. Most of all, she encouraged me, never seemed to judge, and was compassionate in her reactions or questions. I soon found her becoming a friend. There was no pretense, so what she was getting was the real and raw me. It was a time of healing.

Our conversations allowed me the chance to objectively analyze what happened in my past and how I reacted—my victories and my mistakes. Patrice's input was invaluable when there was something I couldn't easily see. I knew I was hiding. My hope was that by the time I left Nice, I would be ready to step outside my protective capsule and move on with my life.

Chapter 65

The time for my departure had come. Though I intended to use the pad in my hand to jot down what I planned to do next, I found myself absent-mindedly doodling. When Patrice came to tell me it was time to leave for the train station, she saw my drawing. "What is that?"

I looked down at the pad and smiled. "It's a phoenix." Studying it further, I realized it might not be soaring yet, but unlike the painting from Australia, its talons were free of the embers. In a way, it seemed the phoenix was beckoning me forward. An enormous sense of freedom came over me like a huge weight had been lifted. I looked at Patrice, hoping she knew how much she had helped me. It humbled me to understand that at my lowest moments, I had been gifted with guardian angels in the form of Amelia, Tara, and now Patrice. I was truly one of the lucky ones.

Our farewell at the station was heartfelt, and I promised Patrice that I'd stay in touch. During the train ride back to Southampton, I had time to ponder what would be next for me. I thought about the migration and how instinctively the animals know to move on. Life constantly moves, so they need to move with it. Maybe it is not so different for me. Life constantly changes. The key is to learn to find beauty and fulfillment within those changes.

I took the well-worn letter from Hans out of my bag and read it once more before letting it float out the window. It was time for my life to move in a different direction.

*****

Eleanor and an excited Harry and Lizzie were waiting at the station, ready with open arms and giant hugs. They were family, and that would never change no matter how far they or I traveled.

187

Seeing the look on Eleanor's face, I said, "Don't tell me." She didn't have to. I knew that Hans had called looking for me. Eleanor had been able to truthfully tell him I wasn't here, and he would not expect me to be here now.

My purpose was to support Eleanor for the wedding. I found Walter, her husband-to-be, and his daughter, Sandy, loving and delightful. Lizzie followed Sandy everywhere, and I knew it would be good for her to have a big sister to look up to. On the other hand, Harry was glued to me, totally obsessed with everything about Africa. He begged me to take him there someday, and I admit I felt a desire to go back and could visualize taking him when he was older.

For now, my plan was to pack up my things after the wedding and move to London. I had a meeting scheduled with Mr. Templeton, and Tara said I could stay at her flat until I found a place. I heard Sam was back at the gallery. I thought his plan was to go back to L'École d'Artes, but I hadn't heard from him since I left for Hamburg. Yvette might have told him what happened. I had no idea what to expect from Sam after all he said after Africa, so I chose to expect nothing, which made everything easier.

The wedding was simple and sweet. Eleanor and Walter seemed truly happy and in love. There was a moment during the ceremony when my heart clenched in regret for what might have been with Hans, but I took a deep breath and it passed. I needed to make a new life and I couldn't help the bubbling of anticipation about what direction it would take!

After I left for London, the house went on the market for sale. I didn't hold a great deal of emotional attachment to it since I had never spent that much time there, but it was surprisingly hard to say goodbye to the children. They were both crying when I left, and I promised to write often. Even Eleanor had tears in her eyes. There were a lot of doors closing around me. Surely that meant another one would open soon.

Chapter 66

Mr. Templeton left a message with Tara for me to come see him at the gallery the moment I got to London. She had been thoughtful enough to get a small storage unit for the boxes I brought with me. Once they were stored and my small bags deposited at Tara's, I went to see what was so important.

I knocked on Mr. Templeton's door, and when he asked me to enter, I saw my painting of *Phoenix Paradox* on an easel by his desk...the very same painting El Amir was supposed to keep safe. He saw the questioning look in my eyes and hurried to tell me what had happened. "El Amir told me he was keeping your two paintings for you while you were in Africa. We knew you would be here, so it was logical to have them stored here for you."

Before I could say anything, he continued, "I had not seen *Phoenix Paradox* or the smaller version of *The Herd*. Sarah, *The Herd* is exceptional, but *Phoenix Paradox* is brilliant! The style and influence of Kenneth Patrick shows. I didn't think there would be any problem hanging them temporarily in the gallery's permanent collection."

My mind was racing. Did something happen to it? Mr. Templeton saw my confusion and pointed to it. "One of my collectors was here while you were gone and saw *Phoenix Paradox*. Sarah, he offered four thousand pounds sterling to buy it!"

I was completely flustered and didn't know whether to be angry that my painting had been put on display without my permission or incredulous for it to have such an offer! Trying to sort through my mix of feelings and find some reason, I finally said, not intending to be somewhat cool, "Mr. Templeton, I was unaware my two paintings would be on public display and had never intended to sell either one of them."

"I understand, Sarah, but a sale of this nature would move you into elite artist status. Let me ask you. Do you think you might want to replicate it?"

"Kenneth Patrick oversaw my efforts to paint this. I believe he made a huge difference in the outcome. It has a great deal of personal meaning to me. I need some time to think about it."

Mr. Templeton then asked if I planned to come back to work at the gallery. I hadn't worked there since before Australia, and somehow coming back felt like a step backward. Suddenly, I felt like I was at a crossroad that was important. The questions flooding my mind were filled with, *What's next?*

I left his office with the explanation I would think about both the sale of *Phoenix Paradox* and coming back to work. I was wandering through the gallery, looking at the various paintings, when I felt myself drawn to the area of replication with the thought of replicating my own painting. There was Sam, seated at his easel, focused on the painting in front of him. It was like he sensed my presence and turned around.

The compassion on his face was only surpassed by his embrace and soft whisper, "I am so terribly sorry about Hans. I know how much you were counting on him." That was the moment the tears started flowing, easing into uncontrollable sobs, all the while surrounded by the comfort Sam was offering.

When I finally broke away to try to compose myself, I looked at Sam with gratitude. "It was such a shock to learn he was married that way. The feeling of betrayal is hard to get past. So many doors are closing in my life, and I don't know my next direction. Mr. Templeton said there is a buyer for my *Phoenix Paradox*, but I just don't think I can give it up."

"You've been dealt a hard blow, and I get that. I care about you, and it is hard to see. But there is no amount of regret or resentment that can change the past. Just be thankful you are here now and able to move forward. I had seriously thought about going back to school, but honestly, after Africa, it just can't compare. Let's go get a cup of coffee."

Sam and I walked up the street to a café and sat down to talk. He started, "El Amir is due here this week, and I thought I would meet with him to see if there is any way to go back. There is so much to be done, and it felt good to me there."

I had to admit it sounded good to me too. "I got such a good reaction from the children with the mural I painted. It would be great to do something similar at some of the other rural schools that are so short on resources. And the Grumeti Girls' Run is coming up in a couple of months. It will bring in women from around the world to support these young girls and have the chance to run in full sight of the moving animals in the migration."

Sam nodded. "That sounds incredible! Now that we know the migration is constantly in motion, it would be awesome to see how their habits change in the different locations. While we were there, I kept hearing how amazing the Ngorongoro crater is and that inside the crater there is its own ecosystem where you can see all the big five animals. It just seems there are endless subjects to be portrayed either on canvas or in sculpture."

I agreed but had no idea how it would be possible. "We were lucky with our month there. It had to have cost El Amir a fortune!"

Sam and I were both concentrating on how to make it happen. He said thoughtfully, "If only there was a way to pay our way. That's what I want to talk with El Amir about."

The nagging idea that the £4,000 from selling *Phoenix Paradox* could go a long way toward getting back to Africa clashed with my desire to hold on to it. I thought about replicating it, but it was one of a kind to me and would always represent my time there in Australia. I asked him, "What made you come back to the gallery?"

"Multiple reasons, I suppose. Yvette told me what happened in Hamburg, and I hated to see you go through it alone. I knew El Amir would be back in London soon, and it seemed a good way to earn a little money."

"Thank you, Sam. You are growing into a remarkable man, and I'm lucky to have you as a friend. I'll see if Mr. Templeton could use me for a few days until we speak with El Amir."

Chapter 67

 F our days passed before El Amir appeared at the gallery. By the time I saw him, he had already heard about the offer for *Phoenix Paradox*. I didn't know how he would feel about that, and I was still rather annoyed he put my private paintings on public display.

Sam and I each had our own agenda with El Amir, but the thing we had in common was our desire to return to Africa and particularly the Serengeti. El Amir must have guessed because he started the conversation at lunch with, "You both did an impressive job during your month in Africa. Actually, the Grumeti managers are interested in having you return." That got our attention, but he switched topics.

"Sarah, you cut your hair! I rather liked it long." Catching me off guard, he continued, "I understand you turned down an impressive offer on your painting. Is that correct?"

I was nervous to give the wrong answer, but on the other hand, I knew I needed to stand my ground. "Sir, if you recall, those two paintings are personal to me and were supposed to be in your care."

Appearing properly chagrined, El Amir answered, "That is true. However, they were in safe keeping here in the permanent collection at the gallery. There was no price tag on them. You received an offer—a very good offer, I might add—but there was no demand that you had to sell it. As a matter of fact, what it did was ramp up the desire and the value for a Sarah Wilkinson original among collectors."

His attention turned to Sam. "The series you did following the lion pride was outstanding. Do you think it possible to convert some of those excerpts to sculptures? I believe there would be a high demand."

Sam quickly answered, "Absolutely, sir! And I would love to go back to expand on the concept with different species."

El Amir, pure business, said, "Am I understanding you correctly that you both would consider going back to the safari lodge for an extended period?" We both nodded with enthusiasm, but it was Sam who brought up the obvious.

"We can't begin to tell you how much we appreciated the opportunity you gave us. And yes, we would love to go back. However, I don't see how that is possible without a sponsor."

"Yes, I thought we might get to the detail of your support. I am sure you both are aware it is a costly venture we are discussing. I was willing to do a month to support not only you both but also the Grumeti managers and their conservation fund. However, an extended stay is an entirely different scenario."

I was not sure if Sam was fidgeting in nervous anticipation, but I knew I was. El Amir continued, "Here is what I propose. I will cover your expenses in Tanzania for a six-month commission. In return, I expect your finest work to come from this time and be ready to feature in your own individual exhibitions here in London. Mr. Templeton was somewhat appeased with not being able to sell *Phoenix Paradox* in return for hosting your exhibitions and receiving a percentage of the sales. I, too, will receive a cut to reimburse me for some of the support I have provided. If that sounds like a fair arrangement, I will work out the details."

El Amir stared at us both. "You are no longer the children I encouraged to learn how to use their talent. You are adults. You will be expected to sign a contract before you leave, outlining our agreement. Shall I have it drawn up?"

I stared at Sam in wonder, realizing we were grown up and that this was a huge commitment. But when he winked at me and smiled, my hesitation melted into thin air, and we simultaneously said yes! El Amir ordered a bottle of champagne, and we toasted to a productive six months. Then El Amir slyly mentioned, "Oh and, Sarah, you might want to take your paintings with you to avoid Mr. Templeton's temptation to sell them behind your back!" We all laughed with the excitement of what was ahead. I looked at them both with a satisfied grin. *A door had opened!*

Chapter 68

The next three weeks flew by amidst contracts, attorneys, collaboration, and preparation for an extended time away. It was decided we would fly there in El Amir's plane again to bring more supplies for us, as well as for the fund.

Sam and I discussed what we were taking in many ways by laughing about what we were missing before. I wanted to bring several boxes of my favorite herbal tea, crumpets, and lots of potato crisps. I hunted for a different bug repellent that was stronger, and Sam found one. He was bringing chocolate—lots of it! We debated what we might need if we did more remote camping, so I invested in a versatile backpack.

The contract for each of us was fair. It turned out the gallery was also making a modest investment into our adventure, so Mr. Templeton signed on behalf of the gallery. Sam and I signed, ready to take responsibility and give the best we could with our art.

El Amir pulled me aside the day before we left to give me an idea. "Sarah, the rangers are building new anti-poaching stations along the northern path of the migration up to the Mara River. The animals most at risk are the elephants for their ivory and the leopards and cheetahs for their skins. I was thinking about the cheetah you painted in *The Herd*. Would you consider doing a series on them? I would like to select one to donate back to the managers to use to promote their cause."

Of course, I said yes, but I had no idea how passionate I would become about the subject of people killing animals for monetary exploit.

I took the time to call Eleanor and Patrice to let them know I was leaving and that it would be hard to communicate, but I'd try when I could. I had dinner with Amelia and her family. She was pregnant again, and it was wonderful to see her so happy.

Tara arranged for the extension of my storage room. That just left Yvette. I hadn't seen her since Christmas in Australia. Our phone call was filled with tearful goodbyes and promises to get together as soon as I got back. She was worried about how I was dealing with Hans, but I had to admit I had been so busy it hadn't all sunk in yet. But I also shared what a help her mother had been. I felt like I had covered everyone...all except one.

We loaded the plane with all the supplies and with instructions from El Amir where most of it would go. He said goodbye with a promise he would come visit in two or three months.

As the plane took off and the whirlwind was behind us, Sam reached over with a smile and took my hand. "We've got this, Sarah. You're not alone. I am here for you, whatever you need, whether it is space, comfort, or more. No pressure. No expectations. Just happy to be here sharing this with you."

I leaned back and closed my eyes, allowing the wash of comfort to surround me. When I opened my eyes and looked at Sam anew, I could see the strength and goodness in the man he had become. "Sam, I want to be there for you too. I'm not sure what that means yet. Let's not jump ahead of ourselves. We have plenty of time to make a difference." I remembered El Amir's words to "make a difference" when we left for Africa the first time and sighed with how life had taken such a series of turns. I was being propelled forward even though I wasn't sure where. Perhaps it was best to not get in the way and allow the journey to unfold.

I think Sam might have been experiencing some of the same feelings. This was a big step for both of us. This time, I could focus on the present rather than a fantasy future. The peaceful quiet between us on the long flight was soothing. My mindless drifting was over, and I intended to move forward with purpose. This time, it was me who reached for Sam's hand and squeezed it.

Our approach to the airstrip was in the daylight this time, and below us were miles and miles of moving animals that had become friends to us. And when we landed, there was Tibu and Mosha, and even Amari, waiting to greet us. They were family now, and it felt like coming home.

Chapter 69

The staff at the lodge greeted us like old friends, and even the Grumeti Fund managers came by to welcome us. We had work to do, and I couldn't wait to get started. All the boxes of supplies were distributed, and my bags and boxes were carried to my tent. It was smaller than last time, which was fine. Sam's was, too, but he was still next door. We reasoned that left the larger tents for the paying guests here for safari.

There was a screened corner of my porch that I dedicated to my easel and paint supplies. I now knew how chilly it was at night and in the early morning, so I was better prepared with layers. It all felt familiar and good being back. I planned with Tibu how to get close to both leopards and cheetahs with their families, which I gathered from him was not the easiest thing to do. Cheetahs hunted during the day to get the most light to help their speed and refrain from competing with the larger predators at night. The leopards, in contrast, hunted at night so they were easier to find during the day resting. With Tibu's help, I began to create a series that would feature these astonishing creatures with their exquisite skin. Tibu was a master and found mostly leopards and some cheetahs, too, but I couldn't help slipping in a few zebras.

Sam was equally immersed with his lions. He had brought a huge crate of the clay he needed to sculpt and planned to create the sculptures in clay and then do the bronzing back home.

Unlike before, I actually decorated my tent and hung both of my paintings in prominent places. I spread more personal things around and made it feel like home. Sam came over, looked around with approval, and asked me to help personalize his. All in all, we fell into a comfortable rhythm focusing on our art and our work in the community.

I was able to become involved in the Girls' Run, and Mosha offered to run with me to train, always carrying his rifle. Sam

196

would sometimes come too. There was always a cruiser follow-ing, ready for us to climb in if needed. It happened but not that frequently, which I'm sure was a result of Mosha's knowledge and skill.

It turned out thirty-five women arrived for the run, which would bring tremendous financial resources to the girls' empow-erment group. I helped them plan the activities and the work fair designed for the girls to apply for work. The run was a great suc-cess, and it was decided that it would be made an annual event.

Things were moving along great, and we were well into our third month. El Amir had not visited yet, but we expected him anytime. Both Sam and I were anxious for him to see how our work was progressing. When the owner of the lodge told us El Amir would arrive the next day, we got busy, making sure we were prepared with what to show him.

What we weren't prepared for was the grim look on his face when he got off the plane. He motioned to Sam to come with him. Sam looked at me with alarm in his eyes and motioned me to join them. "Sarah can hear anything you have to tell me."

"Sam, it is your younger brother. He was with friends and was in a bad car accident. One of the boys died at the scene. Your brother has been hospitalized. Your parents and sister are beside themselves with worry. I am prepared to take you back to England so you can be with your family."

Seeing the shock on Sam's face, I moved to embrace him. He shook his head in regret. "I knew John was hanging with the wrong crowd. There was drinking and reckless behavior. I tried to warn him. Thank you, sir. I do need to get home."

El Amir put his hand on Sam's shoulder. "Yes, the plane will be ready to fly at first light tomorrow. Why don't you pack up your essentials, and the rest will be waiting for you when you return?"

Sam asked, "Should I go ahead and take the clay figures I've completed? They could get a head start getting bronzed." Once El Amir agreed it was a perfect time to take them, Sam headed back to his tent to pack.

El Amir turned to me and said, "Sarah, if you are uncom-fortable staying without Sam here, you could fly out with us tomorrow."

Did I want to stay here without Sam?

I led El Amir to my tent where the series of leopard and chee-tah paintings were lined up next to each other. El Amir, for once, was speechless. He went from one to the other, scrutinizing the technique that he knew was reflected in *Phoenix Paradox*. "They are spectacular! You have outdone yourself. I am amazed at what you have accomplished!"

"I have to stay. I'm not finished and I have a contract to ful-fill. Tibu and Mosha will be close by if I need anything. I was plan-ning to work on another zebra series as well. I am hoping to have all of it ready for the exhibition."

El Amir asked, "Do you want me to take any back with me? I plan to drop Sam off and then proceed to Morocco where I have pressing business. I will return soon, Sarah, and hopefully, I will bring Sam with me. Is there anything you need while I'm home?"

"If it is alright, I'd like to keep the paintings here with me to refer to. I might store some of them in Sam's tent while he is gone." I went to get a package and handed it to him. "These are letters and a package for Harry and Lizzie that I would appreciate your mailing for me. El Amir, how bad is it with Sam's brother?"

"I spoke with his sister. There were some broken bones and cuts and bruises. I think surgery was needed, but she said the prognosis is hopeful. She just felt John really needed Sam right now." I nodded my understanding and slowly walked to Sam's tent.

Chapter 70

Opening the tent flap, I saw Sam seated on the side of his cot, slumped over with his head on his hands. I don't think as long as I had known him I had ever seen him look so defeated. It hit me that pain is somehow inherent in life. People get hurt. People die. And a million other reasons. I'm not alone in the pain I carry.

I thought about how comforting Sam's embrace was when I got back to London, and I wanted to offer him that same sort of comfort now. I sat down next to him and eased one of his hands into mine. We sat there silent, hands holding, for a while. Finally, choked up, Sam spoke. "I love my brother. We have always been close. I just pray he survives this and finds a different direction. Maybe I can help with that."

My arm moved around him, and like a small child, he rested his head on my shoulder. "We are fortunate to have El Amir. If it weren't for him, you would not know about your brother right now. He will get you back there. I never had any siblings growing up. Harry and Lizzie came along much later. That's probably one more reason I always felt so alone. Your whole family, not just John, needs you right now."

Sam pulled me closer so I was facing him. "What about you, Sarah? I feel like I'm deserting you. I can't just leave you here alone."

"You can and you will. I won't be alone. I have Tibu, Mosha, and Tamari. I am going to finish the paintings I need for the exhibition." I realized too late that struck a nerve.

"Geez, I am not going to be able to meet the terms of my contract. Who knows when or how I can get back?"

"Sam, don't worry about anything but your family right now. I will be back in London in less than three months for my exhibition. El Amir promised to come back at least once before then. Just keep him updated on how things are with you and your family." I couldn't help the tears that started to flow. "I will miss you terribly."

We were holding on to each other, and when we got horizontal, Sam was filled with emotion. "I love you, Sarah. I always have." My eyes squeezed shut feeling the pang in my heart, reminding me that it should have been someone else telling me that. But it was Sam, and he was hurting.

"I love you too, Sam. You will be okay. You are a wonderful man with a great talent. We will see each other again soon. I promise." This was a time for comfort, not sexual exploration, so we lay there in each other's arms until Mosha lightly knocked on the wooden frame of the tent flap with two cups of coffee in hand. Instead of going back to my tent, I was content to spend those last moments with Sam. Mosha had brought him a five-gallon bucket of warm water to use for his portable shower. Sam took off his shirt and then filled the bag with the water. He looked rather shyly at me, which was so out of character, before stripping down to rinse off. It had been close to two years since I had seen Sam naked. During that time, he had grown from a slim young boy to a strong and well-built man.

I thought to myself, *Now there is a man worth painting*, remembering with a smile how naïve I had been in my first life drawing class and how I practiced painting Yvette and a very young Sam. He saw my smile and, with a towel around his waist, tossed his shirt at me and asked, "What are you smiling about?"

"Nothing, I was just thinking that you might be an interesting subject to paint."

That got a welcome smile from Sam, and he added, "Back at you! Anytime."

He packed the rest of his gear and boxed the clay figures he had sculpted. In a matter of minutes, he was gone to join El Amir and take the flight home. What was left was a silence that was so palpable I could hardly breathe. I worked to catch my breath and started to listen. There they were, the sounds of the Serengeti making their way to my consciousness. I wasn't alone.

I went back to my tent to find my still slightly warm bucket of water waiting for my shower. As I rinsed my own naked body, I wondered if I would ever again find the intimacy I had with Hans.

Chapter 71

During the next month, I found a rhythm that worked for me. The migration had moved farther north, and if Sam had been here, we planned to follow up to the Mara River and to the Ngorongoro crater. I wondered what had happened at home and how John's recovery was going, but there was no news. I found myself satisfied to spend time with Tamari working with improving the school curriculum, doing the occasional run with some of the young girls I had met during the Grumeti Run, going on game runs or walks with Tibu and Mosha, and spending hours painting. I was gathering quite the collection and was currently working on a zebra series when Tibu arrived to say El Amir was returning! I had written him a note to ask about Sam but had no idea if it reached him.

We all went to the airstrip to meet him, and I was surprised at how excited I was to see him. But that surprise was nothing like the shock of seeing a beautiful blonde woman get off the plane with him! *What!* It dawned on me that in all the years I had known El Amir, I had never seen him with a woman. If he was bringing her here, she must be special.

Even though I searched El Amir's face, his poker face gave me no idea of what this meant. We were introduced; her name was Annie. It didn't take long for us to get acquainted, and I found her story fascinating. She was part Spanish, English, French, and American. She had embarked on an international journey on her grandfather's massive sailing vessel. It was during her stop in Morocco where she met El Amir. They had only known each other a few days before he invited her here to Tanzania.

Her impetuous decision to get on a plane with a stranger startled me. "Don't you think that was a bit reckless, Annie?"

I was immediately contrite when she worriedly asked, "Should I be worried?"

To assure her, I said, "No, I have known El Amir for many years, and he is quite the honorable man." But I couldn't help wondering what his intentions were with this girl. We had to be close to the same age. She might be a little older but not by much.

Annie was so interested in every detail! We took her on a game run which she loved, but when El Amir arranged for a balloon ride, I looked at him and rolled my eyes in disbelief! In all the time I had been here, I had never done that. I wasn't sure if they were doing it alone, but El Amir quickly let it be known I was going too!

Floating over the plains, looking down at the animals gave me a totally different vantage point, and I was busy taking pictures. On the other hand, Annie and El Amir seemed totally engrossed in their conversation. I have to admit Annie was addictive, and her warm nature made it easy to call her a friend.

As if I hadn't had enough surprises, once we landed, a lavish picnic was set up with a white tablecloth and elegant servers right under the acacia tree! Okay, she was impressed. How could she not be? El Amir was obviously taken with her.

But Annie seemed coy with her feelings. She wanted to spend time watching me paint, and I told her about the zebras and how no two zebras have the same pattern of stripes, which made them so fascinating to paint. I was thoroughly enjoying her visit.

El Amir let me know Sam's brother was recovering, and he was spending time with his family to give John support. El Amir had a note to give me from Sam, and I took it to my tent to read privately.

Dear Sarah,

I made it home to be here with John and my family and was here when he was released from the hospital. We are spending some quality time together while he heals. I will always be grateful to El Amir for that. I think about you often and hope to get back to Africa soon. By the way, El Amir said he would extend my contract. They will be packing up my tent and either store it or El Amir will bring the rest of my things back on the plane. I want to know everything, and it is aggravating not to be able to talk with you. Have you gone to the crater? Just know that I do love you and look forward to seeing you soon. You aren't cutting your hair again, are you?

Sam

There was no question I missed Sam. I allowed myself a few moments to think about Hans and how foolish I had been to trust him. Or was it that I had cared so deeply that the hurt seemed so intense? Sam was completely trustworthy, and I knew in my heart he was someone I could count on. *Did that make him a safer person to love?* Maybe, but for now, I had a new friend to entertain!

I asked Tibu where they had gone, and he said down by the river. I started down that way until I stopped when I got close. I had never seen El Amir dressed so informally, and Annie seemed infatuated. Then El Amir handed her a note and turned away. Annie seemed confused, and not wanting to interrupt, I made my way back to camp.

Shortly after that, Annie packed to leave. I had no idea what had happened. She just told me she had been called to Zanzibar, and El Amir had offered her his plane to take her there.

We had just started to get close, and I hated to see her go. We exchanged numbers, but it sounded like she might be away for a while.

And just like that, she was gone, leaving a rather sullen El Amir behind.

Chapter 72

When I tried to ask El Amir about Annie, he rather briskly answered, "There are things going on behind the scenes that Annie is unaware of. It is best she is away from Spain for a while." Then he made it crystal clear he did not want to talk about her any further.

He spent a lot of time studying the paintings I had completed since his last trip. When he finished, he nodded his approval. "Do you think you might have two or three more of this caliber finished in the next month or two? I will schedule a date with Mr. Templeton and communicate the date of the exhibition and date of the plane coming to pick you up through the Grumeti managers. They will let you know."

That sounded doable. I mentioned, "Sam and I planned to go to the Ngorongoro crater before we left. He asked about it in his letter, but I am not really inclined to go without him, or at least Tibu or Mosha."

"Why don't I go with you? My plane should be back tomorrow, and it is a short flight there. I went to the crater once with my father years ago. It is definitely a wonder of nature. I will go arrange it."

A new sense of excitement took over in me to actually be able to do this adventure! Wistfully, I wished Sam was here to go with us.

*****

I should know by now that traveling with El Amir means going first class. The lodge he selected for our short visit rested on the rim of the massive caldera, the largest inactive collapsed volcanic crater in the world! The view overlooked the crater in some places up to six hundred meters deep and a diversity of landscapes that created its own ecosystem within its natural walls.

Our guide, Amadu, greeted us soon after we arrived. *"Jambo!* If you will follow me over to the map, I will show you our plan." We walked over to an expansive map that took up almost the entire wall. "You will find the rich soil and nutritious grassy areas inside the caldera maintains an enormous density of animal life, including over twenty-five thousand of the large Big Five animals, and including the endangered black rhino." Looking at me, he continued, "I heard, Miss, that you were fond of leopards. Right here in this region, there is the largest concentration of leopards on the planet."

I could feel my fingers itching to see and hear more to paint. What an amazing place! Amadu explained, "You may have seen the Masai on occasion in the Serengeti, but here there are over sixty thousand living here as farmers tending their herds of cattle, sheep, and goats. We will see their ancient system to move in sequence with their herds to the watering holes."

Over the next three days, El Amir and I visited the Black Rhino Restoration and Conservation base dedicated to helping restore their population through anti-poaching and relocating them to environmentally friendly areas."

I honestly didn't think I could love this region of Africa any more than I did, but these three days experiencing the caldera were so memorable I knew Sam and I needed to come back and spend more time. Far too soon, it was time to return to the tent camp in the Serengeti, but I knew I returned with a richer understanding of the importance of the conservation the Grumeti Fund was supporting and I found myself proud to be part of it.

Back at camp, El Amir spent one more night before he left, letting me know he would not be able to come back to get me but that the plane would. He had not mentioned Annie again. I was the one who brought her up. "El Amir, I know Annie is on her journey. I met the most wonderful Balinese girl, Mara, while I was in Australia. I thought maybe you might arrange for Annie to meet her." I jotted down her information, along with a note to Mara telling her about Annie. He merely nodded in a noncommittal way and was gone the following day.

One of the managers found me two weeks later to give me the date of the exhibition at the gallery. Immediately I found myself filled with a case of nerves. I had been on my own or with Sam for so long that the idea of walking around a bunch of strangers who were critiquing my paintings was quite intimidating. And El Amir said I had to have a fancy dress! Hopefully he planned to take care of it all, and I could simply show up for a bit and then escape!

Chapter 73

By the time the plane arrived to get me, my case of nerves was full blown. I kept studying each painting, looking for any flaw that would keep it from being acceptable. Each canvas was separately rolled and tied. The framing would come when I got to London and had Mr. Templeton's input.

Since I was taking a one-way ride, there was no reason to meet the plane, and it gave me a little more time to secure everything to take with me. I had no idea if or when I would be back, so everything had to go.

I heard the flap of my tent open and turned, expecting to get some last-minute advice from Tibu. But to my utter shock, it was Sam with that big smile of his! "Hi, beautiful, I've missed you!"

How could it have been just two months? Sam seemed to get more ruggedly handsome with every month. His wavy dark hair was longer, and he was sporting the beginning of a mustache and beard. I couldn't help myself and ran to hug him. He lifted me in the air and twirled me around.

Once I caught my breath, I asked, "What are you doing here? I had no idea you were coming! And I am leaving tomorrow."

"I know, ships passing in the night, right? It was a last-minute decision, and it made use of the plane coming to get you. I put my stuff in the lodge and I am to take over your tent after you leave. El Amir has given me two months here in Africa to finish my contract in time for my own exhibition. I'm just sorry I won't be there for yours." Sam had plopped onto my cot.

"Oh, I was counting on your being there! I am so nervous, and El Amir will be all business."

"Well, I am your biggest fan, and I will be there in spirit. Meanwhile, come here and let me look at you. Your hair is getting long again. I can tell by the length of that ponytail of yours. Let me see." Looking at his devilish smile, I thought, *two can play this*

207

game. I slowly pulled the band out of my hair and shook it so that it fell around my shoulders.

I sat on the side of the cot. Sam was just staring at me. Then, as if he snapped out of his thoughtfulness, he smiled again and reached his fingers to my face. "Why, Ms. Wilkinson, I do believe you are developing the most appealing freckles." I'm not sure what I expected him to say, but that certainly wasn't it. I grabbed the pillow and punched him with it, resulting in a prolonged pillow fight until I finally gave up rather than be battered to death.

Both of us breathless, I suppose it was inevitable that he leaned in to kiss me, rekindling the slow-burning fire between us. His earthy scent drew me in, and I kissed him with a passion I hadn't experienced since Hans. This time, the thought of Hans was fleeting, and I knew I wanted to make this amazing friend my lover. Knowing our time was so limited, a desperation set in to get more and more of each other. This went so far beyond our school-day sexual romps that I found an intensity between us when we were flesh to flesh that was an incredible blend of friends and lovers.

Sam's husky voice urged us on, "My god, Sarah. I have longed for this. You are so damn beautiful inside and out. I can't get enough." He took and I willingly gave and then turned around and took from him. Sam only left the tent once to go gather a few snacks. Even hungry, we knew better than to tempt fate with tasty food in our tent around animals that could make us their next meal.

Late into the night, snuggled into each other, I asked the obvious question. "Do you think we will always be passing in the night?"

"Wait for me, Sarah. After your exhibition, stay in London until I get back. While I was helping out my family after John's accident, I rented a flat near the gallery. Use it while I'm gone. I'll give you a key. That way, I can think of you in my bed, around my things. Stay there. Wait for me." I dozed off, thinking what a wonderful idea it was, hoping his flat had a lingering scent of his earthiness.

Sam helped Tibu and Mosha with all my bags, paint supplies, and canvases to get me to the plane and loaded up. As the plane lifted to the sky, I waved out the window until I could no longer see them waving back.

Chapter 74

M r. Templeton lined up all my canvases on the floor and then moved them around, trying to put them in some sequence that made no sense to me. Thankfully, the phone rang, and when I answered, my initial shock turned into uncontrollable excitement—it was Annie!

When I learned she was coming to London and needed a place to stay, I immediately insisted she stay with me. I was so relieved to have someone here during all this since Amelia was busy with her family and Tara had moved to Wales. The actual show would be in eight days, and there was so much to do. El Amir should be here soon, so for now it was just me and Mr. Templeton.

Annie arrived the next evening, and we talked late into the night catching up. She had been to Thailand, Bali, and Australia since I had seen her in Tanzania. Wow! She told me about the note El Amir got to her about seeking out Mara in Bali. They had become friends, and Mara had actually joined Annie to sail to Australia!

She confided in me that her father was in the British military and had been missing for a long time. She had a lead from a colonel in Scotland and was here in London to find a certain musician. She had gone to the Brasserie that afternoon to look for him. He was there but not very helpful. When she said his name, it rang a bell with me. Very rarely was I around El Amir when he was talking business. But I thought I remembered hearing him talk about that man at the Brasserie. I told her and suggested she ask El Amir about him.

She got quiet and asked, "Have you seen El Amir recently? You two seem so close."

My curiosity about what was between them was further stoked after I told her he would be here in two days. She hesitated for a moment before asking, "Do you two have business together? I never asked, but are you in a relationship?"

I had to laugh out loud. "Me and El Amir in a relationship? Hardly! He has been a longtime patron of the gallery since before I interned in high school. After my painting improved at an art school in Paris, he noticed. My first sale was to him. He has been watching my career and has been a strong supporter. It was about two years ago, before I went to Australia and met Mara, that he became a sponsor. Why do you ask? Are you interested in him?"

"He intrigues me. So full of mystery." I think Annie was watching me for my reaction.

"Well, I never thought to question what he does outside of the causes he supports, but I will tell you this. I have never seen him with a woman before or since he brought you to Africa, and he was spellbound your entire stay. He wasn't very happy when you left so suddenly."

Annie said, "It was odd. Somehow El Amir had received a note for me from an acquaintance actually warning me of some danger, so I left to meet him in Zanzibar. By the time I got there, he was already gone. Very strange." She then left the subject behind and offered to be of any help possible to make my show a success.

True to her word, at the gallery the next day, she met with Mr. Templeton to get the schedule of what needed to happen when. I was stressing over all the details, so nothing made me happier than for Annie to take charge. At one point, seeing me overwhelmed, she came up and shook my shoulders! She said, "Hey, stop for a minute! Now...find a reason to laugh. Laughter is a great stress-breaker. What shall we laugh about? Let's wager whether El Amir will come decked out in full Moroccan attire, or he will succumb to western influences while here."

That was an easy one. "Stodgy old benefactor for sure!" She was right. When we laughed, it was much easier to relax. When I saw him appear, ever the polished businessman, I winked at Annie knowing I had won the bet. But she wasn't looking at me, and El Amir was looking everywhere but at her. Watching them distracted me enough so that I could actually help Mr. Templeton with the frame decisions. Glancing at them when they finally talked, I could see it looked formal and somewhat strained. All I could think of was, *what is going on between these two?*

The following day, Annie said she had an errand to run before coming into the gallery. She and El Amir were both noticeably absent. When Annie got there, she was nervous and edgy, but she plunged right in to help Mr. Templeton start to hang the paintings. The show was just hours away.

At one point during the afternoon, Annie handed me a most beautiful amethyst stone and said, "You've got this, Sarah. The paintings you create are a gift to those fortunate enough to see them. Allow the willingness to expose yourself and your work to the viewer's appreciation. An amethyst is called a metamorphosis stone...an ancient healer of mind, body, and soul. I found it in Bali. The gallery thinks enough of your talent to showcase it. Let this stone help you find a sense of clarity and feeling of renewal as you take this leap of faith. Enjoy this moment, Sarah! Allow the course of your life to take the next step toward its destiny."

Her words brought tears to my eyes, and I knew I would never forget them. I hugged her with the knowledge I had made a friend for life. I could do this. Looking around the gallery at my paintings on the walls so beautifully framed, I marveled at how far I had come.

It was finally time to go change. El Amir arrived at the gallery as Annie and I were leaving, and I even had to admit he looked dashing. Annie and I were dressed and back in time for the doors to open. I took a deep breath with a pat on the back from El Amir for support, and it began.

I wandered through the guests, picking up bits and pieces of their conversation and responding to their questions and compliments. Mr. Templeton had two assistants putting "Sold" signs on paintings as they were purchased. It was almost a total sellout with a list of commission requests. I could not have been any more elated!

There was no way to express my gratitude properly for all that El Amir had done to bring me to this point. And Annie being here to share it was perfect. I pulled a small unframed canvas out from behind the desk and handed it to her. It was a rendering of two zebras in the Serengeti interacting with each other. "Look closely. Although their stripes may be different on the outside, their inner nature is entwined with each other. That is like us,

Annie. You may leave tomorrow but know that I will never be far from your side."

El Amir was watching this tender scene, and I went over to him to say my good night. We both smiled as Mr. Templeton was going through the invoices, obviously a happy man. The evening had been a giant success.

Chapter 75

Annie left early the next day saying she planned to visit her paternal grandparents in Yorkshire to try to learn more about her missing father. I met El Amir and Mr. Templeton at the gallery to reconcile the results of the prior evening. There were only three paintings left. All the rest had sold, and two got multiple bidders and eventually sold well over the asking price. There were seven commissioned paintings that would be unique to the collectors, and I looked forward to doing them. With the funds collected, I was able to pay El Amir back in full for my Africa expenses, make a donation to the Grumeti Fund, and still have a tidy sum left for myself. Mr. Templeton said he planned to take some of the gallery funds to do a small expansion, and it was decided he would keep the three paintings left in his sales gallery for future sales.

With the financial aspects settled, I felt like I deserved a well-earned break. I had access to Sam's flat, and he would not be here for his own exhibition for a month and a half. I gave thought to all the exotic places Annie was visiting and considered going to visit Mara in Bali, but in the end, it seemed like the perfect time to slip away and see Eleanor and the children in the States for a few days.

*****

Jacksonville Beach was a delightful surprise! Sunny Florida weather, sandy beaches, and gorgeous sunrises. Eleanor, Harry, and Lizzie seemed at home there with Walter and his daughter Sandy, who appeared to love being a big sister.

I was fascinated by the swing of the tides and loved walking far out on the sandbars at low tide. When we stopped at a little beach store to pick up more sunscreen, I couldn't help adding a frisbee to my purchase. Throwing it on the beach reminded me of those happier times with Mum and Daddy on Brighton Beach.

We hunted for sand dollars which we then painted and decorated as Christmas ornaments. Harry was the one who loved what he painted. I had a long conversation with Eleanor about the summers I went to art school, and she agreed it was worth exploring for Harry.

Eleanor and Walter looked happy together, although Eleanor confided she often thought of Dad. I think she still carried guilt about not getting him to a doctor sooner. All in all, I have learned from experience to treat each new moment as precious, and that is exactly what I did! Unlike the resentment I felt years ago, my time here was filled with gratitude for this family I might never have had.

It was time to move in a new direction again as I found myself at yet another crossroad. I still had time in London before Sam arrived. I could paint but I wasn't surrounded by my inspiring animals. Instead, I chose to take long walks but missed those afternoons in Montmartre watching the street artists.

Then, as if my thoughts manifested themselves, I got an unexpected call from El Amir. He was in Paris, and Annie had been kidnapped. I screamed in alarm but El Amir assured me that Annie was okay and that her father, who had also been held captive by some Chinese activists, had been rescued. Annie was a bit of a mess, and he wondered if I might come to Paris for a few days to be with her. *What! Back to Paris? Annie needs me?* Without any hesitation, I said, "Yes!"

Chapter 76

During my train ride to Paris, my head tumbled with questions. *Annie kidnapped?* I realized how little I knew about her and her family. And El Amir involved? *How? Why?* My bag was filled with the very few items I had that weren't khaki, and I did love the idea that I might find time for a little shopping. I wondered if I could remember where the little street with the used clothing stores was that Yvette took me to that first year we were roommates.

Yvette and James had graduated from L'École d'Artes. I heard James was doing quite well in New York, and Yvette and Jackson were visiting her father in Milan before moving to Nice near Patrice. So many people and places had moved through my life. Was I destined to be a nomad? Was Africa, its land, its animals, and its people enough to fill the rest of my life? Was marriage and children in the cards for me? *So many questions,* was my last thought before dozing off for a while.

El Amir was there to meet me and took me to his hotel. I suppose I should have guessed but I had never seen such a luxurious living space before. I looked at El Amir with raised eyebrows as he pushed the elevator button to the penthouse!

Once inside, Annie ran to meet me, hugging me so tight I could hardly breathe. She finally let go to introduce me to her father, Alex, a handsome man older than El Amir with a weariness around his eyes, revealing his recent turmoil.

It was clear how much Annie and her father loved each other as they said their goodbye before El Amir left to take Alex to the station where he had picked me up, leaving Annie and me to catch up on what happened. El Amir said in parting that we would make plans once he returned.

I finally looked at Annie in total bewilderment and said, "I want to know everything...from the beginning!"

Annie took me to the balcony to sit and began, "Sarah, it was so scary. I didn't know who to trust to save my father!"

I couldn't keep up. "Whoa! Start at the beginning."

Taking a deep breath, Annie started over. "My father is part of British Special Forces. He is often gone for long periods on missions, but this time he had been gone for over two years. I have been trying to learn of his whereabouts. That is why I was in London, to find that man Earnest at the Brasserie. I had also met a well-known matador from Marbella, Ramone Sanchez. I thought he was romantically interested in me, but he kept disappearing. He is the one who sent the note to meet him in Zanzibar. He was gone by the time I got there, leaving only a plane ticket and commissioned painting of our last evening in Marbella before I set sail on the *Porto Banus.*

"It turns out I was kidnapped by Ramone's father to use me as bait to get information from my father about the British involvement in the scheduled turnover of Hong Kong to China. Sarah, he looked just like Ramone but old and mean-looking. It was eerie. Then Ernest showed up, saying he warned me. It was all very ominous. I was taken to where my father was held captive with the Chinese and who walks in as the interrogator scheduled to use whatever means necessary to get the information they needed? The El Amir I knew had dissolved into thin air! Salvador, Ramone's father, and Earnest put my gagged and handcuffed father and me into a sedan with a stern-looking driver. I was angry at the betrayal, but I was also very frightened for myself and my father!

"Then suddenly, everything seemed to explode! El Amir's driver and Earnest disarmed and secured Salvador. My father was freed, then out of the blue, Ramone walked in! I must have fainted. How these two men were both involved still has me baffled."

El Amir returned and walked out to the balcony with a bottle of champagne. "Annie and Sarah, I think both of you ladies deserve to be spoiled a little."

After the toast, I said to El Amir, "Well done, my friend."

Annie glanced at El Amir and then mumbled, "Well, he was pretty scary yesterday!"

With that, we had another toast while El Amir outlined our plans for the next two days. When he mentioned going to a famous restaurant that night, Annie and I looked at each other in alarm, realizing we had nothing to wear. El Amir, ever astute, said, "Well, it looks like we now have shopping on our agenda!"

I don't think I have ever seen El Amir so light-spirited walking past the Eiffel tower toward the upscale shopping area. Annie and I were having so much fun trying on clothes together, and I realized she was the first real girlfriend I had other than Yvette. One shop owner had served El Amir a glass of champagne while he sat on the sofa thoroughly enjoying our antics, displaying one outfit after the other. Well, until Annie walked out in a certain black dress. Those golden eyes of his were literally blazing as he stared at her. And flirting mercilessly, she turned and dipped, showing a deep side slit up her leg and a great deal of cleavage. Looking in the mirror, Annie smiled and said, "I think I must have this dress!"

To see El Amir's reaction, I totally agreed. "Oh yes, you have to have that dress!" The moment passed, and we gathered a few other outfits for our Parisian holiday.

Chapter 77

Back at the hotel, El Amir said he had some business to attend to and would be back to pick us up. The packages soon arrived, and I couldn't help but say to Annie, "You do know you were shamelessly taunting that man, right? You really should be ashamed. If you are not careful, you will fall into the image Arab men have about oversexed Western women!"

Annie immediately realized she had made a mistake tempting him like that. "Oh, Sarah, you're right! And after all he did for my father and me! I just felt for the first time he might have the same attraction for me that I do for him. One thing is for certain, things are never ordinary around that man."

With that, I had to agree. This trip had shown me an entirely different side of the man who was an artist's sponsor and patron of African conservation. Now I find that he has military intrigue and a serious fondness for a certain blonde.

Honestly, I was relieved when Annie chose a different dress to wear that night. However, by the time we returned to the hotel, I felt like a third wheel and excused myself to go to my room. I am not sure what went on between them that night, but I was happy to see Annie join us on the balcony for breakfast with a genuine smile and El Amir noticeably more relaxed.

By the end of our holiday, Annie had shared what happened with El Amir that night and that he had said his culture forbade him to be with her. She said he practically threw her into the arms of the matador. I reflected out loud, "Excuse me, isn't the matador—Ramone, actually—the same man who betrayed his own father to keep you and your father safe? Do you really think it was easy for him to seek out El Amir for help? It seems to me you have two men very taken with you, but one has declared himself off-limits. Why not explore the possibility with Ramone, Annie? Oh and, Annie? Wear the black dress for him!"

It wasn't until the three of us split up to go in our separate directions and I was back on the train to London that I realized I had never mentioned either Hans or Sam to Annie. Obviously, Mara hadn't either. Perhaps that was just as well. Hans had stopped trying to find me. He was obviously moving on with his married life. And Sam...what about Sam? I know Yvette said that he moved from girl to girl at school while I was in Australia.

Once I got back, though, he was there when I was in love with Hans and once again when my heart was broken. He never pressed, but somehow he has always been a rock that I could depend on. I tried to imagine what a life with Sam would look like. Would we give up Africa with us both so passionate about it? Could we live together in a tent with no privacy? On the other hand, did we seem like we could go back to a mundane city life without the animals?

I thought about the Paris holiday with Annie and El Amir. Did I want more of that? *What exactly did I want?* Just as I came to Paris with questions, I seem to have left it with even more!

Remarkably, the entire time I was in Paris with El Amir, he never once mentioned what he wanted me to do next or the commissions waiting for me to paint. *Hmmm.*

Well, I had time to get started on one of them. Mr. Templeton agreed to let me use the gallery to paint until he began his setup for Sam's exhibition. Before I got started, I wanted to create a photo journal of all my photographs from Africa. I set them up on a drive that I could then project to a screen for an enlarged detail. I hoped to take this setup back to Africa with me to use in the future.

For now, one of the commissions was for a family of elephants moving through the acacia trees. I had seen the actual scene many times and loved how they kept track of each other by connecting their trunk to the tail of the elephant in front of him, forming a line of young and old. This is where I would start.

Mr. Templeton often wandered by, curious how I would translate the requested commission and seemed pleased as I progressed. During one of these times, he let me know El Amir's plane was taking supplies to drop off when it picked up Sam and the rest of his unfinished sculptures. Sam should be here in a few days to begin his bronzing process and go through the sculptures left at the gallery when he was in London on his last visit.

El Amir would be here two days before the exhibition. The gallery began to exude the anticipation of a new exhibition, and I now found myself with a case of nerves for Sam! Too bad Annie wouldn't be around to supervise. Hopefully, I could fill that role somehow.

Just before Sam arrived, I received a letter from Annie. She must have felt me thinking about her. She had returned to Marbella, and things were going well with Ramone. Even with things heating up between them, she was ready to embark on another adventure...this time to the Greek islands. She had asked Mara to join her for part of the trip and asked if I could get away to travel with them. *The Greek islands? Wow!* I would love to, but I didn't see how I could leave and not be here for Sam's first exhibition. I wrote back to explain, hoping she would ask me again some time.

Chapter 78

I wasn't sure the nerves I felt anticipating Sam's arrival were about his show or about seeing him again for the first time since our "ships passing in the night" encounter. I have no idea why I was worried because the moment he walked in the door and flashed that smile of his, all worry was put to rest. Sam had that way about him, whether it be with people or animals. His innate good nature emanated from him, making anyone around him at ease. I was no exception. When he greeted me with, "Hi, beautiful!" I didn't hesitate to go straight into his waiting arms.

The next week was busy putting the last touches on my elephants painting, Sam finishing the bronzing of the new sculptures, and our making love in any and every spare moment. When he and Mr. Templeton began to line up the finished pieces, I went down the line, stunned! They were masterful. The movement captured in the muscles of the lions in motion were incredibly realistic. But one in particular caught my eye...how could it not? It stood about the height of a grown German shepherd! The male lion with his full mane stood tall and regal, commanding the allegiance of his pride. He was breathtaking!

Sam saw my reaction and winked at me just as El Amir walked in. He shook hands with Sam, who then moved aside as El Amir and Mr. Templeton worked their way down the line, discussing the various pieces and proposed prices—that is, until they got to the large one that in my head could only be called *King*. El Amir slowly walked around it, studying the minute details. "Sam, you have outdone yourself on this one. It could very well be in a museum." *Who knew how accurate that prophecy was?*

Sam was obviously proud of it but quietly said, "Thank you, sir. I was inspired. I'm glad you like it." We could both hear the discussion of price, and it was Mr. Templeton who suggested

£15,000. Sam stood there in a state of shock. "Doesn't that seem like an overly ambitious price?"

El Amir was the one who answered, "I don't think so, and if for any reason it does not sell at the exhibition, I will buy it myself. I am very tempted to buy it before the show, but I think it will showcase the other works beautifully and should stand at the entrance. Mr. Templeton agreed wholeheartedly, and they went on to discuss the other details needing their attention.

I took Sam's hand and went back through the sculptures. There were twenty-five altogether, mostly lions interspersed with cheetahs, buffalo, hyenas, and an impressive vulture that made me think about the phoenix. "Sam, you have such talent in those hands! I usually see the clay versions, so I never get the full effect. It looks like the bronzing process somehow differs between them. How do you create the different finishes?"

"After the molten bronze statue cools, it has many imperfections with its many support tubes and pins. After I fix those and polish, I like to add one of the many patinas available to give it a unique look. Some antiquing is helpful to accentuate minute details."

"Although the outcome is totally different, it sounds a little like the process Hans used with his glass." I was first amazed I could refer to Hans in a matter-of-fact manner and, second, grateful Sam wasn't jealous. He merely reflected that they both used a blazing hot furnish to melt either the glass or the bronze. But he explained the difference was that Hans had to manipulate the hot product, whereas he did his original forming in clay.

Everything looked ready, and it was time for us to change for the evening. I decided to wear the dress I got with Annie and El Amir for the evening in Paris. It was certainly more daring than anything I had ever worn around Sam, and his face showed his approval when he saw me.

The drape of the tea-length dress met at a tiny strap over one shoulder, leaving the other shoulder bare. The solid pale lavender was embellished with embroidered iris along the bodice, but Sam seemed particularly interested in the thigh-high side slit. I took all this in while noticing that he, too, dressed up well. I had never seen him in a suit, and to say he looked dashing was quite the understatement. He came over to give me a sensual kiss while his hand found the top of the slit. For a moment, all thought of the exhibition was abandoned...thankfully for just a moment! We readjusted and Sam said in a most sensual voice, "I look forward to finishing what we started later and showing you exactly how talented these hands are...among other things." He took hold of my hand, and we were off.

Chapter 79

Mr. Templeton had turned the gallery into a magical kingdom with each sculpture strategically placed and spotlighted. Sam seemed pleased and sat back a little to view the scene. With the primary lights lowered, it showcased the sculptures perfectly.

I was looking around the room, and Sam was about to go mingle when I pulled his arm back and whispered, "Who is that woman over there? Any idea?"

A perfectly coiffed brunette in a fitted crimson red dress stood out from the crowd. She moved from sculpture to sculpture with an air of confidence laced with arrogance. Obviously, El Amir noticed her, too, and walked over to speak with her. Sam and I glanced at each other with curiosity and kept watching as the conversation between the two of them appeared to get more intense until finally El Amir left...not too happily. The woman, apparently unfazed, went over to Mr. Templeton and, after a few words and a nod in Sam's direction, aimed those piercing eyes directly at Sam. When she began walking toward him, never taking her eyes off him, I mumbled, "Do you want me to stay?" It didn't take long for the woman to answer the question for him.

Even with full makeup, she looked like she was in her late forties or early fifties. Without a glance at me, she introduced herself to Sam as Gretchen Warner from Wyoming. Looking directly at Sam, she added, "Fine collection, Sam. We need to talk." The two of them went to Mr. Templeton's office and shut the door. I went to find El Amir to see what I could learn about this brazen woman. He obviously knew her. The clenched jaw indicated El Amir's displeasure. I asked who she was and if he knew her.

"She's Gretchen Warner, curator of the museum in Wyoming that specializes in natural wildlife. I know her through the Grumeti Fund because the museum is a large contributor, and she sits on the board with me. I knew Mr. Templeton had sent her a pamphlet about the exhibition, but I never expected she would come all this way."

I didn't understand. "If she is part of the conservation effort in Africa, why would you be upset that she is here?"

"Because she wants Sam and the entire collection at the Wyoming museum for twelve months!"

"But there are buyers here. It looks like the majority could sell." My confusion was evident.

"Right, but she told Templeton to halt all sales until she speaks with Sam." He looked at the closed door once again. I was trying to follow. *So if he made no sales, he couldn't pay El Amir back for his expenses or the gallery for all its investment? And wait! Sam would be gone for a year? Would he ask me to go with him?*

"What is Wyoming like?"

"Oh no, you don't, Sarah," El Amir said. "I don't want to lose either of you, but I do not plan to lose you both. I have years invested in you and Sam."

Even though I felt close to El Amir and was grateful for all he had done for me, I didn't care for the idea that he thought he might own me. I reminded him, "If you recall, I am paid in full for the financial advances you made on my behalf."

El Amir was about to answer when the door opened and a rather dazed Sam came out with Gretchen. They shook hands, and then she went to have a few words with Mr. Templeton and abruptly left without a glance at El Amir.

When Sam came over to tell us about Gretchen's offer, no one was more shocked than El Amir. "Gretchen made me an offer I can't imagine refusing. On behalf of the museum, she made an offer to buy the entire collection at the prices marked, which would repay my advances and give the gallery their percentage. In return, she wants me to work in the museum, making sculptures there in the Wyoming habitat. She said Wyoming's national parks are home to over one hundred species of mammals and over four hundred species of birds, all roaming free like in Africa. She also mentioned the museum was a sponsor of the Grumeti Fund."

El Amir was actually speechless. I asked, "She offered to buy your entire collection? Even King?"

Sam answered, "Especially King! The museum already has some large bronzes of bear and bison. She wants me to build on that and increase their inventory of larger pieces. She wants to feature mountain lions, wolves, moose, and bald eagles. I must say it sounds different but in some ways the same. Definitely challenging!"

El Amir finally found his voice only to repeat, "She bought the whole collection?"

Sam glanced at me and then answered, "Yes, Mr. Templeton is spreading the word to the collectors that the collection is sold out. I gather there are some unhappy patrons."

Trying to judge El Amir's reaction, Sam decided to blurt out the next part. "When I mentioned Sarah had been in Africa with me doing her wildlife paintings, she found that interesting and planned to contact the museum board to see if they might add her work to the project."

My eyes grew wide with the potential of such a new experience. It was as if El Amir's disposition flipped like a switch, and he seemed genuinely happy for Sam. "Such an honor to have been singled out like that! With the sellout of this collection, word will spread, and the value of your pieces will take a dramatic increase. This is the potential I saw in you, and I could not be any more proud of how hard you have worked to achieve this." Then he turned to include me and said, "Both of you have surpassed my highest hopes. Perhaps it is time to release the ropes." He gave both of us a rare hug and said he would go console some of the disgruntled buyers and settle up with Mr. Templeton.

Chapter 80

Sam was moving back and forth between total disbelief and a growing excitement for the challenge offered with this residency. On the other hand, I didn't quite know how to react. Gretchen hadn't even given me a sideways glance. There was no question her interest was in him. My own feelings fluttered between pride for Sam, surprise that he had just moved light-years ahead of me in our art career, and pure inconsolable envy.

That night, lying next to Sam, I couldn't help the words that slipped out. "Ships passing in the night, right?" *Was I in for another heartbreak? Would my heart break if I lost Sam? Would I go with him if I wasn't given an offer by the museum? If I went back to Africa, would I be lonely?* Here I was once again with an endless list of questions.

With my "ships" comment, Sam held me closer. He said softly, "I said yes before thinking through what it might mean for us. You know I want you to come with me, don't you? We should hear tomorrow or the next day if they are going to make you an offer. I have three weeks before I leave for Wyoming. Most of it will be spent crating the sculptures for cargo freight to ship. Gretchen anticipated the freight could take up to a month to get to Wyoming." I wasn't sure I liked the way he now so casually referred to her as Gretchen.

There was no call from Gretchen the following day or the day after. My heart sank a little that I might not be offered this opportunity. That was when I decided to ask for a meeting with El Amir. I was not going to sit around sulking—I needed a backup plan!

We met downtown near the gallery for a late lunch. I quickly got to the point. "It is clear Gretchen Warner came prepared to make this offer to Sam. I have done a little research on the museum, and their focus is mostly on sculptures. I don't want to barge in on his success."

El Amir thoughtfully put down his tea. "Sarah, are you and Sam so committed to each other that you would go not to be apart? You know you are a huge talent on your own. What is it that you want?"

"I care about Sam. You know that. If the museum is anxious to have me, of course, I would go. But if not, Sam and I have been apart before. Honestly, I constantly dream of going back to Africa, closer to where the migration is currently moving near the Ngorongoro crater where we went when you were there. If I were to go by myself, I think I would rather be in the lodge where there are other people, not in a solitary tent. Do you think that is a possibility?"

El Amir smiled and said, "I have a philosophy about possibilities. I never think of them as *if* but rather as *how*. There is a gallery in Barcelona doing an exhibition featuring *Birds in the Wild* in four months. Sam arguably said there were over four hundred species of birds in Wyoming, but in the crater, there are over five hundred species, including the great spotted cuckoo, African harrier-hawk, and crested francolin. How do you feel about painting birds?"

Naturally I thought of *Phoenix Paradox* as well as the falcon series I did in school. "I think I would love that. Would I be able to hire a guide to help me find those rarest of birds to present in my series?"

"That's my girl! Of course, you can, and I suspect you will walk away with the highest of awards. Give me the okay, and I will make the arrangements."

"Let me speak with Sam first. Can I let you know tomorrow?" Images of exotic birds were beginning to formulate in my mind.

"You have my number. There is an emergency in the south of Spain, and I leave tonight to lend a hand. Call me when you decide."

Thinking about the south of Spain, I worriedly asked, "Is Annie alright? I thought she was in the Greek islands."

"She is fine, but I need to check on some things for her father, who's back in the States. My plane might be needed." It was evident El Amir did not intend to elaborate.

Back at the flat, Sam was inventorying his pieces with full descriptions, weight, and dimensions. I asked if he had heard from Gretchen yet. Given how he said yes without looking at me told me the museum had not offered me a position. He said, "She wanted to know how the packing was going. I brought you up, and she said unfortunately the museum declined, having used their resources on me and my collection. But, Sarah, come with me. It sounds like Wyoming is abounding with wildlife you can paint, and I'd hate to go without you."

I thought of my trip to Australia. I didn't think twice about leaving Sam or starting an affair with Hans. Taking a deep breath, hoping the decision I was making was the right one, I said, "I met with El Amir this afternoon. He is arranging my return to Africa to stay at the Ngorongoro crater. The migration will be passing through that area while I'm there, and he wants me to do an exotic bird series for an exhibition in four months in Barcelona."

"Do you really want to be there alone? We would be apart all that time."

"Sam, I was alone after you left to be with your brother after his accident. I asked El Amir if I could stay in the lodge rather than a tent so there will be other people around." Sam started pacing, obviously concerned.

"The last time you left me, you fell in love with someone else, and I was left picking up the pieces."

His comment struck a nerve and I had to swallow a nasty retort.

When I could think clearly, I said, "Yes, you did, and it could be you this time who falls in love. And, Sam, if that happens, my hope is that it works out better for you than it did for me."

But an awkwardness arose between us, realizing this separation might not be temporary. The next day, I called El Amir and told him to put the trip to the crater in place, and that I would be ready to leave as soon as possible. I put all my extra things back in storage since Sam was going to give up his flat. Gretchen had arranged for an apartment for him near the museum.

When it came time to say goodbye, Sam pulled me into an embrace. "You know I want only happiness for you, Sarah. I made something for you." He reached for a box to give me. Inside was a necklace, and from the gold chain hung a beautifully detailed golden phoenix. Tears flooded my eyes that he had done such a thing. "Your father saw it. Kenneth Patrick saw it. El Amir saw it. Even your eighth-grade teacher saw it. How could I not see it? Sarah, you are the phoenix. It's time for you to soar. I will try to come to Barcelona to marvel at the bird series you will create. I love you, Sarah. And even if our paths don't reconnect, I always will."

"I love you, too, Sam. You are the most thoughtful person I know, and this opportunity in front of you is so well deserved. Your talent is going to make you famous...I can feel it." I smiled at him and kissed him with all the love I felt for him.

Chapter 81

I had packed *Phoenix Paradox* away in storage, but with the sentiment behind the necklace I was now wearing and Sam's words, I went to retrieve the painting and take it with me for inspiration. At the last minute, I had to wait two days for El Amir's plane. He said he needed to pick up Annie in Crete with the plane and get her to Madrid where he needed to attend a meeting. He would then send the plane on to pick me up and take a commuter flight to Malaga for business.

I wondered about the apparent connection between El Amir and Annie. I thought from our last conversation that she was falling for Ramone, the matador. Maybe something happened between them? *Well, it really is none of my business.*

The plane arrived, and I prepared to board, seeing all the supplies that were loaded into the cargo compartment. How does this man do all that he does? He is a walking superman! They would drop me off at the Arusha Airport before off-loading the cargo in Grumeti. El Amir had arranged my transport to get from the airport to the lodge where we stayed before.

During the ride, I waited for that sense of loneliness, but looking at this incredible scenery around me, I felt nothing but excitement to be here! My guide, Malik, was waiting for me at the lodge. He got me checked in and moved to my room. Since I had been here before, I knew my way around, so we agreed to meet the next morning to devise our plan for the next months.

My room was not nearly as large as my tent, but it did have a hot shower and surely beat a nighttime trek to the outhouse! The lodge owner showed me a well-lit area in one of the meeting rooms I could use as a studio to paint and leave my supplies. I was ready for the adventure!

After ten minutes with Malik the next morning, I knew I was in the right hands to help me select my subjects. The color-coded chart he gave me listed all the species of birds and the codes designated whether they were either critically endangered, vulnerable, or near threatened. With conservation so important in the area, I asked Malik how feasible it would be to concentrate on those rare birds in some state of becoming extinct.

"To find them, knowing the varied habitats of these birds must be combined with the sight of a hawk and the hearing of an owl. Let me see your camera."

I showed him the camera I used in the Serengeti, and he laughed. From his backpack, he pulled a camera body with a separate powerful zoom attachment that he offered for me to use. After a brief instruction on how to operate it, we grabbed the chart and binoculars and ventured out to practice. That first day, Malik trained me to listen to the sounds the various birds made and try to distinguish them from each other. I remembered that small colorful bird on my deck on my first trip to Tanzania and the beautiful song he sang. Malik said I also had to train my eye to look for shape, color, and pattern.

We concentrated on what appeared to be ducks, and I was overwhelmed by the minute differences! He showed me the difference between a red-billed duck and a Cape teal, which also has a red bill. The length of its neck, the shape of its head, and the pattern of its feathers were the distinguishing features. He showed me an African openbill versus a purple heron where I could see no purple. But the gorgeous lines of color sweeping down his neck had no resemblance to the blue heron I saw on the beach during my visit to Eleanor in Jacksonville.

We decided together it was worth using that first week to learn the camera and know how to spot the differences between these remarkable birds. It was altogether fascinating, and I began to formulate a plan. I did not have artists to study this time, so I had to draw from my own experience with the falcon and phoenix. Maybe it was from all the years of painting large animals that raptors, especially endangered ones, seemed like they would be a good theme for my series. Malik approved because with the migration close by, the predator birds would also be in the area. I had no idea at the time the magnitude of how important this project would become.

Chapter 82

M alik was the teacher and I his very attentive student. I was enthralled with my subject of raptors! From the beginning, when he asked me how to distinguish a raptor, I thought about the falcon series, trying to guess the parts of him that cross the various species making them raptors. I got one right—the keen eyesight. I should have known the other two, but I needed help from Malik. All raptors have curved, hooked beaks, and sharp talons, which makes total sense to be able to capture and kill their prey.

He also spoke about habitats and how important conservation was to ensure that the environment remained healthy. I felt like I would be drawing greatly from my study of Rachel Ruysch and her detailed flowers and botany to capture the surrounding area. It amazed me how the influence of an artist I discovered doing a mural in eighth grade, an artist whose painting I had to personally restore at the gallery, and the opportunity to paint under the tutelage of a current master painter could all three intersect to create the painter I was today. I looked over at my painting of *Phoenix Paradox* for the inspiration to accurately capture the souls of these magnificent creatures on canvas!

Malik explained we would see many of the bird species on the chart. However, to remain focused on raptors, they would fall into eight groups: eagles, hawks, falcons, owls, kites, vultures, osprey, and secretary birds. There were many species within the groups. The plan we devised was to spot one from each group to paint, hopefully an endangered one if luck was on our side.

I had never heard of a secretary bird, so Malik decided to start there. He explained the secretary bird lives in the uplands primarily in Southern Africa but can sometimes be spotted here within the crater, and Malik knew where a nest was!

The next morning, we approached the nest area with our vehicle and waited. Just when I was about to give up hope of seeing one, Malik signaled to me he had heard the sound of the mate's approach. I had my camera ready, but there was no way to prepare me for such a sight! The bird in flight had a massive wingspan of over six feet with a huge body! Malik pointed to the snake that was his target, whispering that the bottom half of the long legs are heavily scaled to keep them from getting snake bites. He grabbed the snake and, with swift kicks, made short work of killing it.

Standing tall at almost four feet, it was the most unusual creature I had ever seen. His face seemed to wear an orange mask, and he wore a crown of black feathers behind his head that looked like quill pens. The legs, with black feathers to the knees, gave the appearance of wearing shorts. His grayish-white body was flanked with those impressive wings, half white and half black. He was incredible to behold, and my camera was busy taking photos while my mind was composing the painting I wanted. He was definitely one of my raptors!

Malik was the perfect choice for a guide and instructor, and he never ceased to amaze as one by one he got me close to the rarest of African raptors. When I was ready to begin painting, I had as part of my series the secretary bird, a black-and-chestnut eagle, a Madagascar sparrowhawk, a red-necked falcon, a Verreaux's eagle-owl, and a yellow-billed kite.

L'École d'Artes had taught me well how to create a series, and each painting would have detailed habitat background, an impressive vantage point of the raptor, and an example of its prey. On the eagle-owl, Malik was able to get me close to a nesting mother owl next to her offspring as if comforting it. What an incredible sight to translate to canvas!

Communication was better here at the lodge, so I wasn't totally isolated, and Malik had become a friend. I heard from Sam that he was loving every second in Wyoming, and I had to admit so was I here in Ngorongoro. He said he missed me and was still trying to make it to my exhibition in Barcelona, but the museum was keeping his schedule pretty busy.

El Amir called to see how things were going and to let me know the Barcelona gallery had released the names of all the artists whose works would be presented. I knew some of those names, and one artist had studied with me under Kenneth Patrick!

The next call was from the States. The gentleman introduced himself as a representative of the Peregrine Fund, which specialized in the conservation of raptors. He commented that they heard I would be presenting a series in Barcelona, and he was curious which raptors I had seen and was pursuing. He was particularly interested in the black-and-chestnut eagle. By the end of the conversation, it sounded like he had decided to attend the Barcelona exhibition. It made me wonder about Gretchen and Sam's experience if something like that might happen to me.

Chapter 83

M alik was a constant presence over my shoulder, helping point out any inconsistencies or tweak a particular detail. I did the basic outline on each of them first to be sure there was an edge of continuity between them. Then the painting began. Malik had already filled so many roles, but now he became a cheerleader pushing me to excel.

The exhibition was looming, and I pushed to get the last of the details added to each painting. I was so into what I was doing that the next phone call totally took me by surprise. It was Annie! I shook my head to concentrate on what she was saying.

There had been some drama with Ramone kidnapped! El Amir and her father were involved in his rescue, but Ramone's father had been killed. It had all been dreadfully traumatic, but their families were now on the island of Mallorca, and they had decided to get married there with all the family around them!

"Sarah, we heard from El Amir that you were doing an exhibition in Barcelona. Mallorca is not far from the coast. He said that after the exhibition, the two of you might fly here for the wedding. It would be so great to have you!"

I was shocked and pleased that she was with Ramone, and she confided that she was pregnant. "I would love to be there! Who else will be there?"

"The island is so beautiful! There has been an international sailing regatta, and hiking is the big sport here. We've met some people while we've been here who will be coming, a couple we met hiking and one of the captains in the regatta. Hans actually owns a gallery in Hamburg and is on vacation here. Of course, my cousin, Sabine..."

Annie was still talking, but I heard nothing after the name Hans. When she paused, I asked as casually as possible, "Hans Schuman? Blond, fairly handsome?"

"I don't know that I ever heard his last name, but his first name is definitely Hans, and he is blond. Fairly handsome? More like exceedingly handsome, if you ask me. So you know him?" *How could this possibly be?* "If it is the same man, I've met him before. I think I remember he was an avid sailor." It was as though the earth turned on its axis. Everything was off balance. I quickly said, "I have to go now, Annie. I will be there on Wednesday or Thursday before the wedding. Bye!"

After hanging up, Malik took one look at me and brought a chair for me to sit. "You look like you've seen a ghost, Miss Sarah!"

Surely it's a coincidence. Annie didn't mention his wife. I needed to shake myself out of this ridiculous reaction. I am long over Hans. If it really is him, I will do my best to be there for Annie and ignore him. Maybe I'll sit down to tea with him and Camille. Yes, I still remembered her name from that day she opened the door.

Looking at Malik, whose face was filled with concern, I assured him, "Everything is fine, my friend. We still have work to do. The plane will be here to pick me up next week!"

A streak of stubbornness overcame me. I was a far cry from that timid and wounded little girl who needed to hide behind a façade to get by. I had solid friends in Sam, Yvette, and even Annie. I had the support of El Amir. I had family in Eleanor, Harry, and Lizzy. And now my family extended to Tibu and Mosha, Amari, and Malik. And, most importantly, I was using my talent with purpose. The last thing I needed was to waste my time in regret over a lost love.

My mind was set to handle whatever might come. Then it dawned on me. If Sam came to Barcelona, should I invite him to the wedding? I rubbed the phoenix around my neck. What purpose would that serve? To show Hans I had someone else? How would it affect Sam? I pondered different scenarios and finally decided to call Sam to determine the best course. The nine-hour time difference between here and Wyoming made it a challenge. I waited until early evening, hoping to catch him at work. Luckily, he answered the phone. "Hi, beautiful, I was just thinking about you. Are you ready for the exhibition?"

"Yes, I think so. My guide, Malik, has done an exceptional job. You must come here someday. It is unbelievable! Sam, I want to talk with you about something. My friend, Annie, whom I met through El Amir, asked us to her wedding right after the Barcelona show. I wasn't sure whether to invite you if you planned to be in Barcelona."

"I'm not sure I am going to make it to Barcelona, Sarah. I want to be there to support you, but Gretchen has asked me to attend a fundraising function in San Francisco at the same time."

"Sam, is she coming on to you? She has to be almost twice your age."

"Well, she is a very attractive woman. However, I do not intend to mix business and pleasure, although some pleasure with you would feel good about now." That made me laugh. There was no reason to mention Hans. After all, it might not even be him.

"Don't worry about missing it. I do know someone is attending from another conservation group from the States, and they seem interested in what I am bringing. I'll let you know how it goes. And, Sam, I have been dealing with predators. Don't let that woman snare you!" That made him laugh, and we ended on a jovial note.

So now that Sam wasn't coming, I would focus on my time in Barcelona and supporting Annie in Mallorca for the wedding!

Chapter 84

The Barcelona exhibition surpassed my highest expectations! Unlike in London, this exhibit showcased multiple artists, and the presentation along the pedestrian street of Las Ramblas was lined with artwork. El Amir arrived to meet me. The first thing I noticed were his cuts and bruises. He made light of them and concentrated on picking the right spot to display my series. He selected wisely, right outside the local market, to get the highest foot traffic. I should have recorded the comments, but I knew the oohs and aahs would resonate in my mind for a long time.

Mr. Sullivan from the Peregrine Fund came by and stayed for almost an hour going through the paintings and making notes. He came over to introduce himself and said, "Sarah, these commanding paintings speak well for your talent, my dear. You are destined to be highly sought after. At Peregrine, we are grateful for the contribution you have made toward conservation in Africa which is felt around the globe. Peregrine would like to purchase your collection to serve as ambassadors to help conserve birds of prey worldwide."

Touched beyond words, I looked at El Amir for help in how to respond. He walked over and shook Mr. Sullivan's hand. "Sarah has been obsessed with painting animals in the wild since she was a child. I have been fortunate to serve as her sponsor and mentor. My involvement with the Grumeti Conservation Fund helped pique her interest in conservation, but the rest she did herself."

Mr. Sullivan nodded. "I know the Grumeti Fund well, and although the specifics of our efforts are different, the overall desire for conservation is the same."

I finally found my voice. "Sir, it is an honor to be associated with both of these noble ventures. It is a dream come true to have created works to further your cause."

Many of the artists gathered at the sponsor gallery afterward for a champagne reception. The event had been a grand success for bird lovers from around the world. I had been the only one to limit my work to birds of prey, and it was a pleasure to see all the renderings of the colors and details of the birds represented. I particularly liked the series of hummingbirds. Then there were the Fischer's lovebirds that were a colorful cousin of the small parrot with their two-tone green bodies, yellow-orange head, and red beak. Nature never seemed to stop amazing me, and with a silent thank-you to both Rosa and Rachel, I knew in my heart I would never stop painting it.

Several of us exchanged contact information and promised to keep in touch. Some of them asked if I would go back to Africa. I wasn't sure, and it seemed I had found my way to yet another crossroad. Maybe this time with Annie in Mallorca would be a much-needed break to determine what the next direction would be.

Mr. Sullivan had the gallery pack up the paintings to ship to Idaho where their home office was. Everything else was wrapped up, and we were ready to board the plane to Mallorca the following day. El Amir said he wanted to take me to a late dinner to celebrate but also to talk with me. I assumed it would be to discuss my next assignment. I was wrong.

The waiter brought a bottle of champagne and poured a glass. El Amir lifted it and made a lovely toast to me and the success of the show. I somewhat expected that but was not ready for what came next. "You know I was involved in Annie's father being released from the Chinese. Alex saved my father's life in North Africa, and I have sworn my allegiance to protect him and his family. That is why I originally got involved with Annie, knowing she could potentially become a victim."

He continued, "You probably saw that we had a powerful attraction for each other, but I had to stay true to my traditions and send her back to the matador after leaving Paris." I nodded that I understood that. "Ramone's father, Salvador, who was surrendered to British authorities in Paris, escaped. Alex called upon me to help, which I could not refuse. Unfortunately, Ramone was kidnapped by the Chinese to lure his father, and Annie most likely told you Salvador was killed saving Ramone in a heroic manner. That is why they are all there on Mallorca.

"But this afternoon, I received some very disturbing information that requires Alex's and my attention. You and I will be leaving earlier than planned tomorrow. But, Sarah, when we land, I won't be staying. I will be picking up Alex to go back to Malaga."

"That explains the cuts and bruises, but what about the wedding? Is there a chance her father won't be there? Annie would be heartbroken."

"There is always that chance. Fortunately, her grandfather, Don Marco, will be there. I will do everything in my power to keep him safe and get us both to the wedding. But, Sarah, I need you to support Annie and get her married. Ramone is a fine man, and the sooner they are married, the better."

I looked at El Amir, seeing his pain. Quietly I said, "She told me she is pregnant."

El Amir closed his eyes for a moment. "Yes. I know it must have been hard for him, but Ramone invited me to the wedding himself. You must do me a favor. Annie and Ramone had found a house in Mijas that they fell in love with before all this happened. When Ramone was kidnapped and the family left for Mallorca, I couldn't stand for Annie not to have it." He pulled a photo and a key out of his pocket. "I am giving you this photo of the house. I will keep the key with me, and there is a duplicate with the attorney in Mijas who closed the property. If I don't make it to the wedding to give them the key myself, I want you to give them the photo and tell them about the key. Will you do that for me?"

Tears sprang to my eyes, realizing again and again what a generous man El Amir was but also now fearful for his well-being and that of Annie's father. "I will take the photo, but you and Alex need to do whatever necessary to be back in time for the wedding, okay? What would I ever do without you, El Amir?"

"Sarah, the strength you have developed over the years will always have you land on your feet. You make me so proud of the woman you have become. Now let's get some rest. We have an early flight."

I didn't care about tradition and hugged him with all the love I had for him in my heart.

Chapter 85

El Amir was preoccupied on the fight over to Mallorca, so I was content to keep my rambling thoughts quiet. As we landed, through the window, I saw how distressed Annie was. At that moment, I knew I needed to be here for her just as she had been at my first London exhibition for me. I could tell seeing me was bittersweet since the plane that brought me would take her father.

After hugging her tight, I saw that her mother needed a few moments to say goodbye to her husband. To distract Annie, I looked her soon-to-be husband up and down, trying not to stare at the scars around his eyes, and said, "So this is the handsome matador I've listened to you run on about?"

That, at least, got a smile out of Annie, and I was pleased to see that Ramone had a sense of humor when he retorted, "I am. And I understand you are the artist who lives in a tent and paints zebras!"

I gave him my most charming smile and answered, "Among other things." I relaxed with the easy banter and was thrilled to know Mara was coming. And I was looking forward to meeting all the people I had heard about from Annie.

Considering my living conditions over the last years, Don Marco's villa seemed like a fairy-tale palace. And all the people were so handsome. When I met them, I felt like running to get my camera to capture the moment. Immediately, I was taken with Annie's grandparents, Don Marco and Genevieve. Her cousin, Tomás, had recently married an Irish girl, Meghan. They were there, along with Annie's other cousin, Sabine, who was there with her parents, grandmother, and friend Robert. Then there was Ramone's raven beauty of a mother, Marguerite, and his brother, Antonio, recovering in a wheelchair from a run-in with a bull in the ring.

Sabine volunteered to show me to my room in the casita to the side of the villa. I knew how close she and Annie were, and I welcomed her outpouring of friendship. She asked about Africa and my experience there. Before I said too much, she said the whole group would probably want to know, so I should wait to start. She was right. When I rejoined the group, there were endless questions about Africa, my paintings, and the Barcelona exhibition. Mostly, they wanted to know how I avoided being some predator's next meal.

The conversation was flowing, and I tried to steer the direction back to them and the wedding. Robert and Tomás had waited for Ramone to go hiking. They were about to leave when one of them mentioned they were meeting Stephan, Carmina, and Hans at a certain trail. That made me curious. "I brought hiking boots as instructed. How is the hiking?"

Tomás answered, "The hiking trails throughout the island vary from easy beginner to the most advanced. We are training for a difficult overnight pilgrimage hike Friday night. Stephan normally leads the hikes. We met Hans during the King's Cup Regatta, and he has been training with us since they finished."

I couldn't help asking, "Will they all be at the wedding?"

Annie must have heard my question and came over to answer, "Yes, we invited them, along with several others we've met here on the island."

It wasn't long before it was time to pick up Mara. We left Antonio exercising his legs in the pool with Sabine and Meghan. Meghan was working with him since he was missing rehab while here on the island. The plan was for Annie to take Mara with her the following day to work with the wedding planner to add a Balinese blessing to the wedding. While they would be gone, Meghan and Sabine offered to take me to this picturesque village, Valldemossa, where artists love to paint. It made sense for me to take my supplies just in case, and I welcomed the idea of getting to know these two women.

I heard from Annie that Mara was bringing Jonathan, the man they met on their trip to Australia. I couldn't imagine what kind of man Mara would choose. She was always so aloof in Australia when she wasn't with Hans and me. Just the thought of

Hans made my skin crawl. There had been no mention from any of them about a wife.

Annie's mood saddened as we got to the airport, probably reliving the goodbye with her father that morning. I put my arm around her for comfort. "It will be okay. Let's focus on now. The last time I saw Mara was when we left the art course in Australia. Did you know they were involved? You told me a little about Jonathan, but what do you remember most?"

"Jonathan is different from these other guys. He is a cattle-roping, crocodile-fighting cowboy with his dog Roscoe by his side. He is brawny and rough around the edges, yet he is a serious environmentalist and marine biologist. I always thought he would be more of a fit for you."

When I saw them walking down the stairs of the plane, I had to agree! "This is a joke, right? That hunk of gorgeous man is not with Mara! No way! Look how dainty she is next to him!" There was such a contrast between them. Mara was just as beautiful of a head-turner as she was that day she got on the bus in Australia... tiny frame, China doll-like features. The Western-print sundress looked somewhat out of place compared to her daily Balinese robes. Looking at Jonathan, he had a nonchalant air about him with his ball cap barely keeping his dark blond curls in check and scruffy unshaven face. Rolled-up sleeves revealed bulging muscles over fitted, well-worn khakis. There had to be a good story behind the two of them!

Chapter 86

It was a poignant reunion with Mara. When I hugged her, she whispered, "You know Hans might be here, right?"

"Yes, I heard. I found out the hard way right after I got back from that first trip to Africa that he's married. No worries. It has taken a while, but he is banished from my thoughts." Mara raised her eyebrows but didn't say anything, so I continued, "But look at you with this brawny cowboy!"

Mara actually blushed. "I hardly even noticed him when Annie and I were anchored off Heron Island. He seemed to always be with Annie. Then he contacted me about visiting Bali with the story about some marine project he wanted to check out. We spent some time together and kissed a few times, but there was nothing serious between us. When he mentioned meeting in Capri, I was conflicted. I had always wanted to visit Italy, and I thought it would be casual like before. Jonathan thought differently, and things got awkward between us."

Jonathan had gotten their bags off the carousel and walked over to the car with Annie, ending our brief conversation. Once back at the villa, there seemed to be another awkward moment when Annie returned from showing Mara and Jonathan to their rooms. Annie whispered to me, "Mara seemed concerned that Jonathan wasn't staying at the other villa with Sabine's family. Do you think they will be okay?"

"Of course. Didn't Jonathan say he would be involved with some marine project here on the island? If it is anything like the conservation work I have been involved with in Africa, I should be able to keep him distracted talking about that. He is hiking tomorrow with the guys, and Mara will be with you. It will be fine."

Don Marco was telling one of his stories on the veranda, and I listened, marveling at the way he could flawlessly weave a tale. When he directed the subject back to Africa, he said he was curious how I got there. I smiled. That was a long story, so I gave him the abbreviated version. "El Amir was a patron of the gallery where I interned, and he watched my progress in my art year after year. After I got back from Australia, studying under Kenneth Patrick, he agreed to sponsor two of us tent camping in the Serengeti."

That provoked a lot of questions, so I continued, "El Amir was involved with a conservation group trying to replenish the natural habitat for the animals and work with the communities there. The man traveling with me was an amazing sculptor, Sam Barton."

Sabine was the one curious about any relationship between Sam and me. I paused to think. Rather than go into detail, I said, "Sam is in Wyoming. The series of sculptures he did for his own London exhibition was outstanding, and a representative from a wildlife museum made an offer for the entire collection with a one-year residency for Sam at the museum so he could sculpt Wyoming's wildlife."

Jonathan was listening and asked, "Didn't I hear Annie say you just came from an exhibition in Barcelona? How did that go?" Right about that time, we were called to dinner. Ramone, Tomás, and Robert had returned and washed up, so I went to sit by Annie and Ramone. I gave her hand a squeeze and smiled over at Mara, happy to have these two girls as friends.

The rest of the evening went as well as possible considering the absence of Alex and El Amir. I enjoyed getting to know Ramone better. Having just seen Annie with El Amir, I was happy to see how close she and Ramone had become. He doted on her, and the way she looked at him, it was clear it was reciprocated. I knew Mara would do something special for the blessing at their wedding.

I hadn't expected the warm reception from Sabine and Meghan. They seemed so different from each other, but I could tell they had become close. Annie was lucky to have such a family, and it was clear both girls weren't just being kind. They wanted to know the real me and be friends. It made me smile to think those long-ago days of pretending were no longer necessary.

Chapter 87

Valldemossa was indeed a charming village. I had never seen such a place! The small town was built into the side of a mountain, and its narrow cobblestone roads meandered up the hill to the monastery at the top. The way the roads wound, making an easier climb, also contributed to the fact you never knew what to expect around the next corner. I particularly loved how the villagers decorated their exterior stone walls with flat-back terracotta pots overflowing with colorful flowers.

I wasn't the only artist drawn to its beauty. There were artists perched all along the way, choosing a certain angle or the other to paint. All I could think was, *how do you replicate charm?*

Sabine and Meghan seemed fine walking with me while I searched for the perfect spot. When I finally found it, the girls said they were going to wander around to look for a wedding present for Annie. I realized I hadn't brought a gift and thought about El Amir's photo in my backpack. Hopefully, he would be here in person to give it to them. Maybe a picture of this village would be good.

My portable easel set up, I sketched the basic outline of the scene in front of me in charcoal, noting the variety of shading in the stone walls as well as the cobblestones. It was almost as if each stone was its own work of art. I laughed to myself that it must be Rachel Ruysch's influence that made me drill down on the minute details. I began mixing the paints deep in thought when I was startled by a voice right behind me.

"Hi, Sarah. Long time." I swirled around, and standing there, with his chiseled face and slicked-back blond hair, was Hans Schuman! I had convinced myself I was prepared to see him. Clearly I wasn't.

To compensate for the tears that threatened to cloud up my eyes, I sighed and said as flatly as possible, "Hans...aren't you supposed to be hiking?"

"Ahh, so you knew I was here on the island. Ramone mentioned you might be painting here this morning." Looking at my frayed paintbrush tip, he added, "I see some old habits die hard."

I immediately put the brush down, gritting my teeth that he remembered that annoying habit. "What do you want, Hans? It has been years. Let's just leave our past in the past where it belongs." *Why couldn't he just disappear and leave me to my painting?*

"Sarah, I simply want a chance to tell you my side of what happened. I never meant to hurt you." *Okay, now I'm mad. He was married and never meant to hurt me. Right!*

"Listen, let it go. I have a good life and don't need you to stir it up. I know you have become friends with Annie and Ramone, and we will likely run into each other this week. Let's just call a truce, okay? We can certainly be civil to each other."

Even with my increased discomfort, Hans persisted. "I searched for you after Camille died. It was like you vanished into thin air. When I finally found out you were in Africa, I kept trying to contact you, but every message came back undeliverable."

Camille had died? My mind was racing. "Look, I don't want to hear it! Now please let me get back to my painting." I didn't realize I was shaking when I looked him in the eye and added, "Please."

Resigned, he said, "Alright, I will leave. But I hope you will reconsider and at least give me a chance to explain sometime this week. Bye, Sarah." And he was gone.

Trying to calm down, I hated myself for having this reaction. *He sent messages that were unanswered? Bah! I never got any messages. A liar and a cheat. He doesn't even look like himself, all polished and grown-up. Ugh, I have to forget it and get back to work!*

I finally was able to shake it off and get back to analyzing my color mixtures. There was one point, however, when I realized I was chewing on the tip of my brush that I jerked it out, not wanting a reminder of Hans's mention of my nagging habit.

The foundation of the painting was on canvas, and I was finding my groove, although wishing an animal might appear. Amused at the direction my thoughts were going, I felt someone looking over my shoulder. Convinced it was Hans coming back to annoy me, I turned, ready for a fight.

Instead, there was Jonathan just as rugged as before and a total contrast to Hans's perfect, put-together look. There was something wild about him that reminded me of Africa. Maybe I should put him in the scene, reflecting back to my days of life drawing. *Hmmm.*

"You're staring at my unfinished painting, Jonathan."

"Blimey, you can paint, cobber!" Having no idea what that meant, I chose to take it as a compliment.

"Did you decide to skip the hike? Weren't you going with the others?"

He sat down on the half wall next to me. "I had a good walk for sure, but I am not as serious about it since I won't be doing their overnight hike. Anyway, I have to work at the aquarium all day tomorrow, so thought I would look around. Mara will be here for lunch, right? Do you know where we meet?"

I looked at my watch and answered, "We are meeting at the family restaurant up the hill in about an hour. Everyone except the hikers should be there."

"Alright, then, I'll leave you be and go wander a bit." Jonathan strode off with a swagger that left me with another subject to ponder. I made a promise to myself to find out more about his relationship with Mara and learn a little more about that man. *There...perfect way to get my mind off a certain blond German.*

Chapter 88

Antonio was the highlight at lunch. There was nowhere for Annie's car to park by the restaurant, and they couldn't manage the wheelchair going down the cobblestone path. Mara came in to ask for help, and both Jonathan and Francoise, Sabine's father, jumped up from the table to offer. By the time Antonio got to the restaurant with the two men on either side, he was actually bearing weight! Meghan, who was working so hard rehabbing him, was ecstatic. The overall mood was joyful, and Don Marco made a toast praising the local saint. Jonathan seemed pleased he could be part of it and had found a way to fit in.

The conversation shared a little of what Mara had planned for the Balinese blessing part of the wedding. Genevieve insisted we all call her Gennie, and she told us about the party planned at the villa tonight. It sounded like it would be a full house. I would have a chance to meet Stephan and Carmina, his girlfriend who was planning to take us girls on a coastal hike. Also at the party would be Marguerite's new friend, Paulo, along with others. I could only assume that included with others would be Hans.

Later that afternoon, I found a moment to speak with Mara privately. I told her about Hans showing up in Valldemossa that morning and that he would probably be there tonight. "Honestly, I don't want to hear anything he has to say. I just want it to stay in the past."

Mara confided, "I have to say I am a little anxious about being with Jonathan tonight. I am not sure he got the message that I do not want to pursue a relationship with him."

I tried to reassure her and mentioned, "Sabine hinted she had connected with Antonio. Not sure where that leaves Robert."

Mara said, "I like Robert. I should ask her if it is true about her and Antonio. I wonder if Robert knows?"

An idea popped into my head. "How about if you talk with Robert and I talk with Jonathan? Hopefully that will create a shield for us."

Mara smiled and gave me a hug. "It really is good to see you again. I know you have downplayed the Barcelona exhibition, but I heard your raptor series was spectacular."

"Thanks. They are such an intriguing group of birds, and I learned so much. Are you still designing clothes? The designs you made in Australia made me envy such talent."

Mara explained, "When I got back to Bali, I was approached by one of the batik designers in the area. I worked with him for about a year creating block prints. Recently, though, a fabric maker hired me to paint a design on silk that is replicated on various fabrics to mass produce. I am hoping the fabrics get picked up by some of the major designers."

"I knew right away you were a serious talent when you started painting on silk. Kenneth Patrick was a genius for helping you discover it! Speaking of Australia, do you think Hans pursued glassmaking?"

Annie found us then and asked us to join them at the pool before getting ready for the evening. While they were all marveling over Antonio's victory at lunch and improvement in the pool, I had the chance to slip away for some moments of alone time. I hadn't realized how comfortable I had become living on my own with only the sound of the animals to keep me company.

The reality is that Sam and I had not spent that much time together, and I found myself slipping away from him. Even though I said differently, deep down it hurt that he did not come to the Barcelona event and been there by my side for such a momentous moment like I was for his.

Rosa Bonheur had found two loves in her life that were genuine and lasting. Do I even need that? *Could I visualize myself as an aging spinster in Africa under the care of Tibu or Mosha or Malik? Should I give Hans a chance to explain?* Yet again, questions flooded my mind.

Rarely did I take special care in how I dressed, but today was an exception. I wistfully thought about the fragrance I had worn that day in Hamburg...Hans's favorite. It got thrown off the bridge in Nice the day I got my hair cut. It seemed strange to connect hair to intimate moments. It was long again, normally up in a ponytail. Today I made

8

an exception and brushed it until it shined and fell in natural waves. Did I have the right clothes? Not too dressy, not too casual. *Why was I making such a fuss? Was I harboring some deep hope that there might still be a connection between Hans and myself?*

I chose a casual long khaki skirt with a white off-the-shoulder knit top and then, at the last minute, added a red belt now that I knew the theme color of the wedding would be red. When I heard voices indicating people were gathering, I ventured out, leaving the safety of my room behind.

Annie was over to the side, quiet, so I saw it as a chance to connect with her. With the wedding, there were many people around who cared about her. It wasn't easy to find one-on-one time. She was looking out at the people on the veranda. I put my arm around her. "Hey, what's going on? Are you okay?"

I could see the contemplative look in Annie's eyes when she quietly shared with me, "So much has happened, Sarah. Ramone was kidnapped by Chinese political outlaws and roughed up badly. His father, Salvador, was shot right in front of Ramone as his father tried to rescue him. Salvador had always been opposed to his sons taking up the family tradition of bullfighting. Just as Ramone thought there might be hope to reunite with his father, Salvador was taken from him. This has been weighing heavily on him since we got here, and I just hope we are not moving too fast with the wedding."

I hugged Annie tightly, understanding her struggle. Then I looked her in the eye and said, "Every time I see the way Ramone looks at you, there is no confusion in his eyes. He loves you, Annie. And he desperately wants you to be his wife."

She nodded, then told me about a note she received from her father saying they were delayed but were still trying to make it back in time for the wedding. She sounded almost resigned when she said, "I should be used to it by now. Throughout my life, he has been away more than at home. And I do know how lucky I am to have Dom here to walk me down the aisle if Dad doesn't get back in time. I am just really praying he will be here."

A catch formed in my chest that made its way to my throat, realizing I had no father or grandfather to walk me down the aisle if a wedding ever happened for me. It was as if Annie read my mind and looked at me with compassion. "It will be fine. Let's go join the others."

Chapter 89

The moment Ramone saw Annie, he was by her side. Their love for each other was so deep it was clear for anyone to see. I said a little prayer that Alex and El Amir would make it back in time to make her special day perfect and that El Amir be resolved to see Annie and Ramone marry.

I fought the magnetic pull that told me Hans was close by. How could he still have that effect on me? I forced myself to not look around and headed straight for Mara, who was getting a glass of wine. When she saw me coming, she ordered a second one for me. We walked over by the pool with our wine, and I asked, "He's here, isn't he?"

Mara took a sip of her wine and said, "Yes. Sarah, I had a chance to talk with him. You should hear what he has to say."

My stubborn streak was back. "I don't want to make a scene, but I have no desire to hear anything he has to say."

"Remember the shark you painted that day on the beach? You regretted it, didn't you? Don't paint yourself into a corner, okay? Give him a chance to explain. Then you can better sort through your hurt."

Jonathan waved us over to join him where he was talking with Meghan and Tomás. They were discussing their plans for the next day, Jonathan working for the Aquarium and Tomás hiking with the others, training for the overnight hike. Meghan looked at Mara and me to confirm our joining the coastal hike the next morning. I answered, "I talked to Mara about possibly going back to Valldemossa to paint. In the end, we agreed it was important to stay with the group, so yes, we'll be hiking."

Meghan was in the middle of telling us the route when I saw Hans approaching. I tried to look as uninterested as I could, all the while feeling that familiar tug. "May I speak with you, Sarah."

This was the moment I had dreaded. Mara, Meghan, and Jonathan were watching me. I had nowhere to go but to say, "Sure." Hans led me to a small garden terrace area on the side of the villa and asked me to sit. Before he said a word, I said through gritted teeth, "I told you I didn't want to talk about it!"

Trying not to show his frustration, Hans replied, "Just hear me out. I know what happened seemed heartless. You left Hamburg in such a hurry I never had a chance to explain. By the time I got to the train station, you were already gone, and I had no idea where."

I ignored the part that he had tried to find me. "What, that you embark on a love affair in a faraway country and all the while you are married? Nicely done." That was enough of this torture. I got up to leave.

Hans pulled me back down and softly asked, "Please, Sarah. Let me tell you. I wasn't married when we were in Australia...far from it! The feelings we shared there were real. The love I felt for you was beyond anything before or after that time together. It was just...I had a close friend back in Hamburg, Camille. I had known her since we were children, and she was like a sister to me. When I got the opportunity to study with Kenneth Patrick in Australia, I knew she was ill. She didn't have any family. My father didn't want me to miss this chance, so he said he and my mother would look after her while I was gone. I was selfish, Sarah. Any remorse I felt about leaving her with no one but my parents was overshadowed by this amazing opportunity for me. Then I met you. From that first day, you captivated me with your spirited eagerness to hone your skills as an artist. I never saw the shyness you often spoke of except around me during those early days, and all I wanted was to protect you and show you how I felt."

An unwelcome sob built up in my chest with the memory. Hans continued, tears in his own eyes. "By the time I returned to Hamburg, Camille had just been diagnosed as terminal. She had no insurance and was facing death alone. My parents insisted I do the right thing, and I knew I could not live with myself as a human being if I neglected to help her. I didn't think through the impact it would have on you finding out before I could explain. I wanted to tell you in person, not in a letter. When I discovered you came to Hamburg, I tried to find you, but you seemed to vanish."

Silent tears were falling from my eyes, remembering. "I went to the South of France for a while. Later, I was at my stepmother's wedding before she and the family moved to the States. I felt sick and betrayed. Then I had the chance to go back to Africa to paint and prepare for an exhibition. I didn't think I had anything to lose, and I found work with the managers working on conservation in Tanzania fulfilling, so I went."

Hans shook his head sadly. "I thought you might have gone back to Africa. I was a mess, Sarah. It wasn't easy seeing what Camille went through in the end, but I won't ever regret being there. My father could not understand why I wasn't pursuing my art, and there were many heated discussions. Nothing felt right. After she passed, I desperately tried to find you. Through the London gallery where you had that first exhibition, I learned you went back to Tanzania. I wrote you numerous letters in care of the safari lodge in the Serengeti. Each time they were returned unanswered."

"I moved from the tent camp in the Serengeti to Ngorongoro, so the letters would never have gotten to me. But I wouldn't have opened them anyway. I thought you were still married."

His face showed his frustration, and I tried to grasp what he was saying. "If you had read the letters, you would have known differently. When I found out you were planning to be here for the wedding, I could not believe that fate had allowed us to cross paths again. Don't you think we should at least try to get to know each other after all this time to see if that connection might still be there?" Hans reached over to put his hand on my face, wiping away my tears.

My tough façade began to melt. I was stunned by what he told me and ashamed at how wrong I had been about him. "I'm so sorry for all of it. That I never gave you the chance to explain and that you had to go through all that you did for Camille alone."

Hans stood up, pulling me into an embrace. "There is no pressure and no agenda. It just gives me enormous happiness you finally know the truth." With his arms around me, I pulled him closer, vowing to look at him anew with fresh eyes.

Chapter 90

There was little sleep for me that night, and as we started the hike the following morning, I was still sorting through all that Hans had explained, trying to make sense of the situation we were now in. When Mara tried to question me about what happened, she quickly got the hint that I was in no mood to talk. She quietly pulled out her sketch pad to capture beautiful vistas along the way.

With the others chatting and occupied, it gave me a chance to realize how I had rashly judged Hans over the years without giving him a chance to explain. When I thought about that time he spent watching Camille wither away, I cringed guiltily for letting Hans go through it alone. I remembered how frail she looked and that I thought she had the face of an angel.

Not surprisingly, it was Annie who walked over and matched her pace to mine. "I had no idea that you and Hans had a past, Sarah. He seemed like such a nice man with an unhappy history. I never would have invited him if I thought it would make you uncomfortable."

With Annie, it was easier to verbalize my thoughts. "We were just college kids in Australia. We parted, and El Amir sent Sam and me to Africa for a month to get involved in the conservation programs there. All I did the whole time was talk about Hans. We had only been apart six weeks when I made that impulsive decision to go to Hamburg and surprise him." Annie put a hand on my shoulder. "I guessed we were both surprised. When Camille opened the door and said she was Hans's wife, I went numb. Annie, I met Camille. It is impossible to imagine what the next year was like for them."

Annie tried to make sense of it and replied, "You have both experienced a great deal in the time you have been apart. You are not young students anymore. Your career has sprinted forward during that time. It seems to me Hans is the static one having a difficult time to move forward. Honestly, do you think it could be feasible to rekindle those old feelings and carve out a life together? What about Sam? Where does he fit into all this?"

"Sam is in Wyoming, and he is a talent to be recognized. I thought he would be at my exhibition in Barcelona, but he was too busy. Sam has always been the rock I could count on. I just don't know if he is still that rock." I knew I was keeping Annie from the others and lightened the subject. "Enough of all this! As Hans said last night, there's no agenda."

Carmina was up ahead stopping the group for a break. While we went into the restaurant, it was clear Carmina and Ramone wanted to join the serious hikers to get in a little more training before the pilgrimage hike. They left after a quick appetizer. Celeste ordered champagne, and Sabine called Meghan to come join us for what had turned into Annie's bachelorette party!

As the champagne flowed, so did the disclosures. Sabine was first when she sheepishly shared she might be in love with Antonio. Annie asked, "Are you thinking of pursuing things with Antonio?"

The most genuine smile came over Sabine's face. "I think the feeling might be mutual. We didn't want anything to take away from you and Ramone. We can wait."

Before Annie could respond, Mara looked at Sabine and asked, "You and Robert aren't together?"

Meghan arrived, wanting a recap. I had never been part of a lively girls' gossip session and found myself shaking off my serious mood and just having fun.

Annie seemed to be keeping score and, with a smile, loving all of this, responded, "Well, Sabine is not with Robert and is now with Antonio. Mara is not into Jonathan. She thinks he sees her as one of his specimens. Sarah, what about you?"

Yes, what about me? I didn't want to change the lighthearted mood. "Well, as Mara and Annie know, I have a past with Hans. After speaking with him last night, I know I misjudged him. He wants another chance, and I am very tempted. But I'm no longer that shy and timid girl he knew." Looking at Mara smiling, I added, "But for whatever reason, I am also drawn to Jonathan. I think it is the time I have had in Africa. But if he is looking for a specimen to put on a shelf, that is not for me either." Mara agreed.

Meghan, always the rational one, looked at me and said, "Why don't you take the time to find out if that spark you felt for Hans is still there? For that matter, perhaps you should also get to know Jonathan a little better."

I took another sip of champagne, taking a relaxing breath. "Yes, and then there is Sam. Maybe I should just be a feather in the wind and not fight the paths that might open in front of me!"

After the expected jokes about choosing between three men, the conversation moved easily back to Annie and Ramone, the overnight pilgrimage hike, and the wedding.

Chapter 91

Back at the villa, the high-spirited camaraderie remained from lunch until Celeste showed Annie the note from her father saying they were still delayed but trying to make it back for the wedding. Mara and I decided against going back to Valldemossa to remain with Annie. With Meghan and Sabine busy in the pool with Antonio, it gave the three of us time to visit and speculate about Alex and El Amir, and when we would see each other again after the wedding. Annie was now five months into her pregnancy, so we pledged to meet once the baby was born. When Mara offered to paint a mural in the baby's room, they both looked at me.

"Ah, the ABC mural. Of course! And with the talented help of Mara, we should be able to complete it in no time!"

That was when Annie got quiet. "If there is a wall to paint. Ramone and I found the perfect home in Mijas. When everything happened to get us here, he wasn't able to finalize the purchase."

It took every ounce of strength I had not to run get the photo and tell Annie what El Amir had done. But this was his surprise to share, not mine. Instead, I tried to encourage her. "You still have plenty of time before the baby arrives. I know the ideal home is waiting for you!"

We were just enjoying the time together when Jonathan arrived back from the aquarium and joined us. We asked about his day and he answered, "We went out to the seagrass beds looking for sharks. I was able to share with them the important role that sharks play in the ecosystem, along with the work we are involved with in Australia protecting the shark population. The sharks create a balance by removing the weak and sick to maintain a healthy ocean."

I was fascinated at the similarity between two completely different means of conservation. "It is like that on the plains of Africa with the predators like lions, leopards, cheetahs, and hye-

259

nas. They prey on the weak, quickly eliminating them. When I'm there, I often marvel at an early-morning kill of a zebra, gazelle, or some other weak animal that sets into motion the hierarchy of animals who partake in devouring it, so by nightfall, all that is left is a slight dent in the grass. Nature is magnificent with all its intricacies, don't you think?"

I think Annie and Mara could see this was a subject Jonathan and I had in common, so they decided to go for a swim. Jonathan turned his attention to me to explain the aquarium's role here in Palma doing great work around the Balearic Islands, and they had asked him back the next day. Since he wasn't participating in the hike, he had agreed. Then he asked me, "Sarah, you just came from an exhibition. Barcelona, right? Were you featuring anything in particular?"

"It was an intriguing series of endangered raptors. These particular birds of prey are threatened, and my series caught the attention of an organization in the States dedicated to the preservation of these birds. Their representative actually flew to Barcelona to see the series for himself and bought the full collection. I have a pamphlet with some of the pictures if you'd like to see it."

"I would love to take a look!" I went to my room and got it, finding a bit of a thrill that someone might actually be interested in my subject matter.

I handed him the brochure which had four of the featured paintings, including the secretary bird, which Jonathan was studying. "Blimey! I don't think I've ever seen such an animal. He has the height of an ostrich but look at the distinctive black and white coloring and those plumes! What does he eat?"

"See the snake in the painting? Snakes, lizards, and insects mostly."

Jonathan and I found we had a lot in common and thoroughly enjoyed our conversation. The hikers came in and, after dinner, called it an early evening to prepare for the overnight hike coming up. Mara seemed relieved when I joined Jonathan and her to spend a little more time out on the veranda over a nightcap.

Hans did call to tell me he was turning in early, as well, and would see me tomorrow morning to take Mara and me to Valldemossa to paint. None of the hikers planned to do anything strenuous during the day because the hike would take everything they had to finish. Fifty kilometers up increasingly higher mountains to get to the monastery at the top seemed unfathomable to me, but all seven of them seemed intent on not only doing it but also making it to the end.

Chapter 92

The day of the hike finally arrived, and Hans picked us up after breakfast. He looked a little different this morning, not so polished and perfectly put together as the other night, with tousled sandy-blond hair, unshaven face, and white shirt rolled at the sleeves and partially unbuttoned. I swear Mara looked at me with a twinkle in her eye. Hans noticed and said, "Sorry, I plan to clean up later."

I shrugged and mumbled, "You look okay to me. Right, Mara?

Nodding her approval, Mara said to Hans, "This morning, you look more like you did when we were all back in Australia!"

Arriving in Valldemossa, Mara squealed, "Oh my! This village is breathtaking. We obviously aren't the only artists here. I can certainly understand why!"

I found my spot from before and pulled out my easel and unfinished painting. I had brought an extra canvas and makeshift easel for Hans, and he got himself organized where he could reach my paints. Mara seemed to want to investigate her own spot a little further and said, "No reason for us all to paint the same scene."

Once Hans and I had made a truce, I realized I had many questions to ask him. I started with, "What made you give up painting and open a gallery instead?"

Studying the scene in front of him, Hans answered, "I was so honored to have been accepted for the course in Australia and especially honored to be around such talented artists as you and Mara. It was my father always pushing me to paint like my grandfather. In Australia, I became passionate about the glasswork I was doing, with 'but although my father seemed to support it, I could tell he felt it was not making the best use of my talent. Geoffrey tried to reason with him without any luck.

"Life turned around so suddenly back in Hamburg with Camille. Between the wedding, securing insurance, and doctors' appointments, there was hardly a moment to think about painting, much less the glassblowing. With everything spiraling, I didn't have the energy to fight my father anymore. As you know, Geoffrey offered to establish a place at the gallery for my glass collection. My position was assistant manager. He offered me flexibility when Camille needed me, and they provided great insurance. Eventually, I found I enjoyed discovering new talent and helping young artists become better known. After Camille passed, Geoffrey retired, and I decided to buy the gallery. It seems to pay the bills pretty well. Most all of the glass pieces sold a while back."

"You haven't made any glass pieces since?" I found it hard to believe that Hans hadn't painted or worked with glass since Australia.

"My life took a turn in a way that nothing seemed right. I turned down an offer to apprentice on the island of Murano. For the last two years, I have taken the month of August off to travel, sail, and surf. Those are the months I feel I truly live. Now I seem to have gotten into hiking. The rest of the year I seem to just exist. I do think you should do an exhibition there sometime, Sarah. I think my collectors would love your work."

That was a shock. "You've seen my collections?"

"As a dealer, I received materials on a couple of your exhibitions. I saw your zebra series and lion series. They looked incredible. I thought about coming, but the timing wasn't right. Also, I wasn't sure how I would be received since my letters came back unanswered."

I took a deep breath. "I owe you an apology, Hans. It must have been horribly difficult for you." I looked at the scene in front of me but without focus. I must have been chewing on the tip of my brush because Hans looked over and smiled at my familiar habit.

"I will never regret being there for Camille. It was the thought of how I hurt you and how betrayed you must have felt that put a dagger in my heart. Sarah, please believe me when I tell you from my soul you were the love of my life. There has never been anyone close before or after you."

I thought about all the choices I had made since that fateful day when Camille opened that door. "If things had been different, I would never have moved to Africa and had my amazing experiences there. El Amir's sponsorship has paved the way for my success and my newfound support of conservation in Tanzania. That probably would never have happened either. The paths we took moved in different directions. Perhaps it was destiny we did not end up together."

Hans turned to me and stared in disbelief. "Then why do you think we are here together now? Do you not think this is destiny? Maybe we both had other things to fulfill. Shouldn't we allow ourselves to consider that fate might have brought us this second chance?"

When he pulled me toward him, a chill went down my spine... the magnetic pull between us was still there. His kiss was gentle at first, willing the memory of our blissful days of kissing in the past to come forward. Slowly, as if awakening, my body pressed into him. Hans felt it, too, and deepened his kiss, willing me to give him a chance. We can't change the past. *Was it possible to go into the future inspired by the past and not be burdened by it?*

Chapter 93

The reality of the challenge involved in the annual *Des Güell a Lluc a Peu*, or Night of the Pilgrims, had not sunk in with me until we arrived at Don Marco's reserved flat overlooking the Plaça des Güell. Thousands of people were gathering in the park. Hans came in with Stephan and Carmina wearing their registered bib numbers. Ramone, Robert, and Tomás brought Roff from the crew of the *Porto Banus* with them. I learned he had raced with Hans during the regatta. Second-in-command on Don Marco's sailing vessel, Roff had subbed for an injured sailor on the *Nautilus*, and they had come in second place! I could tell Hans and Roff had developed a great deal of respect for each other.

There would be seven of them hiking with ten thousand others. It was stressed over and over how most of the hikers wouldn't make it to the monastery. Shuttles would be going throughout the night to bring any back to Palma who had to quit. There seemed to be a strong bond between our seven hikers as they ate a good meal together with plenty of water. Since Antonio was wheel-chair-bound, he and Sabine planned to shuttle along the route to offer support at the major stops.

Before he left to join the throngs, Hans came over to me. "This is one of the biggest things I have ever attempted. I am not going to give up. And, Sarah, it is just as I am not going to give up on us. Be at the finish line, okay?"

I looked at him with a new conviction and assured him, "I'll be there."

I had no concept as the hikers left the park and we were wined and dined at the flat what courage, strength, and endurance would be required of them through the night. We drove to the monastery the next morning to wait at the finish line. Antonio and Sabine arrived weary from their overnight with no sleep but filled with inspiration. They reported some of the intense hard-

265

ship Hans and Tomás, in particular, were going through. They said at the last stop where they saw them, each hiker had pledged to the other they would only cross the finish line if they all did together.

After waiting for what seemed like forever, they showed up, coming around the last corner. Hans and Tomás could barely walk and were practically being dragged by the others, each of them exhausted beyond reason. But they made it over the finish line together. There were tears in my eyes absorbing the enormity of the moment when Antonio stood out of his chair in victory like he had finished the race with them. Jubilance surged through the crowd and even the hikers who collapsed at the finish line. I went to Hans, regretting I hadn't done more to support him.

I was worried about the cramp in Hans's leg. Roff came over and said he needed to stretch it and drink lots of water. Annie, Meghan, and Sabine planned to tend to their men for the day before the sunset cruise that night. I just didn't feel that was my place. So Hans went to clean up, tend to his legs, and rest, agreeing he'd meet me on the *Porto Banus* for the sail in the late afternoon.

While the group rested, that left Jonathan, Mara, and me to come up with something to do. We decided to have lunch at Fornalutx, a little authentic village that Meghan told us about. It did not disappoint, and I knew Mara was itching to pull out her sketchpad. The surprise of the lunch came when Jonathan said, "The aquarium seems to like what I have to contribute and have offered me a two-bedroom apartment on the bay if I would stay and work with them for another week."

"Are you going to do it? Do you have the time off?" I loved the opportunity for him. From personal experience, I had become a firm believer in taking advantage of opportunities laid at your feet.

He said, "Yes. I have an extra bedroom if either of you ladies would like to join me. I've got the room. We might as well take advantage of it."

Mara was quick to answer, "My flight back to Bali is on Monday. I have to get back to work."

Jonathan looked at me. "What about you, Sarah?"

I could see how inspiring this island was. I had just finished a huge undertaking ending in Barcelona. I could take a break, right?

"Possibly, since I finished my latest project, I should have some downtime. And I love the idea of painting some of these vistas. Let me think about it, okay? I have no idea what El Amir has planned for me next. I should speak with him but I don't think Celeste or Annie have heard from Alex or El Amir since Thursday, and the wedding is tomorrow."

Chapter 94

It seemed Hans had gotten the hint to soften his polished and reserved self. Gone was the gel that slicked back his hair. He seemed much more approachable, which made him very hard to resist. As always, even though I was already on board the *Porto Banus*, I knew the moment he arrived. That connection was still there. I turned and saw him in a new light. I knew now how hard it was for him to make it through that hike. The respect I gained for all the hikers was immense.

He came up to me and possessively put his arm around me. He pulled my ponytail loose and nuzzled my neck, whispering, "God I've missed that hair. You are so beautiful!"

I pulled away and laughed. "I should have taken a picture. I left Hamburg and went directly to Nice, to my friend Yvette's family home. While I was there, I cut my hair to spite you and threw the fragrance that you liked off the bridge!"

"Sweetheart, I am so terribly sorry you went through all of that. There will be other fragrances, and I am thrilled to see your hair grown back out!"

Ramone and Annie came over, and I could tell Ramone was scrutinizing Hans to see if he was okay from the hike. Once Hans told them the cramps were gone and he had rested, Ramone asked, "What are the odds you two would meet again so randomly on this tiny island of Mallorca? Do you have any plans from here?"

Hans answered, "I would love to have Sarah come to Hamburg to do an exhibition at my gallery. Beyond that, we have agreed to take it one day at a time." Right as he said that, Jonathan came over to join them.

Looking directly at me, knowing the others were listening, Jonathan asked, "Have you given any more thought to staying next week?"

I tried to ignore the startled faces and answered, "I said I would think about it, and I am. But I am leaning toward staying."

Jonathan smiled at me, oblivious to the stares, before he parted with, "That's great, cobber. I'm going to find Mara."

Annie was the one to jump in first. "What was that all about?"

I could tell Hans was listening closely. "Jonathan seems to be a hit with the aquarium, and they have asked him to stay for another week. They've given him a two-bedroom apartment by the bay to stay in, so he asked if either Mara or I wanted to stay."

I knew what was coming when Hans asked the obvious. "Is Mara staying?"

"No, her plane leaves Monday morning. She has to get back to work." Annie nudged Ramone for them to move on and left me to work this through with Hans.

"So you are staying on the island with this man you hardly know for a week at his apartment?" His tone had gotten a little louder, which caught the attention of those near us, so I suggested we walk up to the bow to talk.

"Hans, I have worked nonstop for the last four months to produce the pieces for the Barcelona exhibition. Did you even ask me how it went? Never mind, it's alright. I just need a break. This island is gorgeous and its vistas inspiring. Seeing you again, I need to find some order in my feelings right now. Jonathan is obsessed with his work, and he will be gone every day, giving me plenty of time to wander around Mallorca. I hadn't made up my mind until this moment. But now I have and I plan to stay, Hans."

He pulled me close, and it was unclear whether it was a promise or a threat when he whispered, "I said it and I meant it. I don't intend to let you go again, Sarah."

Chapter 95

For the rest of the cruise, spirits were high. The victory of the hikers crossing the finish line, Antonio standing on his own, and the upcoming wedding the next day were all being celebrated with free-flowing prosecco. It was impossible not to get swept up in the moment. It felt natural to have Hans's arm around me or holding my hand. It seemed as though things were becoming more comfortable between us. *Then why do I have a feeling nagging my mind that something isn't right? Something feels out of place. Did I feel in some way I was cheating on Sam?*

Maybe I was just overtired. I looked over at Annie, surrounded by Sabine, Meghan, and Mara. Although there had been no word from Alex or El Amir, she looked happy, and Ramone could not take his eyes off her. Her gaze caught mine, and she motioned me over to join them. I happily did, cherishing our friendship that accepted each other for our true selves without any pretense.

*****

Sunday, the day of the wedding, arrived. I had seen the location at the pavilion high in the mountains overlooking the sea, and the vista was breathtaking. I could only imagine what it would be like at sunset for the wedding.

Celeste was steaming the dresses. The wedding planner, Veronica, came by to give us the schedule. She asked to see what Mara would be wearing for the blessing, so she went to get it and brought back her full Balinese garb that complimented Sabine and Meghan's red dresses perfectly. Mara also unwrapped two beautiful hairpins for the girls to use. It was when Annie looked at Mara and said, "Thank you for being here, my friend. You have added so much to this day!" I realized the painting of Valldemossa might not be personal enough. Geez!

Frustrated, I thought about what I could do at this last moment, then remembered the photo El Amir gave me. There had still been no word from them, and I felt both Celeste and Annie were disappointed but resigned to their not being at the wedding. That would mean I would have to give them the photo. I slipped away to my room to find the picture.

Just as I found it, there was a knock on the door. It was Celeste. "Sarah, are you all right? You know no one is trying to exclude you. Annie is so happy you are here."

"Annie is lucky to have you, Celeste. I lost my own mother when I was ten. It was a tragic accident."

Celeste, with a sympathetic tone, said, "Let me help. What is going on? Is it Hans?"

"There was such an awkward moment on the *Porto Banus* last night. Jonathan is staying another week to work with the aquarium and asked if either Mara or I wanted to stay. Mara has to get back to work and can't. But I just finished my exhibition in Barcelona, and for once, I don't have El Amir pushing me." Celeste smiled and I continued, "I find this island an artist's dream. I can see why Chopin composed brilliant works while here. I think I'm staying. When Jonathan came up to me to ask if I had decided to stay, it caught Hans by surprise, and he misunderstood. It seems misunderstanding is a pattern with us. I tried to explain that I was not staying for Jonathan, but in my deepest heart, I wonder if that is true. So much time and so many experiences have passed since I was with Hans. I question whether he is chasing a dream of the past. And I still have feelings for Sam."

Celeste, talking like the mother I wished was still with me, said, "Sweetheart, you do have a lot going on with these three men. Unfortunately, you can't save today for later. It is here, and the things you do and the choices you make can either create the future you deserve or regrets that might be hard to overcome. Think about the choice you made when you left Hamburg, not giving Hans a chance to explain. How different would your life have been? Take time to choose wisely, dear, to get the future you envision for yourself."

She hugged me, and in that instant, I felt what it might be like if my mum was alive. *Were any of these men matches for me? Would I even want my life to have been different during this time?* Celeste shook me out of my reverie by asking about the photo I was holding. "It is something I want to paint for Annie. I think I can finish in time to give it to her as a wedding present. Will you just tell her I am working on a surprise? Tell her I will be there in time to help Veronica and the florist." I made a quick call to Hans to ask if he would pick me up later and set up my easel to get to work!

Chapter 96

Vista Hermosa could not have been a more inspiring location for the wedding! The white pavilion with its columns stood at the end of a stone peninsula projected out from the mountain, giving the feeling of being suspended high above the sea. The lowering sun began to reflect the colors of sunset bouncing off the surrounding mountains and sky. Simply awe-inspiring.

I left the painting of the Mijas house in Hans's car to somehow determine when to present it. Hans was being particularly sweet, and as I left him to help the florist and check on Annie, he asked me to sit with him during the ceremony.

Both Sabine and Meghan were wearing their red dresses, and Mara had given their eyes a little more exotic look with extra eyeliner. Annie was radiant in her simple white sheath that gave but a small hint of the child she was carrying. Don Marco came by the room looking as dashing as ever in his formal suit, full of compliments and ready to walk Annie down the aisle. I had been so sure Alex and El Amir would make it in time for the wedding. It had to be disappointing, but both Celeste and Annie seemed prepared to make the best of it.

People were beginning to arrive and take their seats. I gave Sabine and Meghan a hug and then held Mara at arm's length, marveling at what a beautiful picture she made with her Balinese attire. When it came to Annie, she also had a dramatic pointed outline to her eyes, and the slight blush on her cheeks gave her a glow. As I hugged her, I whispered, "Your matador won't be able to take his eyes off you! You are gorgeous, Annie." Her smile spoke a thousand words that we both understood, attesting to the friendship between us.

I left to join Hans, walking through the two pillars of colorful Balinese offerings and saying a silent prayer for Annie and Ramone, adding an extra for the safe return of Alex and El Amir.

The deep resonant ring of Mara's bell signaled the wedding was to begin. Once everyone was silent, Mara proceeded to the altar where the minister was waiting, tossing rose petals along the way. Tomás and Antonio were first down the aisle. There was a brief hesitation before Ramone made his entrance in his full black-and-white bejeweled matador regalia! No one was expecting that. He must have made his decision to go back to the ring! Sabine and Meghan were next registering their surprise when they saw Ramone.

All of the guests, including myself, turned to see the bride walk down the aisle. Hans took my hand. The anticipation rippled through the guests. Instead, what we saw was Don Marco coming down the aisle alone. A look of worry crossed Ramone's face until Dom winked at him and found his seat next to Gennie. The suspense was thick in the air.

El Amir slipped into the back row next to Jonathan. His arm was in a sling. I smiled at him, so happy he had made it here in time. Jonathan must have thought I was smiling at him because he winked back. Hans caught that and looked none too happy.

The wedding march began, and Alex was there to walk his daughter down the aisle. There were tears of joy in Celeste's eyes as Alex took Annie's hand and placed it in Ramone's. The shock of seeing her father and then Ramone's choice of attire seemed to leave Annie somewhat dazed. However, Mara's blessing and their participation seemed to calm her.

After the sentimental wedding, the guests moved to a different area for the spreading of Salvador's ashes off the mountain. There was a solemn quiet when Ramone began to speak, ending with his announcement that he would be giving up his bullfighting profession for good. I could see on Annie's face her questions whether he was making this decision for the right reasons, but this was not a time for debate.

The music began again to signal the transition to the reception. While champagne was poured in celebration of the couple's marriage, I found a moment to seek out El Amir. I first asked how he was and learned he fractured his arm in an accidental fall. Not sure I believed that I chose to accept his answer and tell him about the painting. He seemed pleased, and when I returned to show it to him, he nodded his approval.

El Amir clanged on his glass for everyone's attention. "Annie and Ramone, your sudden departure from Marbella caused you to leave behind something important to you both." Annie and Ramone were suddenly curious. "I know how important this was to you and to the child you will soon bring into this world. Please allow me to hand you this key and all that it opens for your future together." That was the signal for me to step up and hand them the painting. El Amir had just handed them the key to the house in Mijas!

Chapter 97

Tears sprang to Annie's eyes in disbelief! To El Amir, she asked in wonder, "You did this for us? Oh my gosh! I can't believe it." Looking at the painting, to me she said, "It is exactly like I remember. I couldn't be any happier!"

Ramone was more reserved when he patted El Amir on the back in lieu of shaking hands with his broken arm. "That was far too generous to handle such a transaction on my behalf and secure it for us."

I think El Amir could sense Ramone's hesitation and told him, "I'm just pleased I could do it. We can talk about the details later."

Ramone looked at the painting and, knowing how happy it made Annie, hugged me tight with a whispered, "Thank you, Sarah."

The dance music began, and Hans took me into his arms. Whether I was giddy from the feel of being in his arms or how happy Annie was, I wasn't sure. With El Amir back, I gave some thought to whether or not I should stay the week with Jonathan after all.

It was Hans who brought up the subject. "Sarah, we have finally found each other again. It doesn't seem right for you to stay with another man for a week."

I was about to try to find the right words to respond when El Amir came over and asked me, "May I have a few words with you alone?"

Nodding, I got up to go over to the side. El Amir said, "I heard you planned to stay on the island for a week. Is that true?"

"Yes, I thought I might take a break. It is so inspiring here!" El Amir looked so serious. Surely he didn't want me to go right back to painting.

He pulled two envelopes out of his jacket and handed them to me. "I planned to give these to you on the plane tomorrow. If you are considering staying, I thought I should give them to you tonight."

It was too dark to see the return addresses. Curious about who these could be from, I asked, "Should I open them now?"

"They could be important, and you might want to talk about them. If you'd like, you could wait until we get back to the villa. I will be available tonight or in the morning."

Thanking him, I put the two letters in my bag and made my way back to Hans. I must have been absentmindedly rubbing on my necklace because Hans noticed and asked, "The necklace that you're wearing...I haven't seen you without it this week. It must be important. What is it?"

"Do you remember the painting of the phoenix I did in Australia, *Phoenix Paradox*? It carried a great deal of meaning from Dad's last letter to me. The necklace is a phoenix that was sculpted by a friend. Its symbolism has become a life goal to have emerged from the difficult childhood I had to find my way through my art to a freedom from those early restraints."

"Ah yes." Hans held it so he could see it better. "I remember now. Your father wrote something about letting the phoenix soar. Do you have any idea what that would mean to you?"

"Honestly, that is one of the things I want to consider during next week." I showed him the two envelopes. "For some reason, I have a strange feeling these letters are important. The raptor series I did for the Barcelona exhibition got a great deal of notice. El Amir suggested I read them back at the villa."

Hans raised my hands to his lips. "I lost you once, Sarah. I have told you I won't easily let you go again. I love you. I have since that first day on the beach when I saw you running toward me. I understand that you might have choices to make. All I ask is that you consider including me on whichever path you take. He kissed me there on the bench. As the kiss turned more passionate, he led me out of the light to an area more secluded. There was no denying the familiar magnetic pull was there with Hans, but somewhere in the back of my mind, a certain dark-haired sculptor was saying, "Come home to me."

Chapter 98

It was hard to imagine it was already time for the festivities to be over. Jonathan had picked up a rental car for us to use over the next week. Hans planned to turn his in first thing the next morning. I was to drop Jonathan off at the aquarium and pick up Hans for breakfast before coming back to the villa to take Mara and Robert to the airport.

Sabine's family was flying out that afternoon, but Sabine planned to sail with Antonio on the *Porto Banus*, joining Annie and Ramone and her family for the trip back to Marbella. Alex and El Amir had made it back to the island for the wedding, but they still had unfinished work in Malaga. I wasn't the only one staying. Marguerite, Ramone's mother, planned to stay for a while on the island with Paulo, the man she had met here in Mallorca. Tomás and Meghan weren't leaving until Tuesday to secure the villa after everyone's departure and would take the ferry to Barcelona to fly to Meghan's hometown in Ireland.

Everyone would be parting to go in different directions, and there were promises made to reconnect when Annie and Ramone had the baby.

Hans and I were quiet on the ride back to the villa after the reception ended. Finally, I asked, "I know I asked this before. How could you give up your art? You had such talent, Hans. Your whole being lit up when you made a new glass piece! And to have had the opportunity in Murano!"

"I have thought about it. Probably the misery surrounding that time with Camille combined with my father's dismissal of the glassblowing made me lose the passion I had found."

I thought about the excitement he had in Australia when he was working the glass. Tentatively, I treaded further into this subject. "Do you think the gallery was the easy route? When you saw the glass pieces that you worked so hard to create sell, one after the other, did you never want to replace them?" I knew it was a hard topic, but it was important to me to know where that fire went, so I took one more step. "You say you still have a fire for me, but what if something happens to make it fade like the passion you had for your art?"

I could tell he read the direction of my thoughts. "It is a great deal to consider. My father grew frustrated once he thought I would never become the artist he pushed me to be. I compensated by helping other artists find their way through the gallery. I had lost you. I had lost my art. Except for the one month of the year I took to be me, the rest of the time was simple existing. I am not trying to make excuses. I want that passion in my life again...for you and my art." He took a deep breath. Moving to a subject we both knew could be important, he asked, "What do you think is in the letters?"

By this time, I had seen the return addresses. One was from Sam in Wyoming and the other from Kenneth Patrick in Australia. "At first, I was curious how El Amir even got the letters. But in the years that I have known him, I have learned whenever he is involved, I can expect the unexpected. He was very cryptic when he gave them to me. It was like he already knew what was in them." We were pulling into the driveway at the villa, and I added, "I will open them when I get to my room and let you know if they are anything important tomorrow morning when I pick you up." He kissed me, and I huskily said, "And, Hans, I do hope you find that passion."

Hans parked the car and looked at me with such a sad face. "I never thought I would see you again, Sarah. Now that I have you within my reach, we are saying goodbye. That doesn't make sense to me. I thought about staying, but I have to get back to open the gallery and decide what I am going to do with it."

Why wasn't I as disheartened as Hans by being separated again? "Hans, I didn't know how I would feel seeing you again. I'm glad to know the truth after all this time and realize I misjudged you. I just need time to think and somehow decide what is next. I will see you again. I promise."

Hans lightened his mood a little and said, "I will take you at your word. I love you, Sarah. Let's find a way to be together. Why don't you stay with me at my hotel tonight and let me show you the passion I know we can rekindle?"

"It is certainly tempting, but I am not going to do that to Annie and Mara. I'll see you in the morning. Good night." I slipped in the side door to get to my room in the casita. I heard voices in the side garden and stopped. Not meaning to eavesdrop, I listened to see if it might be Annie or Mara. Instead, it was Alex and El Amir that I heard...then wished I hadn't.

It was Alex's voice speaking. "If he is alive, they obviously have him deep undercover."

El Amir said, "How can we not tell the family? Marguerite is getting further involved with Paulo, and Ramone has given up his profession..."

I didn't want to hear any more. *Salvador alive? How could that possibly be? How do I erase that from my brain?*

Chapter 99

Even thoroughly rattled, I knew I wasn't supposed to hear them. I looked at the two letters. *Focus, Sarah!* I opened the one from Kenneth Patrick first.

Dearest Sarah,

It has been both inspiring and gratifying to follow your time in Africa and the incredible series of paintings you produced! This most recent raptor series in Barcelona was reminiscent of the Phoenix Paradox. *I wonder if it influenced your work? Each of these rare, endangered birds is a miracle to behold, and you bring their very soul to the viewer.*

There is no doubt you have the opportunity to achieve great fame and a comfortable life as an artist. I have a hunch you are at a turning point in your career, if not in your life. I'm reaching out to you to encourage you to take care in your choices. Let your achievements set the stage for greater achievements. Set your sights on an upward trend for the higher good.

I am aware you have an impressive sponsor in El Amir who allows you the resources to move your career forward. I would like to offer myself as a second sponsor to further those opportunities. My proposal is to have a meeting between the three of us to discuss future possibilities. There is a conservancy conference in three months in Khuh Nuur, Mongolia, known for its grasslands. I would like you and El Amir to be my guests.

Best of luck to you, Sarah. I will await your reply!

Kenneth Patrick

Mongolia! There is no question I found a passion for conservation while working with the Grumeti Fund in Africa. *Kenneth Patrick a sponsor?* A wave of shock went through me followed by a chill of anticipation. I liked the sound of working for the higher good. Conservancy around the globe? *How could I help?*

The second letter from Sam turned out to be just as mind-blowing!

Hi, beautiful!

Well, girl, you are a hot topic over here with Gretchen and the museum. Although the wildlife museum and the Peregrine organization have many of the same ideals and support some of the same causes, there has been an unspoken rivalry between them.

Gretchen is ruing the day she and the museum passed on bringing you in-house. I think they are prepared to make you a fairly incredible offer, although I don't know the details. Gretchen is concerned they might have offended you, so she asked me to write to you to see if it might interest you to come over this way.

I know I would be deliriously happy to have you back in my arms! On the other hand, I only have about six more months on my contract, and I am not so sure the Wild West is the place I want to stay.

I think of Africa and Tibu and Mosha a great deal and often consider going back to Tanzania to stay. I don't think I could picture a better life than the two of us together surrounded by the magnificent plains of the Serengeti.

Consider it, Sarah. Just six more months and we could be together for good. And if you would like to hear their offer in person, I would be thrilled to make up for lost time in the passion department! The lon-

ger we are apart, the stronger my love for you grows.
Don't forget me, sweetheart.

Sam

PS. Is that phoenix still around your neck?

I chuckled to myself. I could almost hear Sam talking. It was ironic to me that both Hans and Sam were such talented artists, but that is where the similarity stopped. Sam had the passion. Could Hans get it back?

There was a soft knock on my door, and when I opened it, there was El Amir. "Have you opened the letters? Shall we walk out by the pool to talk?" I nodded, and as we walked, I was flooded with the debate of whether to tell him what I overheard.

It was late, and the sounds from the villa had quieted. I had to ask, "How is it you seem to know what is in the letters?"

"I don't know the specifics in your letters. I, too, got a letter from Kenneth Patrick telling me of his proposition and hope to meet in Mongolia. What do you think about that?"

"Kenneth is quite the character but with an incredible talent. I suppose it wouldn't hurt to hear what he has to say. He said we would be his guests. It is in three months." *Maybe I needed to chart out a timeline.* After all, Annie's baby was due in less than five months, and Sam still had close to six months in Wyoming. Bringing my attention back to El Amir, I asked, "So you also know about the wildlife museum?"

El Amir nodded. "Gretchen Sullivan called me herself. She was concerned you might have been offended when they didn't offer you a position. Her offer is a good one. Does that appeal to you?"

"Sam mentioned going back to Africa after he completes his residency in Wyoming. There's something else. Do you remember the boy I fell in love while I was in Australia, Hans Schuman?"

El Amir asked, "The one you found out was married? Was that him at the wedding?"

"Yes, it was. He was married, but there were extenuating circumstances that I never gave him a chance to explain until these past few days. He wants to rekindle what we had before. Honestly, it has been so much time, and our lives have moved in vastly different directions. Him following me around to who knows where doesn't feel right, and me sitting at a gallery in Hamburg doesn't make sense either."

"What about this man you plan to stay here with?" I could tell his interest was piqued.

"Annie and Mara met Jonathan when they were in Australia. He is a dedicated scientist with a rough exterior. All three men could not be any more different from each other."

"Well, Sarah, it sounds like you have a lot to sort through! You may not realize it, but there is another option on the table. There is an organization planning to take over management of the Grumeti Fund. They have approached me about your being their spokesperson to help generate funding and through your art enlighten the world about the impact of conservancy. It would not have the glamour or the pay scale of these other positions but..."

I finished his sentence. "But it would be for the higher good."

"El Amir, there is something else. I hate to mention it because it was totally unintentional. When I came in through the side door tonight, I overheard you and Alex talking."

El Amir froze, searching for what to say. What he finally said had an ominous ring to it. "If word got into the wrong hands that you heard what we said, you could be in a great deal of danger. For that matter, anyone you might inadvertently mention it to might also be in danger. This is not good."

Chapter 100

"You can't stay here, Sarah. It is too risky that you might unintentionally say something to Jonathan, or, worse, to Marguerite. Why don't you go back to London to give some thought to these incredible offers. I will get back there as soon as I can."

"El Amir, I never realized the danger you put yourself in. You have a broken arm! What would I do if something dire happened to you?"

He put his hand over mine and gently said, "When it is my time, so be it. I promise you I won't be foolhardy. But look at you, Sarah! You don't need me anymore. Consider how far you have come from that devastated little girl with the hidden paint set in the closet. I believe in you. I have since I first met you at the gallery and bought *The Migration*. Now it is time to believe in yourself. You have been gifted with a great talent. Truly enjoy the opportunities that you choose and then go beyond enjoyment. Expand and share, magnify and multiply those opportunities to make a difference. You have two men of substance in love with you. You are a lot like Annie in that regard." El Amir gave a resigned smile, and I could feel his loss of Annie. He continued, "When the time comes to choose a man, be certain it is someone who will allow your star to shine. Don't be afraid to want it all, Sarah. You deserve it."

By the time we said good night, it had grown very late. It wasn't long before the alarm went off to give Jonathan a ride to the aquarium and break the news that I wasn't staying.

I found him loading his bags in the rental car. He came in to retrieve his cup of coffee and offer me one. "Well, cobber, here is the key to the flat. It's walking distance from the aquarium, so I should be there by five o'clock."

I didn't want to take the time to have the conversation here in the kitchen, so I made my way to the car to get going. Jonathan drove. It was the first time we had been alone, and I let the fleeting question cross my mind of what a relationship with Jonathan would look like. As quickly as it came, it was gone. I liked his strength, but there was no tenderness. I took a deep breath and told him. "Jonathan, I won't be staying after all. I have to get back to London. As a result of the Barcelona exhibition, I received three offers last night that require serious consideration and possible negotiation. I hope you understand."

"Hey, you showed me the pamphlet with the pictures of a few of your paintings. They were magnificent! That's great news."

"You know, we are both involved in conservation...you under the sea and me out in the plains. It would not be surprising if our paths crossed again at some point. I might be working with Kenneth Patrick some, and he is practically at your back door."

We pulled into the aquarium parking lot. He asked, "Are you planning to visit Annie and Ramone once the baby is born? I promised them I would try to come."

"Yes, Mara and I plan to paint a mural for the baby's room, so we will be there. I am taking the afternoon ferry to Barcelona to catch a plane to London. Should I leave the car at the flat?"

"The Aquarium is closer to the ferry dock. Just bring it back here and leave the key at the front desk." I came around to the driver's side and hugged him.

"Keep up the good work, cobber. I have a feeling you are on to something big!" He flashed that big grin and left.

Something big. Hmmm. I had a little time before I was due to pick up Hans. He was too important to me to hold back. What I knew was that sitting in a gallery in Hamburg was not one of my options. I hoped he would understand that. But was I willing to see him pass out of my life again entirely just as I rediscovered him? *God, I hope not.*

He was waiting with his bags on the sidewalk. I was pleased to discover his slick, polished exterior was nowhere to be seen. This softer, more easygoing look appealed so much more to my senses. He got in, and I asked, "If it's okay, I have a lot to talk to you about, and I wondered if we could skip breakfast and go somewhere a little more private?"

Hans picked up on the seriousness of my tone and quickly agreed. "Sure, I would like that. The sailboat I used for the regatta,

286

Nautilus, is still docked at the marina. No one is currently using it. We could go there."

The marina was relatively quiet. *Nautilus* was tied up at the far dock. Its sleek, streamlined design was engineered for racing, but there was ample room to sit and talk.

"Sarah, are you alright? Was there something in the letters that has you so serious?"

I tried to let the various subjects drift into some order but finally just blurted out, "I have decided not to stay on the island for the week. I'll be leaving on the late afternoon ferry to Barcelona to fly to London!"

Chapter 101

The shock was clear on Hans's face. "What! Has something happened?"

"Hans, I don't want there to be any secrets between us. I would like to tell you about the two offers that arrived with the letters, as well as a third that El Amir told me about." As I told him about Kenneth Patrick's potential sponsorship and the meeting in Mongolia, Hans's eyes widened in amazement. I told him about the new management overseeing the Grumeti Fund and that they had requested me as their spokesperson. The pay would not be great, but it would go a long way in helping the conditions in Tanzania.

With a deep breath, I continued to the third offer. "Hans, you know about El Amir's other sponsored artist, Sam Barton. He and I have known each other since we were teenagers working at the London gallery. You knew we were going to Africa after Australia. We have had an off-and-on relationship through the years." I watched for Hans's reaction and only saw the flinch of his jaw. "It was never even close to what we had in Australia. However, over the past year, it has grown more serious. Then his entire exhibition was bought by a wildlife museum in Wyoming with an offer of a residency there for one year."

I shifted, determined to continue. "Sam tried to get them to make me an offer, but they refused. Now they have heard the Peregrine Organization has bought my entire raptor collection in Barcelona. That has made them reconsider making me an offer. They have reached out to Sam and El Amir to be sure I wasn't offended by them passing me over six months ago, and they are willing to make me a very impressive offer. Sam wants me to take it to be with him or wait for him and return to Africa."

Hans got up and paced as well as possible on a sailboat. He then sat back down. "First of all, each of these offers is a testament to the talent you possess and the artist you've become. And secondly, you are a beautiful woman. It would be insane on my part to think there had been no other suitors. Sarah, tell me the truth. Are you in love with Sam?"

"I do feel strongly about him, and he supported me on that first African trip when all I talked about was you and also when I came back with my heart broken. But no, I have never felt the intensity with him that I felt with you. But he is a passionate, talented artist, who loves me." The magnitude of admitting that to Hans formed a lump in my throat.

His eyes glistened. "I envy Sam for all the time he had with you that I missed. He has that advantage. I don't know if I can ever make it up to you. All I can tell you is the moment after Camille told me about your visit and I couldn't find you, the candle in my heart stopped burning. The gallery never had my passion. I realize that now. I was there for Camille. She knew about you, Sarah. Right before she died, Camille's remorse that she had somehow split you and me up encouraged me to look for you after she was gone.

"Somehow, destiny has intervened to allow us to find each other here through Annie and Ramone. If it weren't for the friendship we both have with them, this chance might never have happened." He took my hands. "My place is beside you, Sarah. Nowhere else is home to me. You have three remarkable offers and a great deal to consider. And, I understand you have Sam wanting a life with you. Allow me to make you a final offer. Let me love you, Sarah. What you have accomplished certainly makes you a phoenix rising. I don't want to compete with you. Let my love, support, and devotion encourage the phoenix to soar!"

Tears were flowing down my face. All thought of making his flight was gone. So many things in my life had led me to this moment, and I thought about Rachel Ruysch, who had a husband and ten children yet still maintained a noteworthy career as an artist.

Hans moved to one knee. "Sarah Wilkinson, be the wife I have always wanted and the mother of our children. Reignite my candle and make me whole again. I love you beyond any words could describe."

Dare I hope this was real, that I could find my true love again? "What about the gallery and Hamburg? That is not one of my options."

"The gallery has served its purpose. When I weigh having you by my side and finding my artistic path again versus running the gallery, the gallery loses. I want you, Sarah...wherever that takes us. I don't need the push from my father to pursue the artist in me. You inspire me to do it."

It was time. I threw all of the doubt, caution, fear, and lack of trust to the wind! I cringed realizing the hurt Sam would feel but that magnetic pull had never left, and I answered, "Yes, Hans Schuman, I will marry you and give you that same love, support, and devotion you so generously offer. I then kissed him with all the passion that had been dormant for far too long. I knew in that instant the phoenix had been set free! I was ready to face what the future brought with Hans by my side.

And the journey continues...

About the Author
Nina Purtee

Nina Purtee is a worldwide traveler, philosopher, and adventure romance novelist. Growing up in Atlanta, Nina's father ignited her travel obsession with lavish family trips to exotic locations. Some of those experiences have found their way into her writing. Island-hopping with her family through the Greek islands on a 95-foot sailboat, the *Eleni*, gave Nina the inspiration for Don Marco's vessel, the *Porto Banus*.

While on safari in East Africa, she met a woman artist with her companion, a sculptor, living in tents, immersed in their artwork. They inspired the characters of Annie's friend, Sarah, and the sculptor, Sam, whom we meet in Sarah's book.

Nina draws from her travels to embrace multicultural characters and couples seemingly from different worlds and allow them to compromise, co-exist, accept each other's traditions, and even find love.

Emma Megan with *Readers' Favorite* describes *Finding Sarah* as "the kind of book that breaks your heart and then mends it, and you will finish it with a smile and a long, satisfied sigh."

Nina now lives in Florida surrounded by family and friends when she is not traveling the globe seeking new experiences to write about.

www.ninapurtee.com

Moroccan Sunset

DAWN OF A NEW BEGINNING

Elena: El Amir's Long-Awaited Story in the *Annie's Journey* Series

It is time for El Amir to move on with his life. Annie is happily married to the Spanish matador, Ramone, with their child on the way. Honor and tradition dictate the mandate of his Arab culture that he only seek the hand of a suitable Arab woman. Will following tradition override his chance of love?

Elena Al-Farouq, a beautiful young Arab heiress, is far from the stereotypical dutiful bride. As she seeks to assert her independence and defy the old-world traditions, she sees El Amir as the perfect path to the life she desires. She intends to make El Amir forget any lingering feelings he might have toward Annie.

Can El Amir find the traditions of the past evolving into a future that includes the love and passion he craves? Or will he reject Elena's defiant spirit and possibly lose the love of his life?

Coming in the Fall of 2024.

FINDING SARAH: A PHOENIX TO BEHOLD
Book Club Questions

1. Who are the supporting characters that play an important role in Sarah's life and how do they shape her artistic journey and personal growth?

2. How do Rosa Bonheur and Rachel Ruysch, real-life artists from different centuries, fit into Sarah's artistic development?

3. Sarah spends time living alone in a tent in the Serengeti. What challenges and revelations did this time bring for her?

4. Sarah's father refers to her as a phoenix in a letter. How is this symbolism woven into the story?

5. Finding Sarah digs deeply into themes of loss, resilience, and the transformative power of art. How do these themes intertwine in Sarah's story?

6. What does the ending of the story signify in a broader context of second chances in love?

#

Printed in Great Britain
by Amazon

58921910R00172